THE
AND (

LUCIE DELARUE-MARDRUS (1874-1945) was born in Honfleur in Normandy, the youngest of the six daughters of an advocate. In 1900 she married the Orientalist Joseph-Charles Mardrus (1868-1949), a marriage which endured until 1913, but the union was confused from the outset by Lucie's apparent preference for women as sexual partners. She was a member of Natalie Barney's coterie of female poets and was rumored to have had affairs with more than one of them. A prolific author, she produced more than seventy books, including the collection of poetry *Ferveur* (1908) and the novels *L'Acharnée* (1910) and *Amanit* (1929).

BRIAN STABLEFORD'S scholarly work includes *New Atlantis: A Narrative History of Scientific Romance* (Wildside Press, 2016), *The Plurality of Imaginary Worlds: The Evolution of French roman scientifique* (Black Coat Press, 2017) and *Tales of Enchantment and Disenchantment: A History of Faerie* (Black Coat Press, 2019). In support of the latter projects he has translated more than a hundred volumes of *roman scientifique* and more than twenty volumes of *contes de fées* into English. He has edited *Decadence and Symbolism: A Showcase Anthology* (Snuggly Books, 2018), and is busy translating more Symbolist and Decadent fiction.

His recent fiction, in the genre of metaphysical fantasy, includes a trilogy of novels set in West Wales, consisting of *Spirits of the Vasty Deep* (2018), *The Insubstantial Pageant* (2018) and *The Truths of Darkness* (2019), published by Snuggly Books, and a trilogy set in Paris and the south of France, consisting of *The Painter of Spirits*, *The Quiet Dead* and *Living with the Dead*, all published by Black Coat Press in 2019.

SNUGGLY BOOKS

LUCIE DELARUE-MARDRUS

THE LAST SIREN
AND OTHER STORIES

TRANSLATED AND WITH AN INTRODUCTION BY
BRIAN STABLEFORD

THIS IS A SNUGGLY BOOK

Translation and Introduction Copyright © 2020
by Brian Stableford.
All rights reserved.

ISBN: 978-1-64525-041-8

CONTENTS

INTRODUCTION

LUCIE DELARUE-MARDRUS (1874-1945) was the first female journalist to be recruited to the stable of writers formed by the Parisian daily newspaper *Le Journal* to supply its daily "Contes du Journal" feature with copy on a regular basis. The most prolific contributors to that feature, including Jean Lorrain, Edmond Haraucourt and Paul Adam, supplied material on a weekly basis, or very nearly, while others delivered an item once a fortnight; Delarue-Mardrus was in the latter category. She began that work in July 1906 and remained associated with the newspaper until her death, but the nature of her contributions changed very markedly over time. Initially, however, she wrote a series of short stories interspersed with a handful of satirical articles, which appeared at near-regular intervals until February 1908: thirty-five stories in all, which were never collected in book form in France, but translations of which constitute the present volume.

Short stories were an important feature of several of the French daily newspapers of the 1890s and early 1900s, including *Gil Blas, La Lanterne* and *L'Écho de Paris*. Some of the papers concentrated such material in weekly "literary supplements," as *Le Journal* had initially done when the paper was launched in 1892 by Fernand Xau, but when it was taken over following Xau's death in 1899 and Henri Letellier took the helm, the new editor deliberately cultivated greater literary pretentions than his competitors, and soon made the Contes du Journal the most prominent feature of his paper, establishing it as the lead item on page one, except when truly important news required it to be displaced—a position it maintained until 1904. By the time Delarue-Mardrus began writing for the feature, however, it had been moved to form the lead item on page three (of four or six).

The Contes du Journal were longer than the short stories typically featured by its direct competitors. Although short fiction did not usually appear in the feuilleton slot, below the line ruled at the bottom of a page, where all the major daily newspapers ran serial novels in episodes of between 1200 and 1800 words, following a tradition that went back to the 1840s, most of their editors applied similar word limits to short fiction, or even accommodated briefer lengths of 500 to 1200 words. In keeping with Letellier's greater pretentions, the Contes du Journal had a standard word-length of 2000, and frequently went as high as 2500, or even 2800, even though those greater lengths required extending the layout of the story to a third column (of five). That gave writers a little more narrative space in which to operate, but it was still relatively narrow by comparison with the scope routinely offered by monthly or weekly periodicals that had far more space to fill than a four-page daily newspaper printed as a single sheet; it was not until 1907 that *Le Journal* expanded routinely to eight pages as the volume of advertising it carried increased to require that permanent modification.

Stories of that length had, of course, existed for a long time, and writers had developed narrative techniques adapted to their formulation, but from 1890 onwards the marketplace for such material expanded vastly as newspapers proliferated, in the wake of more efficient printing presses and cheaper methods of paper production, and such fiction increasingly came to be seen as a significant selling point. For some twenty years the mass-production of such material by professional writers became a very attractive option, and numerous writers took it up, with varying degrees of success, for various lengths of time, although it required particular skills and an artistry of which only a few were capable, and even those who proved expert tended to run out of steam eventually, as their ability to invent new stories was stretched to the limit.

The great pioneer and exemplar of that kind of literary mass-production was Catulle Mendès (1841-1909), and many of the writers who followed in his footsteps, usually temporarily, took some inspiration from him regarding the methodology of writing such stories. The most successful included Octave Mirbeau, Maurice Leblanc, Jules Richepin, Jean Lorrain, Paul Adam, Léon Bloy, André Theuriet, Maurice Level, Edmond Haraucourt and Hugues le Roux, most of whom were regular contributors to *Le Journal*, that being one of the key criteria defining success in the medium. Although Mendès was the great pioneer of mass-produced short fiction, he naturally appropriated and developed the viable narrative strategies developed by earlier writers, of which the most important, by far, was what had come to be titled, after an 1883 collection by Auguste Villiers de l'Isle Adam, *contes cruels*: terse narratives whose "cruelty" generally consisted of a cynical view of life and a regretful observation of the fact that the dreams and ambitions of hope and optimism are ever vulnerable to abrupt shattering.

One of the key features of longer fiction is, of course, a frequent denial of that inevitability, or at least a compromise with it. When novels began to be mass-produced in the nineteenth century, their writers rapidly developed a narrative strategy that proved capable of pleasing large numbers of readers, whereby possessors of hope and optimism struggle against adversity at great length, but eventually reap the few rewards possible in a world in which, as everyone eventually has the opportunity to observe, "life's a bitch and then you die." It quickly became a cliché that in order to please the maximum number of readers, novelists were well-advised to provide endings in which evil characters come to a sticky end while good ones achieve, at long last, a happy marriage and financial security. It is, however, very difficult for short fiction to achieve that kind of story arc, which requires space if it is to develop the necessary complication and tensile strength. Hence, the natural pattern of the short story, in the constricted length favored by the French newspapers of the Belle Époque, is not a shrinkage of the pattern of the novel, but rather a kind of ironic counterpoint to it. Although "happy endings" are by no means impossible in short fiction, it is far more difficult to inject them with sufficient narrative energy for them to be effective, whereas the instantaneous deflation provided by a *conte cruel* ending is not only easier to contrive but tends to provide a greater, if calculatedly perverse, satisfaction to the reader.

When Lucie Delarue-Mardrus embarked upon her brief career as a mass-producer of short fiction for *Le Journal* she inevitably followed the precedents that had been set by her predecessors—which is to say that almost all of her productions in that vein were *contes cruels*—but her works nevertheless have a certain distinction, which differentiates them sharply from the general run of such productions. That distinction is to some extent a product of her unique personality and circumstances, but also, inevitably, reflects the fact that she was the first female recruit to the Journal stable, possessed of a viewpoint that was thoroughly feminized, and also somewhat feminist. The short stories were written at a particular point in the author's life when she was envisaging the imminent irreparable decline of her career as a "professional beauty" in Parisian society—an anxiety that forms the subject-matter of one story and is obliquely reflected in several others. The particular feminized attitude engendered by that point in time could not endure for long; like "Princesse" Mina's dresses in "L'Armoire de Barbe-bleu" (tr.

herein as "Bluebeard's Wardrobe"), the collection represents a temporary aspect of her soul, which was not replicated in her subsequent literary endeavors.

Delarue-Mardrus was not the first female writer to attempt to dabble in that kind of short story mass-production, nor the first to exhibit feminist tendencies as well as the inevitable feminization of their viewpoint. Marie Krysinska, the only female member of the Hydropathes, had made a half-hearted attempt to work steadily for *Gil Blas* and *La Lanterne* in 1890-92, some of the stories she produced in consequence being reprinted in *Amour chemine* (1892; tr. as *The Path of Amour*) and Jane de La Vaudère had made a much more sustained effort, supplying material regularly to the pages of *La Presse* from 1897-1901 and *La Lanterne* for some years thereafter, although her fictional efforts in that medium, like Delarue-Mardrus', were never collected in volume form, in spite of her novels attaining best-seller status. Krysinska and La Vaudère were, however, working to more restricted word-limits for less pretentious outlets, and that added to the distinction between their endeavors and those of Delarue-Mardrus, which are, if seen as a compact set, highly unusual.

There are, of course, many kinds and shades of cruelty exhibited in *contes cruels*, and if the genre is viewed as a whole all of them are repeated incessantly. Delarue-Mardrus' contributions inevitably participate in that repetition, but in spite of their loyal generic affiliations, the literary cocktail contrived by the thirty-five stories in the present collection has a flavor that is unique, and piquant. The collection has no original in volume form, but it could and perhaps should have had; it is a ghost twice over: a translation of a book that never existed, but which, had it existed, would undoubtedly have been one of the author's finest works, and arguably her most interesting.

✳

Lucie Delarue was born in Honfleur in Normandy, the youngest of the six daughters of an advocate, and although the family relocated to Paris when she was six years old they revisited Normandy routinely, and Lucie retained a strong nostalgic attachment to the region. That affiliation is very evident in several of the stories in the collection, one of which, "La Mort du furet" (tr. as "The Death of the Ferret") is even presented as an item of autobiography, although its detail is manifestly fictitious. Later in life, she served as a nurse in Honfleur during the Great War, and eventually, while still living and working in Paris, she acquired a property there. She eventually died in the town, in difficult circumstances, overwhelmed by debts run up and long sustained by a slightly extravagant lifestyle.

Delarue-Mardus recorded in her actual autobiographical writings that her older sisters teased her a great deal when she was a child, with ostentatious contempt, and the children who feature as protagonists in many of her stories, the termination of whose childhood illusions is routinely featured as the most poignant cruelty of her *conte cruel* endings, are invariably described as being "different", by virtue of being more imaginative than their fellows and more inclined to be self-indulgent in the uses of their imagination. She later considered, however, that she had obtained a due revenge on her prosaic sisters when her physical youth became an advantage and she acquired a reputation in her late teens and twenties for exceptional beauty, and became, in the terminology used herein, a Parisienne "princesse." Her admirers included Philippe Pétain, eighteen years her senior, who asked for her in marriage but was refused. (She does not appear to have regretted that refusal when he became a hero during the Great War of 1914-18, or when he headed the Vichy government during World War II. She provided a great deal of copy to *Le Journal* during both conflicts, in spite of her military duties during the first and her failing health during the second.)

In fact, Lucie married rather late by the standards of the day, to the Orientalist Joseph-Charles Mardrus (1868-1949), in 1900. Mardrus was a great traveler, a lover of flowers and precious stones, and an enthusiastic photographer—all interests that his wife shared, and which assisted her to further her burgeoning career as a journalist; the couple's frequent visits to North Africa provided raw material for several of the short stories in the present collection. Although the marriage endured until 1913, it was confused from the outset by Lucie's apparent preference for women as sexual partners. She was a member of Natalie Barney's coterie of female poets and was rumored to have had affairs with more than one of them, with the knowledge and apparent approval of her husband, whose esthetic appreciation of her allegedly extended to not wanting her to have children lest it spoil her figure—although that anxiety might have been as much hers as his.

Given those circumstances, it is unsurprising that one of the most remarkable features of the fictional world contained in the stories in the present volume is its attitude to amour and marriage. Whereas the stories produced by Krysinska, La Vaudère and many other writers for similar markets routinely feature characters whose primary obsession is amour, in which it is routinely imagined to provide the most powerful incentives and the most precious possible rewards in life, Delarue-Mardrus almost makes a fetish out of its irrelevance to many of her characters, and the minority who fall victim to infatuation in her stories are not merely disappointed but devastated or destroyed in consequence. In her literary universe, love is a disaster best avoided, marriage and adultery being incidents of little importance to those who can succeed in being uninjured by them.

The fictitious amour in question is invariably heterosexual, alternatives being difficult to mention, let alone celebrate, in the pages of a newspaper, in spite of the fact that some male writers of the era, notably Catulle Mendès and Pierre Louÿs, were fascinated by the notion of lesbian lust, featuring it explicitly in some stories and hinting at it with salacious obliquity in many others. She was not unaware of a certain intrinsic paradoxicality in her work of the period—clearly exhibited in "Le Bâton" (tr. as "The Stick")—and perhaps an element of conscious hypocrisy, and that awareness is occasionally evident in her work even without reading between the lines.

The extent to which Delarue-Mardus' preference for ignoring the existence of lesbian sexual attraction in the phase of her work reproduced herein was a marketing decision, a defensive concealment, or a reflection of an actual conviction of its relative irrelevance, is an intriguing question, but in real life she does not seem to have made much attempt to conceal her sexuality and it is interesting that in introducing "Princesse Patricia," a character clearly but unflatteringly based on herself, in the first of four stories featuring her, "L'Auto Fantôme" (tr. as "The Phantom Auto") virtually the first thing the narrative voice says about her is that her "pose" is pretending to have been "badly brought-up." Patricia's husband is not given an active role to play, even when he is present, and her unspecified multiple lovers are only mentioned dismissively in passing.

As befits the productions of someone proud of having been an eccentrically imaginative child and insistent on remaining an unorthodox adult, many of the stories in the present set are fantasies, including the first and the last. "La Dernière Sirène" is a title that had been used before on short stories of the same kind by Bernard Lazare and Maurice Magre—and was to be used again by Pierre Mille—and the theme had featured in several more, including a lachrymose story by Catulle Mendès. It was also used in the poetry of the Symbolist Movement; it was a frequent motif in the work of René Vivien, another member of Natalie Barney's coterie, who included lightly-disguised transfigurations of Mardus and Lucie in the first version of her quasi-autobiographical fantasy *Une femme m'apparut* (1904; tr. as *A Woman Appeared to Me*), but removed them from the second version published a year later, perhaps because Mardrus complained about the nasty depiction of him. The plaintive nostalgia of Vivien's depiction of sirens—always in interaction with female protagonists—is, however, very different in tone from the bitter sarcasm of Delarue-Mardus' appropriation of the notion, which is the most brutal of the entire set.

The subsequent fantasies in the sequence, by contrast, often shun well-worn themes and strive for originality, frequently achieving it, as in "Une Femme aux enfers" (tr. as "A Woman in Hell") and "Le Fantôme dans la rose" (tr. as "The Phantom in the Rose"), which are equally remarkable in different ways. Although uniformly cynical, the stories are otherwise variable in their attitudes, the blunt misandry of "La Dernière sirène" being countered by the sly misogyny of "Lise et les chimères" (tr. as "Lise and the Chimeras"), with various shades of sympathy and antipathy represented in between. The naturalistic stories, however, are more uniform in their antipathy to mature women, female characters over the age of fourteen generally being represented with a ferocious lack of sympathy—although, in fairness, several male characters over that age receive equally unkind treatment and even the one who ends up literally smelling of roses is not as fortunate metaphorically.

The predominance of fantasies within the set is unusual as a feature of work done for the Contes du Journal, which featured occasional fantasies by the likes of Jean Lorrain, Paul Adam and Edmond Haraucourt but generally gave preference to grim and stubborn naturalism. Although fantastic apologues can easily be fitted to restricted word-lengths, most of the writers mass-producing work for such slots found it more comfortable to produce work in quantity of the anecdotal "slice of life" variety, in which an incident trivial in itself becomes a paradigmatic example of the entire fate of a character and of the essentially

15

disappointing, disabusing and disenchanting nature of life's accidental collisions. It is not surprising that the pattern of Delarue-Mardrus' stories—reproduced here in chronological order of appearance, and presumably that of composition—shows a marked development in that direction, perhaps spontaneous and perhaps responsive to editorial suggestion.

The fact that the series signs off with "Le Revenant marin" (tr. as "The Ghostly Mariner") is significant, not merely because it is a trifle weary by comparison with the earlier fantasies, but because it seems to be bidding an explicit adieu to that kind of imaginative work, to which the author never returned, even though she continued to work within the Contes du Journal slot for several years more before her journalistic work for the paper broadened out considerably, eventually becoming completely transformed during the Great War. Once the ghostly mariner had returned symbolically to the sea, turning his back on his beloved Honfleur, Delarue-Mardrus rarely made much room in her work for the flamboyant figures of the Romantic imagination, and when she did, it was usually in an ironically apologetic manner.

Delarue-Mardus was by no means the first writer to suffer imagination-fatigue as a result of producing short stories in a fixed format at fortnightly intervals. Very few who started the game showed the same versatility and stamina as Catulle Mendès, Jean Lorrain and Edmond Haraucourt, and even they "cheated" routinely in order to meet the obligation with reduced imaginative enterprise. The principal problem with the policy adopted by the stories in the present volume is that of maintaining variety, of finding a different, and preferably original, idea for every single story. In any such sequence, repetition eventually creeps in, as does the temptation to link stories together with continuing characters, settings and themes.

Jean Lorrain had already begun arranging most of his Contes du Journal in groups long before 1906, sometimes stringing together sequences of episodes in which the same characters simply move from one location to another, recounting and participating in anecdotal incidents. Two such sequences, "Astarté" (1899) and "Coins de Byzance" (1901) extended to become novels, the former published in volume form as *Monsieur de Phocas, Astarté* (1900; tr as *Monsieur de Phocas*) and the latter being reprinted in *La Lanterne*'s feuilleton slot as "Les Noronsoffs" in 1903 as well as providing the bulk of the substance of the book *Le Vice errant* (1902; tr. as *Errant Vice*). That example, developed in parallel by Octave Mirbeau, was eventually followed by Edmond Haraucourt, who varied his unitary *contes cruels* with groups and serials of various lengths, two of which became the bases for his two finest novels, *Dieudonat* (May-November 1906; revised in book form 1912; tr. as *Dieudonat*) and *Daâh, le premier homme* (December1912-May 1913 and May-June 1914; revised book version 1914; tr. as *Daâh, the First Human*).

Delarue-Mardrus' employment of her Contes du Journal slot after February 1908 abandoned all pretence that her work there consisted of independent short stories. After a four-part novelette devoid of an overall title serialized between 28 February and 3 April 1908 she simply began to serialize novels there, beginning with *Marie, fille-mère* (April-September 1908) and continuing with *Le Roman de six petite filles* (October 1908-April 1909)—both developed from ideas first trailed in short stories in the set translated herein, "Conte de Noel" (tr. as "Christmas Story") and "La Mort du furet" respectively.

There was, in textual terms, no reason why those novels should not have been featured in *Le Journal*'s feuilleton slot, but in practical terms, there is a considerable difference, from a writer's viewpoint, between supplying copy for a daily serial, at a rate of more than 10,000 words per week, and delivering material for a fortnightly slot of 2,000-2,500 words. Serials produced and published in that relatively leisurely fashion, however, have to be much more episodic and discontinuous than stories that are assumed to be read every day in a continuous fashion, and if writing Contes du Journal required the development of particular narrative techniques and artistry, writing novels for stringing out in the Contes du Journal slot posed a more extreme challenge, which even writers of the caliber of Jean Lorrain, Octave Mirbeau and Edmond Haraucourt had difficulty meeting even sporadically. Delarue-Mardus met it almost continuously, for some years.

Delarue-Mardus did write more independent short stories later in her long career writing for *Le Journal*, but they are markedly different from those in the 1906-08 sequence, and the majority of the individual items with which her serials were interpolated consisted of factual reportage, mostly derived from her travels, especially her travels in the Middle East, before the outbreak of the Great War, and almost exclusively concerned with the war and its aftermath from 1914 until the early 1920s. By then, the person who had written the stories translated in the present volume had been completely transformed, and so had her work, further emphasizing the fact that the stories herein represent a distinct and self-contained phase in her oeuvre.

Lucie Delarue-Mardus' novels were successful, without ever attaining best-seller status or receiving very enthusiastic critical attention. Her literary reputation was largely formed and defined by her poetry, much of which she wrote before diversifying into prose fiction, although that literary reputation was always confused with her temporary reputation as a notorious beauty who posed as having been, to put it euphemistically, "badly brought-up." Because the material translated in the present volume was not reprinted in book form, it became effectively invisible, impossible for anyone to consider and judge as a whole, and thus to see as a significant phase in the author's literary development, until the Bibliothèque Nationale made its archive of *Le Journal* available on its *gallica* website. Indeed, it was not until *gallica* took aboard the Biblothèque Nationale's collection of old newspapers that it became possible for anyone fully to appreciate what a vast wealth of unreprinted material such newspapers had contained, or the context in which it was written and published.

Delarue-Mardrus' short fiction is by no means the only interesting treasure-trove thus revealed, but it is one of the most interesting, because of its originality and enterprise. Although decidedly idiosyncratic, she played an important role in the development of women's writing in the latter part of the Belle Époque, which deserves more recognition than it received at the time or has been given since. She began work too late to be immediately pigeon-holed as a Symbolist or a Naturalist, so she felt free to be a little of both, alternately and simultaneously, and something of a Decadent too, while plowing her own furrow at an angle to those excavated by her contemporaries. A handful of the stories in the present collection qualify as forgotten masterpieces, but all of them contain features of interest and originality, while offering valuable oblique insight into the author's character, and they add up to a magnificent kaleidoscopic whole, which I am pleased and proud to have collated for the first time.

These translations were made from the copies of *Le Journal* reproduced on the Bibliothèque Nationale's *gallica* website.

—Brian Stableford

THE LAST SIREN
AND OTHER STORIES

THE LAST SIREN
(*Le Journal*, 8 July 1906)

NO one spoke the delightful name of the people who had died in the abandoned property, the grand old gardens of which went all the way down to the sea. For decades no one had passed that way any longer. But perhaps *something* passed that way? The sea, which has so many stories to tell, doubtless wrote this one in the sand of the little creek with the tips of her waves, which left secret white traces behind every day when the tide ebbed. But whether the beds of wrack sometimes remained hollowed out at low tide, as if haunches had rested there, no one would ever know. The dramas of an absolutely solitary tiny terrestrial and marine area did not concern anyone in the world.

A day came when the property was bought. The house was horribly renovated, the gardens turned over and shaped; nothing more remained of the abandon slowly amassed among those things like an unknown treasure. That real being, a monsieur, came to sit down, banal and content, in the midst of the past, and his family, around him, broke all that silence with the noise of human life.

One of his first cares was to descend alone to the creek, with the intention of fishing with a net. He was having a house-warming party the following day and he wanted something caught with his own hand to fry for the morning meal he was giving his friends.

He was seen, red-faced and amused, his feet bare, advancing toward the retreating sea. His large net, disposed over a wooden square, was weighing upon his shoulder at the end of a long pole. The light of the setting sun splashed the sand, the mud and the pools around him. The world glistened at his feet like Chinese lacquer. At sea, the sun was dying. He was dreaming of little soles, dabs, plaice and shrimp. He searched for a nice hole of troubled water, and found one: a hole as large as a pool; in truth, as wide and deep as the pools of important persons of old.

Suddenly, turning crimson, the man stared with eyes bulging from his head, because he had just thrown his net effortfully and saw it filled to breaking point by a long scaly body, the frantic lashing of whose tail shook his arms terribly. But did he not also divine, caught in algae, mesh and hair, a human face whose frightened pale eyes were looking him? Were there not two little hands clenching and struggling?

He made a movement to flee, but pulled himself together very quickly, because marvels never astonish ordinary people, and such an adorably terrifying thing as finding a siren in his shrimp-net cannot disturb for long a monsieur who is fishing for a fry-up, without thinking about anything else. He only exclaimed: "What a funny eel!"

He would have been more charmed by an encounter with one of those mussel-fishers whose complaisant bosom one could evaluate from the corner of an eye, than the sight of a fabulous creature, frightened, wet and gilded.

That is why he only uttered a loud burst of laughter when the siren spoke.

"I was afraid of you," she said, "and yet I waited for you. You're the charming human that my mother saw from afar wandering at the end of the gardens, and whom she told me so much about when she died, when I was still as small as a gurnard."

Her head was raised. Drops of water were still streaming over her livid cheeks, all the way to her crimson mouth. Her nostrils were palpitating like the delicate gills of a fish. When she moved she spread a strong perfume of iodine and salt. In addition, the sea had ornamented her. Her hair was still extended by the seaweed that was mingled with it; her forehead was coiffed with starfish, and a few pearls were nested in the complicated hollows of her ears. Necklaces of seashells and coral were sliding around her neck.

But was not the most beautiful of those ornaments, displayed between the breasts imprisoned in the threads of the net, the luminous violet flesh of a jellyfish, like an unexpected item of glassware?

She could not free her hands. She repeated: "I waited for you."

As he did not say anything, she considered him at length with her immense eyes the color of water, in which the patch of the pupil flowered like a black nenuphar.

"You see," she said, "your fishing-trip, this evening, is a cast of the net of destiny. For such a long time I've been coming at low tide to lie in this bed, in order to watch for you. Soft and floating wrack carpet the bottom, and I often go to sleep here, my head in my arms, by virtue of gazing toward the land without seeing anyone come. Sometimes I risk myself at the very edge of the waves and, crawling over the mud and the sand, I drag myself to the shingle of the shore, in spite of my precious body being wounded by it. I stretch myself out on the wrack, still moist, and I gaze at the shining sun. I've even dared to sing to appeal to you. Do you know that no one in the world has yet known the taste of the oyster of my mouth? Why didn't you come? But now you've found me, and I shall no longer utter my great cry of appeal along the strand. You'll lie beside me in my bed and we'll espouse one another in the shifting submerged shadow of algae. And I, the last of my race, will give birth in my turn, as my mother did, and thus, the sirens of the sea won't die forever with me. Don't you see how richly I've arrived for you from the depths, streaming with maritime ornaments? The waves dress me with a robe of light, and I'm drawing behind me the entire sea for a mantle. Come! I am your nuptial siren, your wife, O king of lovers!"

The poor man pointed a finger at the changing scales and sniggered.

"What do you take me for?"

But the salty lady did not understand. She displayed the blue perplexity of her eyes to him. "Listen to me! Listen to me! Doubtless you don't yet know the marine secrets; but I'll teach them to you. Think that I'm alone, to populate the sea. Can I not know it entirely, I who only have its waves for companions? It is the waves that have rounded my breasts like the shingle that they roll. It is the waves that have deposited these pearls in my ears. They love me. I lie down softly in them, and it is for having cradled my body that they arrive so hollow on your shore. They have told me everything. I know the days of calm in which their glaucous and succinct skin barely swells, and the days of tempest when, black with storms and white with foam, they run in furious folly to charge the cliffs terribly. I know exactly the meaning of the changing sea, warlike and retractile. Its monstrous rumor is in my blood. I have seen its ripping rocks at close range, but I have also known long slumbers in its saline puddles, amid a little sand, mud and shingle, between a few shellfish and algae, and also profoundly drowned repose, when strange fish come to look at me with all their phosphoric soul, and the scales of my tail shine like gold in the silent obscurity. I've known the spring mornings when young women throw a few flowers into the bitterness of the sea, a few flowers to sweeten the sea, and the electric evenings of summer when boats draw a fiery wake behind them. I know everything! I'll teach you everything! Like me you'll understand the abyss and the surface, and the great evenings in the open sea when the acute dolor of seaweeds streaks the sky and my hairy head, cleaving the immensity, emerges in the sunset, in order for me to extend insensate arms toward the horizons of flame and desire, in the utmost depths of my being, to drink the sea and eat the sun!"

She had finally disengaged her little hands, which she raised above her head, her mouth wide open, her eyes turned to black.

And the man suddenly cried: "But it's true that she has breasts!"

Then, his hands forward, with a happy smile, he advanced toward the siren, and his two large palms were plastered in a single thrust upon the firm and streaming bosom.

She uttered a great chromatic clamor, like that of steamers in distress. Her entire body writhed in indignation, and in a moist frisson, turning round against him, she suddenly dug her ten fingernails into the ruddy cheeks, while, with a sweep of her furious tail, she pricked his legs with all her defensive spines.

Blinded, frightened, washed by the algae and the tresses, wounded by the fingernails and the spines, he was nevertheless able to seize her by the shoulders. She writhed in his fingers, struggled amid the gleams; but with an effort, he caused her to tumble back into the mesh, which he closed with an abrupt movement. Then, dragging her behind him furiously, he returned with long strides to the darkened strand, howling and still trembling with fear:

"You're nothing but a fish, after all! To the cooking-pot! To the cooking-pot!"

And his coarse laughter, through the rising marine night, drowned out the unusual cry that the last siren, as she died, directed toward the sea, and liberty.

THE ARCHANGEL IN THE CABARET
(*Le Journal*, 24 July 1906)

SHE was some child in a garden, a little Marie or a little Berthe, who was playing silently in the corners, who never had the cross, and whose large ringed eyes, when they dreamed, prompted people to say: "She's idle." People also said: "She's a liar." And people repeated to her every day: "Your guardian angel is watching you!"

But she smiled mysteriously at that, because she knew full well that her guardian angel did not have the soul of a schoolmistress. And without being able to explain such a complicated thing to herself, she knew, with the certainty of instinct, that the unpleasant faults that made her a shameful and scolded child could not trouble in any way a certain place in her soul, a place unknown to all, chaste and cold, where seraphic whiteness held sway.

In any case, and although she was often told that one could never see him, she often distinguished her angel. She was not unaware that, on Sunday, he mingled with the children of the choir and gazed at her from afar with luminous eyes, magnificently changing, and which understood everything. Other people mistook him for a sunbeam or confused him with the ornaments of high mass, the gold of the censers, the linen of the surplice or the statues of saints, but Marie was ecstatic, immobile. Then someone jabbed her severely in the ribs, and whispered to her: "Read the mass!" And her poor little face rapidly plunged back into the open book. Thus she was forced to the boredom of the Roman parishioner, instead of being allowed to follow her own liturgy.

Now, as the unpleasant faults and the punishments actively pursued their parallel work, it happened that, from school to apprenticeship and from apprenticeship to the sidewalk, the little girl, mutated into a prostitute, became the same Marie or the same Berthe and walked in the bad places of Paris, her large eyes a little more ringed.

In order to arrive there she had passed through many chagrins and many humiliations, but she had not complained, because she was very meek. Furthermore, those things had simply seemed to her to be the continuation of the idleness and lies, the scoldings and punishments over which her childhood had wept so many warm tears. All in all, she did not find the life of grown-ups very different from that of little girls . . .

And then, what it is necessary to say above all is that the supernatural that had flowered in the soul of the culpable little girl had not abandoned the woman of ill repute. Without her experiencing the need to talk about it to anyone, wings continued to beat around her heart. Her child angel, who had once been no taller than a petty clerk, with the wingspan of a swan at the most, had grown with her in proportion to her height. He had become an archangel, of tall stature.

In the evening when she chanced to be alone in her poor prostitute's room, he came in with the sunset through the closed windows and, standing in a corner, gazed at her.

His wings, although furled, filled the entire room. Their great cumbersome and white pinion feathers trailed around him, stretching as far as beneath the furniture. And doubtless the odor of high masses of old remained in his hair, for his head, when he moved it, smelled good, like a censer. As for his face, it was perfectly handsome. But how would Marie have had the leisure to study him in detail? Since she had known him, she had never been able to detach her gaze from his eyes. Their formidable and charming gaze entered into her, and there was, without terror, without embarrassment and without even a blink of the lashes, an absolute communication with the mystery. There was also something simple, like the gazes exchanged between animals, and something pure, discreet and honest, like a sharp dagger plunging into the soul all the way to the hilt.

When someone knocked on the door, the winged adolescent flew away with the loud noise of a fan that frightened seagulls make. And Marie, opening the door to the monsieur, tottered a little, because the archangel's eyes had left her with spots in her eyes, as when one has looked at the sun. And the monsieur thought: "The kid has had one absinthe too many!"

One evening, for the first time, Marie spoke to her archangel.

She had come back from a little cabaret on the edge of the Seine, where she habitually touted for custom in summer. Her heart was beating with a great emotion because of what had happened. Some kid with made-up eyes, one of her comrades, with whom she was chatting, had suddenly started weeping on her shoulder; and Marie had felt at close range the spasms of the great feminine sob that, without one knowing why, always in reserve, waits even in the depths of those who are only prostitutes, as if all women were born with a heavy heart.

She had interrogated the child delicately, and had found out what was doing harm to her life. But she had perceived that neither she, nor the others, nor any of those in whose midst they moved had, as she did, a white relationship with some vesperal friend, in the eyes of whom to recover intact the immaculate conception of the interior soul. Then, an idea had come to her, as spontaneous and simple as those that are born in humble hearts. That was why, that evening, she waited, quivering, for her archangel.

He came. She greeted him respectfully as she was accustomed to do; then, without looking at him, for fear of absorbing herself immediately in his eyes, she said: "We've never talked. But this evening, it's necessary that I tell you something. You must know what I do with my days and my nights, since you've often been obliged to fly away to leave the place to clients. So I'd like to ask you this: Would you like to come with me this evening to the café? It's on the edge of the Seine, under the arbors, and although there's a fête today, it won't be very well-lit. No one will recognize you. But there will be a lot of people there, and I'd like to have you with me, solely because of your eyes. A great desire has come to me for you to gaze at my comrades. They're unhappy, even though they make merry. And if your eyes open even once in their midst, they'll be consoled for the rest of their lives. Do you understand? I'd like to lend them your eyes . . ." She uttered a little intimidated laugh and added: "What is your name?"

There was something like a harp arpeggio in the room when he replied: "Domination."[1]

She clapped her hands.

"Domination! What a lovely name! My name's Marie. So, Domination, would you like to come with me this evening?"

The archangelic voice spoke like a song; it said: "But what are we going to do with my wings?"

---

1 This name might have no significance other than the literal meaning of the word, but it is probably not irrelevant to observe that that Lucie Delarue-Mardrus' name was often coupled by contemporary observers of the Belle Époque with that of the notoriously beautiful poet Comtesse Anna de Noailles, one particularly notable coupling being in Robert de Montesquiou's essay "Deux Muses" in the significantly-titled *Professionelles beautés* [Professional Beauties] (1905). Anna de Noailles' novel, *La Domination*, was also published in 1905, featuring the exploits of an exceedingly handsome and perverse young man, a model of contemporary ennui. Delarue-Mardus and Noailles apparently loathed one another—Montesquiou's coupling was deliberately mischievous—but they surely kept a sharp eye on one another's work.

Abruptly consternated, Marie lowered her head. "That's true! What are we going to do about them? We can't walk in the street like this; we'd be taken to the police station right away."

Suddenly remembering the days of her apprenticeship, rediscovering the gestures of a seamstress, she advanced tranquilly, with neither fear not effrontery toward the innocent and brilliant being, and her hands manipulated the giant wings with hasty movements.

"Perhaps by turning them like this . . ."

But there was no means of dissimulating them. The great plumes always overflowed, fluffing up like the white wheel of a peacock-tailed pigeon. The archangel mingled his fingers, like lily buds, with Marie's poor hands. They both shook their heads like embarrassed young women.

In the end, Marie had a sudden inspiration.

"I'll put one of my dresses over them!"

And then, without laughing, she fastened a wretched skirt over the sacred body puffing it up complaisantly. Then, as the plumes still overlapped, she went to look for her beautiful stole with three long tippets and arranged it over the winged shoulders.

"It doesn't suit you very well," she said, while adjusting a boater and a veil on the head embalmed with incense, "but there's no means of doing otherwise. As for these few long feathers that are still trailing, they'll be mistaken for the lace of your petticoat."

And they both went out into the black night, in quest of the train that would take them to the little cabaret of vicious nights.

Marie made recommendations: "Above all lower your eyes, Domination! Lower your eyes. You understand that if you only open them slightly, everyone will come to look into them, and there'll be five hundred people around you right away, like moths around a candle. When we've arrived, only then will you

32

open them, suddenly, and you'll gaze. And, you see, it will be as if happiness were letting two stars fall into the middle of all those people . . ."

They went. The nocturnal cabaret, because of the nearby Seine and its grassy banks, had a simultaneous smell of fish and hay. Oil lamps were hanging here and there, with a few Venetian lanterns, and under the arbors, amid two or three sunflowers, there was a great noise of diners finishing their meal. The immeasurable shadows of the diners moved behind them against the walls, amid the coming and going of a few waiters in blue aprons. A rusty piano was tapping out a waltz.

And as soon as she went in, Marie shouted in a clear voice to everyone: "I've brought you a new kid!"

She shouted with the soul of the Precursor in the desert. And because people had been drinking adulterated alcohol, their eyes were shining and they were ready, on no matter what pretext, to become overexcited. That is why they quickly flocked around Marie and her companion. And people also came through all the doors of the little guinguette, regulars and others, rich monsieurs and well-dressed women who had come to amuse themselves on that festive evening with the poverty and the vices of the poor. All the classes were there, rubbing shoulders, hoisting themselves up on tiptoe in order to see. And the hats of the socialites quivered with all their plumes between the reflections of top hats, the kepis of soldiers, the hair of the prostitutes and the white berets of apprentice bakers.

Then Marie removed the veil from the head of her archangel. Glorious and prophetic, with the great tremor of those who make revelations, she murmured: "Open the eyes."

And, the archangel having lifted his eyelids, the fulguration of his pupils spread around him like a burst of sunlight in the middle of the night.

But in the circle of people there was neither a surge nor a recoil. The majority, having not noticed anything, were already going away, thinking about something else. A few men and a few women sniggered. Some came, with a dirty gesture, to look at the supernatural face at close range. Alone, the child with the made-up eyes who had wept on Marie's shoulder formulated the vague sentiment of the crowd. She stopped behind the wings hidden under the double and unusual protrusion, crossing over beneath the cloth of the stole and deforming the three capsized tippets; and gently, in order not to disturb Marie, brushing the archangel's back with an eloquent finger, as she might have done that of a hunchback, she muttered between her teeth:

"You know, she has rather pretty eyes, the kid, but it's a pity that she's crippled . . ."

THE TOWER ON THE MARCH

(*Le Journal*, 9 August 1906)

SINCE it had four feet in order to walk, why did it stay so meekly in its place?

The languages of the five continents of the world had jabbered in it during the years of the Universal Exposition like a flock of variegated birds in an iron cage. Standing upright at the center of the cardinal points, it had tempted all the human crowds as a candle attracts cockchafers. It had received princes, kings, emperors and presidents. Its glory had shone on postcards, watch-cases and pin-cushions. It had even had the supreme consecration of being imitated. The second city of France had wanted, following the example of Paris, to honor its river with such a lofty presence, and the foggy hill of Lyon took pride in also being stabbed by a fake Eiffel Tower.

But why recall all those triumphs? It is only necessary to say that the magnificence of its success had wearied it. It was bored. In vain it made the great complicated eye of its searchlight rotate. The four horizons no longer had any novelty for it; and as for the atmospheric phenomena that might have distracted it, it was scornful of them, because it did not like nature. In any case, it had the sentiment of its superiority. It was not unaware that its lightning-conductor was stronger than the lightning, its lens larger than the stars, and that its flag clattered better than a hurricane. If the inflamed sunset struck it obliquely, it produced fireworks more beautiful than any red evening, and if the mists of the Seine sometimes made it a phantom tower, it knew projections even more gripping. As for the swirling visits of swifts and other birds, it did not even pay attention to them. It considered that sort of thing good for trees.

However, one capital concern made it supercilious. It suffered from its entourage. It knew full well that it was above them all, but it suffered a considerable irritation in seeing the monuments of Paris, especially the towers, profiled against the sky. Were they not as many personal insults, those silhouettes that permitted themselves to dominate in front of it? It would have liked a universal leveling at its feet, something egalitarian, like a freshly-trimmed hedge. If even the plaster of the stucco-work that it distinguished on the nearest houses obfuscated it, what could be said about the cathedrals that permitted themselves to be perforated, sculpted, incrusted with stones and equipped with steles? Why were those personalities, which disrupted the orderliness of the city, opposing its geometry in all directions? It could almost have forgiven the Petit and Grand Palais and other Alexandrian bridges. They, after all, were only held in place by an arrangement of clockwork. And then, they were new, and everyone knew what purpose they served. But those old antiquities, for the existence of which no one any longer knew the reasons, all the Tours Saint-Jacques and Notre-Dames, what were they doing on the horizon, taking up so much good building land unnecessarily?

Now, having meditated those grievances for a long time, it finally decided. One night, when no one knew what was happening, in the brief absolute silence of sleeping Paris, it shook its metallic spine formidably, darted a circular glance of its searchlight over the city, and started to walk.

The fashion in which its four awkward feet maneuvered, after being paralyzed by sixteen years of native immobility, no human would ever know. The moon alone saw its enormous

36

shadow agitating over the city; the moon alone perceived the four irregular thrusts of its limping gait hammering the urban silence, the moon alone received in the face the splash of the Seine when, punctured by the four iron legs, its water leapt up into the sky with a vertiginous din.

There was also a poor sergent de ville astray in the night, who raised his white stick toward it at the moment when it set foot in the water, but, in trying thus to reestablish the order troubled by the three-hundred-meter passer-by, it goes without saying that he and his stick were reduced to negligibility, without the tower even perceiving him.

Meanwhile, it had traversed the Seine. As heroic as the queen in a game of chess, it ran first at its principal enemy. Negligently, almost in passing, it knocked down both towers of the Trocadéro. Satisfied with its first exploit, finding vengeance so sweet and facile, it pursued its course with long strides, determined to cast everything down. It ignored the Louvre; that was of scant interest. It was in haste to arrive at the object of its rancor: Notre-Dame.

When it was in front of the double tower, which, solemnly surrounded by moving clouds and moonlight, seemed to be advancing vigorously into the night, it stopped.

It was not afraid of priests, but—it did not know why—that old godlover of a cathedral, seen at close range, intimidated it. It suddenly seemed it that the steeple of that dwarf surpassed it, the Eiffel Tower, by an incalculable number of meters, and it took account of the fact that it could not dispose of those towers like those of the Trocadéro. That is why, disguising its humiliation beneath an arrogant attitude, it insulted its rival in these terms:

"Hey, down there, little one! Can't you see me?"

Its voice being as hard as iron, a sort of musical growl rose by means of resonance from the depths of the great organs asleep in the interior of Notre-Dame . . . and that was all.

"What did you say?" said the astonished tower.

Then, suddenly, furious at the effect it had produced, it gave the parvis a gigantic kick, and in a single burst, spilled everything that its hatred and vanity had to formulate.

"Fundamentally, why are you so stuck-up? What is it that you represent? Why were you built? Yes, I've heard mention of the *Ave Maria* that the little girls of old used to recite, but what is that, in sum? One knows her, the little Jewish woman to whom you're dedicated. I saw heaps like her in 1880 and 1900. Of what are you proud, then? Me, I'm something else. Me, I'm the modern spirit, the giant bell-tower of modern piety. I'm the iron cathedral of this era. I have the air of a blast furnace. When the sun sets around my head, one might think me a factory chimney. And then, you see, I'm new. But you? Look at you, then, seasoned like an old pipe. Your stained-glass windows? But haven't you seen me on feast days? Oh, my electric flames, my girandoles, my confetti, my serpentines! Your masses? Your organs? But don't I have a barrel-vault where people sing little songs in vogue? You, you're only a church. Me, I'm a theater and a beacon, a tower and an elevator, an observatory and a lightning-conductor. Your history of France? Your Saint Louis and your Napoléons? Me, I've sheltered Félix Faure and Tsar Nicolas, and many others. So you don't know who I am? Look at my legs! I give birth to all of you, weary of churches and monuments. I give birth to all of you every day. I'm the Mère Gigogne of Paris, I am!"

Even the organs had fallen silent. Although every gargoyle had a sardonic crease at the corner of its mouth, the abused Notre-Dame continued, as in the past, to enclose its immemorial heart in its hypocritical and gilded reliquary. It knew that it was something other than a little Jewish woman, something other than the gospels, something other than the priests. It knew the races that it had eaten and the crowned heads and feet in clogs—workers, kings, thinkers, artists—who, in the triumph of the *Te Deum*, had advanced toward the sublime countries of its rose windows.

And the great new tower, on its splayed base, stamped its feet with anger and impatience, without daring to decide to approach any closer.

Finally, the cathedral took pity on it. Through the triple mouth of its doors, it said:

"If I were you, I'd return very quickly to my post. You just have time before dawn, and thus, no one will notice your absence."

"What about the other towers?" said the giant, with humility.

"The other towers will remain in place," said the cathedral, severely.

"It's just that," said the poor three hundred meters, "I thought I ought to pay them a visit . . ."

"They can do without it," replied Notre-Dame. "As I'm their elder, it's sufficient that I've seen you. And then, one knows you sufficiently from a distance."

But the tower did not go away. A thought was torturing its exceedingly small head.

"I'm obliged to agree that you have more experience than me," it said. "So I want to ask you for some advice. You understand that I belong to the era of the auto and old crocks, and I sense that I can no longer remain still. It's absolutely necessary that I travel. Where should I go?"

The cathedral had a ferocious response:

"Why don't you go to see the Sphinx?"

And the tower, not having understood the irony, took possession of that idea violently and started dancing on its feet joyfully.

"Thank you!" it cried, "And *au revoir!*"

It knew, vaguely, the Sphinx was a celebrity, that it was a cousin of the obelisk, and that it lived in Egypt.

An Arabian, it thought, *isn't very difficult to flatten.*

And it rejoiced in advance, thinking of the beautiful revenge that it was about to take, after its disappointment. That is why, limping along, it pursued its nocturnal route, going bravely toward the Sphinx.

The story of its voyage would be too long. Let us only explain how, throughout France, it was prudently scornful of the likes of Notre-Dame and Sacré-Coeur, contenting itself with overturning in passing a few new towers of villas, how it marched on the sea-bed, how the entire Mediterranean traversed its framework, and how the fish in the depths, mistaking it for the wreck of an ironclad, came to look at it ironically with owl-like eyes.

The sea rusted it and poeticized it. Shellfish and algae took root on it. Coiffed with coral and seaweed, it came ashore one day in Egypt, and immediately, a few storks had the desire to build nests in its head. But it shook itself indignantly and resumed its march. And as it approached the region where the enigmatic Beast lay, its footsteps sank deeper in the sand, like those of a colossal elephant.

Now, before introducing itself, because it knew how saucepans are scoured, it took care to roll in the sand for a long time, in order to get rid of all the marine rubbish. It wanted to be as new as possible again, and painted yellow. When it judged that it was a little brighter, and decent, in three strides it was before the Sphinx.

Night was descending around it. Its head was bathing in the sky and its loins were buried in the sand. As the rising moon crowned it with a tiara of light, the goddess slept invisibly between its claws. And before the sixteen-year-old tower that was considering her stupidly, her millennial attitude, on her face of stone, expanded like a rose the youth of eternity.

In any case, the tower did not consider her for long.

Is that it? it thought. *It's that big cat that doesn't even know how to purr? It gives the impression of being shrewd because the full moon is over its head; but me, I have a hundred moons in the evening when my electric globes are illuminated!*

And suddenly cheered up by its long sea bath, it gathered itself and, pouncing on her, it cried, facetiously: "Check to the king!"

But it recoiled quickly. It had bumped its leg violently.

Then, vexed, remembering as it faced that sacred smile the vocabularies of Paris, it cried in the hoarse voice of a market-worker: "Camel!"

The Sphinx, like a spitting cat, simply blew on it.

Carried away by the simoom, the unfortunate three-hundred-meter tower, the nail of Paris, found itself rolled over in an instant, dislocated and buried in the sand. And it was no more than a carcass in the desert, less beautiful than that of the camel it had invoked, like the wretched debris of iron bridges dragged away by floods, at which their discouraged builders come to gaze, with folded arms, along the Saharan wadis.

THE SECRET FAY
(*Le Journal*, 23 August 1906)

THE little orphan and her charming grandfather took their places every evening near the large fireplace. There was as much space there as in a bedroom, and the fire changed form according to the season, from the logs of Christmas to the two or three brands of summer, arranged like chestnuts under the ashes.

There, one sensed the patrimonial house living around one, under its hat of ivy, and the somber garden that only ended in the sea.

From one end of the year to the other, the old gentleman told stories to his frail favorite; and in that custom he had ended up almost believing his own tales. That can happen. There are little girls who are so mysterious when one sees them holding things in their apron, coming back from the garden, their eyes announcing treasures. One leans toward them and perceives, in the apron, red berries, leaves or little pebbles; and without smiling, one remains silent, because one has understood that all of that is enchanted.

The girl, on her grandfather's knee, listened with a five-year-old's gaze, hypnotized by the fire, and sometimes the wind cried at the door like a desolate beast; or it was only the sea that was heard in the distance, occupying the horizon. But other evenings were so calm that the first nightingale of spring replaced them entirely. An odor of rain on the verdure, or warm hay or dead leaves, slid through the gaps as epochs passed. Then it was a cricket that was manifest, close by, or the little spirit of the logs that suddenly whistled.

When the tale was concluded, the child kissed her grandfather, without speaking, and allowed herself to be taken to bed. However, she never forgot, by way of conclusion, to put a kiss on the ring that the old man wore on the little finger of his left hand; for between the two of them, there was a convention on the subject of that ring. By virtue of gazing into the worn opal, they had ended up deciding together that a fay inhabited it. It was that fay who, when she moved, caused the colors of the opal to vary. She displayed her changing robe and her strange pale eyes there. And from the depths of that little universe of precious stone, omnipotent, hidden and minuscule, she protected them.

Now, after several years of that life, the inevitable happened. Because the child was still only a gamine and the grandfather had become too old, death separated them unexpectedly: a little cough and oppression for three weeks, and in the fourth, he was extinguished.

Had he understood that he was going? On the eve of his end, when he found himself alone momentarily with his little accomplice in the marvelous, without a word, he had passed the excessively large ring over the red and swollen index-finger of the little girl with a sign that meant: "Keep it." And they had then exchanged a gaze in which they expressed everything.

Is it necessary to specify the kinds of successive circumstances and affairs of inheritance following the death that changed the destinies of the old property? Beneath its ivy hat, it was obliged to sense its ancient and delightful soul abandon it when the dead master crossed the threshold in his long bier, and the little girl, in mourning and sobbing, went elsewhere.

She ended up in a black quarter of Paris, in the home of a poor aunt. False daylight stagnated through two narrow rooms. Through the windows one could only see the wall of the courtyard and a section of roof. The only patch of sky lost in those green-tinted things was no bigger than a handkerchief. And as the vague noise of the streets rose, affirming the ugliness of positive life, from the very first minute of her new existence, the sobbing child understood that she would never talk about fays again.

The aunt was a "good person," in accordance with the impression provoked by that term. By means of a few clichés regarding reverses of fortune and the loss of loved ones, she did her best to console the dolorous child. Then, without wasting time, she informed her of the secrets of restricted life, sent her to the local primary school and, since the girl was approaching her tenth year, made her darn socks and do the housework between lessons.

In addition, one could scarcely see in the evening. And because, around the oil lamp under which they ate and sewed, the conversation had the color and form of the days, the orphan with the disconcerted eyes, without knowing why, did not tell the story of her opal. She even avoided wearing the ring. She kept it enveloped in cotton wool in a little wooden box at the very bottom of a drawer in which her effects were arranged. To the first interrogation on the subject she had responded, weeping, that it was a souvenir of her grandfather, and it had never been mentioned again. The aunt thought: *That child keeps things to herself*; and that was all.

However, when, by chance, in the evening, the old woman went out for one of her meager excursions, the niece ran to her drawer. Blushing like a culpable individual, her swollen heart began to beat very rapidly; and as soon as the opal was on her finger, one might have thought that its gleam illuminated the entire dark quarter. The child no longer knew anything of the facing wall, the section of roof and the patch of sky. She sat down in a corner alone with her ring, alone with her dream. For a moment, her heart-rending nostalgia calmed down. The evoked fay acted as good godmothers do, and the frail little girl rediscovered in the color of the versatile stone everything that she no longer had.

Had not the sunsets that were once contemplated beyond the fields taken refuge one by one in that narrow space? Was that not their flame brooding there in that burning dot? Suddenly, a twitch of the hand capsized the nuances, recreating another world. It was moonlight over the garden, with droplets of clarity falling through branches. Then it became one of the brands in the fireplace where grandfather told tales. It was the rainbow they had seen one day, after the rain, above the house. And suddenly, it was the sea. By putting the opal to her ear, as one does with seashells, perhaps she would have heard the voice that occupies the horizons.

But what was certainly distinguishable most clearly in the incendiary stone were the costumes of the fay. That slender lady drew through the opal, sumptuously, the robes of Peau-d'Ane: a robe the color of time, a robe the color of the moon, a robe the color of the sun . . .

Joyfully, the little girl burst out laughing. "Quickly, quickly, where are the dark glasses?" And abruptly, to the sound of her own gaiety, she woke up from her dreams. The treasures were extinguished. The opal was no longer anything but a single eye, a discolored eye like those of the dead, which stared at her, devoid of a pupil.

Then the aunt came back. At the sound she made it was necessary to hide the ring rapidly, with a last furtive kiss on the varicolored stone, the dainty and magnificent palace of the marvelous.

A day came when the child fell ill. She was approaching the age that is called ingrate because it renders one slightly ridiculous, and is in reality that most pathetic. An ingrate age, a return of the age of childhood, a sad reversal of the first existence, in which the poetry innate in the commencing years is going to sink in puberty and be lost forever in the prosaicism of "grown-ups." In truth, the only poets are those in whom childhood is not entirely dead.

Having become, therefore, a little paler, the mysterious child took to her bed. In spite of her poverty, the frightened aunt called the doctor. Then, in the two wretched rooms, at the same time as the great drama of the child's soul—which had not revealed itself to anyone since the death of the grandfather—the paltry tragedy was played out of a lack of money in face of the costly malady, and the bill to pay: all the hidden peripeties that generally compose the existence of poor people and sculpt, at length, their habitual bleak visages.

Now, as the cares augmented, it happened that one morning, the aunt went out clandestinely, leaving the little invalid somnolent in her bed.

By means of what interior warning was she aware of that momentary solitude? Raising herself up from her pillows for the first time in a week, she looked around, and a weak smile distended her little absorbed face. Feebly and slowly, holding on to the furniture, she tottered as far as her drawer.

The wooden box trembled in her hands. She opened it.

The ring was no longer there.

In what state did the aunt find her on reentering the house? Having returned to her bed, the child seemed assassinated. At the first words, suddenly recovering her strength, she started crying out with such insensate tears, demanding her ring with such vehemence that the aunt ran to fetch the doctor.

"She's delirious! She's going to die!" she repeated, between sobs.

And the worthy physician ran downstairs, shaking his old head sympathetically.

Sitting on the edge of the bed, he interrogated her with a good deal of kindness, but he was a stranger to the destiny of the child. Without seeing anything, without hearing anything, she demanded her ring recklessly, howling toward her dream, toward her grandfather, toward her great fires, toward her past. All her soul, for the first time, expressed itself, while the two incompatible and desolate witnesses of that soul were unable to understand anything of the great appeal that she was hurling at them.

Finally, the blushing aunt was obliged to admit to the doctor the poverty of which she was ashamed. She had gone that very morning to take the ring to the Mont-de-Piété. Weeping, she showed him the receipt. As the mount of the ring was gold, and fairly heavy, she had been given forty francs for it. And her unconscious and sacrilegious mouth sadly pronounced this blasphemy:

"As for the stone, it appears that it has no value . . ."

One can imagine the fine gesture of the physician handing two louis to the poor woman, telling her to go and recover the ring and come back quickly.

Leaning on the foot of the bed, he waited patiently. The invalid, no longer looking at anything, no longer saying anything, was shivering. As soon as she heard the door open again, she exclaimed: "My ring?"

And the aunt, opening her hand, held it out to her like a star.

Then, that child, so gentle, made a brutal movement. Seizing the ring in silence, she bore it to her mouth with so much rudeness that the faded stone split against her teeth, and her feverish lips, cut by the impact, began to bleed. And then, gazing with crazed eyes at her cracked and bloodstained opal, she resumed crying out, saying: "Blood! Blood! They've killed the fay! They've killed the fay!"

That is why, losing patience, the doctor and the aunt thought it good to scold her a little. To the funereal cry she uttered, they responded with reason, that bleak thing:

"Come on," they said, "what are you saying? Are there such things as fays? It's necessary, in sum, for you to remain tranquil. You're no longer a child, you know."

And the little girl, as if struck by a great blow, shut up. Her hands fallen back, she looked by turns at her ring and the two irritated gown-ups with eyes in which the marvelous was dying.

For she had just understood that her realm was lost, the realm of childhood that everyone has to renounce one day. It was necessary to enter into the banal dolor of living. And because of that, her heart of a little woman broke in her breast, like the damaged opal in which the fay was quietly dying.

THE ROMANCE OF THE LITTLE SHOE
(*Le Journal*, 16 September 1906)

THE shoe-cupboard, as pretty as a drawing room, brought together a charming company.

The members of that society, quite renewable, were varnished or mat, with laces or buttons, black, chamois or yellow, or even red-heeled or golden. They conversed a great deal in the shoe language, by means of little creaks full of delicacy. They were very worldly. They had vanities, jealousies and disappointments that they did not talk about, but they told one another delicate lies. Above all, they gossiped.

In turn, each couple, on reentering the circle when their service was finished, recounted what they had observed of life. Thus, as soon as the door opened and the hands of the chambermaid deposited some shiny seigneur and his double in the middle of the crowd of other shoes, each one awoke from the somnolence of long days and was all ears, fully extended.

But no one had a success like two black twins, with a low neckline and varnished tips. Was it because the little toes, the masters of the cupboard, found themselves particularly comfortable in their supple kid-leather? The pair of those preferred shoes went out more often than the entire company put together. In the evenings, a circle formed round them. They knew so many things! One can imagine what stories a pair of shoes might have to tell, being the base and support of that adorable, important and complicated edifice: a lady!

Their existence went by in delightful emotion. They alternated between the carpet of the dressmaker, as thick as a lawn, and the green grass of the Bois, as neat as a carpet. They knew the footstep of the coupé and the asphalt of the sidewalk. They knew the rustle of skirts, the fragile reliquary of juxtaposed underclothes, and spider-silk stockings, in which the dear ten digits that they contained lived like roses. They knew the beautiful log fires before which the little clandestine feet allowed themselves to be warmed, when a trembling hand held them naked in its exact palm. They also knew what happened under the table at meals, and many other things, in detail.

Their correctness would perhaps have suffered from that, had it not been for the two severe shoe-trees that, after each excursion, inflexibly remade their character. They had, moreover, so much verve, in spite of their impeccable manners, that the slippers, which never went out of the apartment, loosened their stitches, laughing when they listened to them, showing their teeth of thread, all the way to the soul.

A day came, however, when their fine appearance felt tarnished. That was because of the extraordinary glare with which the cupboard was illuminated by two new green velvet shoes that no one had previously seen or imagined.

It was early morning. They arrived still warm from a famous costumed ball, the last of the season, where the little feet had danced all night. What did the costume signify of which they were the complement? That scarcely touched the society of the cupboard. It was only necessary to know that they were perched high on their heels and as shiny as young leaves, with a certain something archaic and complex in the cut, which gave them an infinite aristocracy, and explained their haughty attitude.

No one dared interrogate them. But there was whispering around them, and the shoes that were literate immediately thought about Cinderella and her slipper of *verre* or *vair*—the orthography does not matter.[1] Those two words were fused into one alone, and that quite naturally became *vert*, like the newcomers. Green shoes, enchanted shoes; one sensed, merely by looking at them, the peripeties through which they had just passed; for the fulguration of the ballroom chandeliers remained among their reflections, making of them, in truth, a couple of unforgettable suns.

It was just at that moment, before having known the identity of the marvelous velvet visitors, that the black twins were apprehended by the hands of the chambermaid and taken to the apartment of their mistress.

The poor things did not know that they were going in that fashion to their destiny.

In fact, having arrived before the trunk in which they were about to be packed away for the annual departure to the country, they heard the voice to which the little feet belonged. It said, quite distinctly: "No, Joséphine, not those. You can keep them for yourself."

And that was such a horrible speech that the pair fainted, with a single similar movement.

How long did they remain inert? They were in the country when they woke up again, one after the other, under the impression of a sharp pain: Joséphine was wearing them.

From then on, they knew a tortured life. Their narrow points revolted the maid's toes. There was a long dolorous struggle. The new feet, not finding sufficient space to lodge their lumpy form, molested the unfortunate shoes to the extent of wounding them grievously. Disfigured and split, they no longer know

---

1 Pseudoscholars suspecting Charles Perrault's tale of a folkloristic origin—in fact he stole it from salon tales improvised by Mademoiselle l'Héritier and Madame d'Aulnoy—suggested that an original slipper of *vair* [fur] might have been replaced by one of *verre* [glass] by tellers ambiguous in their pronunciation.

51

the unctuous unguent with which their somber elegance was coated every morning, not the rigorous shoe-trees that raised their morale so vigorously every evening. And what spectacles, during the days, what promiscuities!

They were the same mores, however, but in cotton stockings and in corners of mansards, or even the kitchens. One day they knew the supreme shame: under the table in the servants' parlor, a man's clogs, reeking from having been treading the stables, made them propositions.

That was an adventure such that one of them, unable to overcome the humiliation, committed suicide. With the particular science that objects possess for gestures of that sort, it escaped from the maid's hands, and before she had time to catch it, let itself fall in the middle of the fireplace, before which a roast was turning.

Joséphine's wrath was the only funeral oration of the desperate individual; after which the remaining shoe, useless henceforth, was thrown brutally on to the rubbish heap. Buried in an unknown world of rags, broken crockery, shards of glass and detritus, it found itself alongside the garden wall in an alleyway. The cherished, advantageous, successful shoe was expelled from the house henceforth and alone in the world. Nothing of its former splendor subsisted. Veritably, it seemed to belong, from birth, to the sad race of beggars.

That is why, passing by, some vagabond, one of those who drag themselves around behind a caravan, immediately took possession of it. One of her brown feet was naked, and she shoved it swiftly into the unpaired shoe, and, almost joyful at her find, resumed her route less painfully. Her other foot was clad in an old masculine boot.

It was necessary to walk for months in that company along roads of dust or mud. And the unfortunate shoe did not take long to comprehend that, in the time of Joséphine, it had still been fortunate. Had it not had, in that epoch, its partner in misery, its fellow, to whom to communicate its chagrins? Now, next to that surly soldierly boot, obliged to roam the roads like a trooper, it had to suffer the conversation of that boot, led relentlessly by temperament to make coarse jokes, and whose language was bristling with revolting leather.[1]

A day came, however, when, without the brown foot even having perceived it, the shoe was abandoned. It mattered so little! It remained alone in the corner of a road, definitively lost, forgotten forever.

The road had no traffic. It knew complete solitude there, on the edge of a former ditch, as tragic as a scar. The seasons passed over it. It contained, by turns, dead leaves and ordure, gravel and fallen chestnuts, in the very place where the little toes of its past had throbbed. It felt viler than a threadbare slipper, finished, like a formerly pretty woman overflowing with experience and bitterness.

It was a desolate time to remember. The brilliant companies of its youth passed through its memory, the cupboard as pretty as a drawing room, the tender and adventurous excursions of little feet full of audacity, and like roses. Its reminiscences persisted above all on the last vision of its happiness, those green velvet shoes, high on their heels, like young leaves, which, still warm from the ball at which they had danced, were shining with all their reflections like a couple of unforgettable suns.

In the regard of the two marvelous visitors, what had it become, the lamentable once-black shoe? It thought that it had, for a minute of its life, envied their green magnificence; and it established the difference between what one dreams of being and what one is . . . the comical aspect of that disparity! It had a desire to laugh as loudly as the slippers of old. Now, as the damp had penetrated it to saturation point, it could only weep large tears, in silence. That was, moreover, a relief.

---

1 The French word *cuir* [leather] is used familiarly to refer to incorrection in speech, especially when salacious.

After many seasons and after-seasons, it found itself one morning in the middle of an April shower. Under the rain that soaked the road, a puddle gradually formed alongside it. And as embellishments follow bad weather, it saw in a fugitive sunbeam everything that was reflected in that puddle. There was a large swaying branch with its birds, a patch of blue sky, and a round, white cloud. The shoe was distracted by all that momentarily. Then, as the rain had returned, the puddle grew, menacing it.

And it said to itself, with the bitterness of the old and disabused: "There it is! I'm not wet enough! That puddle is going to cover me and I'll be a little more unhappy. Life is decidedly something that goes from bad to worse . . . What was I thinking, to envy the green shoes? I would truly be too content, at present, if I still belonged to the old gypsy, following the wheels next to the worthy boot. Now, paralyzed in my place, I no longer have any shape . . . and that accursed water is going to submerge me and freeze me! If only it could drown me . . . at least then I'd be finished with life."

Suddenly, a prodigy was produced. As the water reached it, it perceived its reflection in the puddle, a fugitive natural mirror. And it was a green velvet shoe, shining like a young leaf, as splendid as an unforgettable sun!

For in the silence and the darkness, moss had covered it; and it understood that it was dead, and that its afterlife was commencing. Green shoe, enchanted shoe—because, like the bird, the branch and the cloud, it had entered into the rhythm of universal life, because it had become vegetal, like the plants, and immutable, like the stones; changing destiny could no longer attain it. Henceforth, on beautiful evenings, the glowworm would take up residence within it; the toad would sing its unique note there, and a thousand golden insects would burrow through its adornment.

The finished shoe, the beggar, the rag, was now glorious and alive—immortal.

THE PHANTOM AUTO
(Le Journal, 12 October 1906)

A moon rising in the forest of Brothonne announced the summer night, so pure that even the footfalls of the game would not have dared to disturb the enigmatic, as if submarine, life of the moonlight. The invisible red deer confounded, without moving, its animal branches with those of the ferns and the trees, and twelve-hundred-year beeches, enchanted by the blue night, were able, in the absolute immobility, to resume their Merovingian dream.

But who could know whether, at that sacred moment, a quiver might run through the beech groves, and whether, on the horizon, wheels were already growling and two menacing points of light, quickly growing, might not annul before them, as they approached noisily, the moonlight ecstasized in its balsamic silence?

It is thus that one night, through lunar Brothonne, the long veils of women, stretched by speed, trailed and writhed behind a vertiginous auto. It had just been precipitated down a hill, and in a single bound, the portion of humankind contained in the machine was allowing itself to be carried away, as if to the abyss.

The mind blurred by having seen too many things in one day, without the time necessary to classify them in passing, one has traversed four départements. Having departed at daybreak, one is drunk on geography and wind, in order to end up now supping in the forest by the glare of the headlights. And since, for hours, in the disorder of meager baggage and fallen blankets, young people have been huddled together in the packed vehicle, doubtless the atmosphere of slight amorous adventure that slyly and delicately envelops almost every social gathering has taken on for some, excited by that sort of heroism of speed, a more passionate and grave character . . .

The severe old comte, the driver of the vehicle, absorbed in some dream, did not know what was happening, nor did the little comrade clinging to him, the seven-year-old child whose large naïve eyes were slightly dilated, magnetized by the moonlight.

The entire complex deceit of salons was therefore palpitating, packed into that narrow space. From time to time, the shrill voice of the child traversed the hypocritical silence. It was a candid little refrain, a childish obsession: "Tell me, Monsieur, do you think that we might see King Dagobert?"[1] And the old comte replied with words that no one heard, good and jolly things such as it is necessary to say to little girls. They only perceived that there was mention of fays and Saint Eloi. Thus their little poetic romance continued through the evening, so sensual and enervated for others . . .

Oh, the race to the abyss, the race to amour! When the eyes of women are languid behind large goggles and their mouths, alone naked under the masks, are red with the desire for a kiss already consented, which might possess them more entirely because those instants when speed and desire are only a single vertigo, when someone holds them against an abandoned self,

---

1 Dagobert I (c603-639) was the last king of the Franks of the Merovingian dynasty. His name was familiar to French children because of an allegedly-ancient nursery rhyme in which he accidentally puts his trousers on backwards, in the presence of his chief counsellor, Eloi, or Eligius, who subsequently attempted to Chistianize Flanders and was canonized in recognition of that effort. Skeptics suggest that the song was actually a satire composed during the 1789 Revolution to mock the divine right of kings.

when they sense themselves, in the furtive grip that enlaces them, finally carried away as they have always wanted to be . . .

Another descent. A frisson passes. The eyes are closed as if in a faint. And the shrill voice of the child repeats, hallucinated: "Might we encounter the king, Monsieur? Are we going to encounter him?"

Then, suddenly, they have arrived. It is necessary to get out, astonished to resume being on foot so abruptly. A woman stretches herself. To break an awkward silence, Princesse Patricia,[1] whose pose is to have been very badly brought up, makes boorish quips. They plunge into the wood on foot. And as there are little round-dances of light in the moss, the skirts give the impression of trailing through stars.

When they were sitting in a circle at the chosen spot, illuminated by the headlights, facing the disposed victuals, they perceived that they were very hungry. Around the laughter and cheerful remarks that bubbled with the pink champagne, the forest seemed to draw nearer and close in. Through everything, they sensed around them an immense propitious living mystery. And as the wide eyes of the little girl dilated a little more regarding the possible apparitions of the night, those of the grown-ups allowed deep gazes to filter between their lashes, for they were thinking about moonlit beds and black branches in the depths of which, under the simple sky of August, the kisses so long in preparation could finally be exchanged furiously.

At midnight, the champagne having gone to the heads and completed the intoxication of the clandestine engagements, the headlights were switched off. That was a caprice of the women. Abruptly, the moonlight had taken possessions of people and

1 When Lucie Delarue obtained her revenge on her older sisters for their teasing in becoming a "professional beauty" she was nicknamed "Princesse Amande." Princesse Patricia, who is an exaggerated and rather unkind self-portrait of the author, viewed from an older and wiser viewpoint, presumably acquired her honorary title in a similar fashion.

things again, extending its large neat shadows over the moss and making bright patches through the foliage, organizing its insidious games of light everywhere.

The old comte raised his sparkling glass, which was suddenly illuminated by a glacial blue reflection; and, turning to his little seven-year-old friend he said: "I'm drinking to King Dagobert."

Nervously, the little girl huddled against him. For a moment, already, she had thought she was seeing things. It seemed to her that singular individuals were among the guests; but she dared not say so out loud. However, she noticed that two ladies had planted their lorgnettes on their noses; then there was Sir Welly, who was sticking out his chin and blinking; and finally, Monsieur Ernheim, the young billionaire collector who, outside museums, was not passionate about anything; even Princesse Patricia and her beautiful friend, the old comte's niece, appeared to be prodigiously interested in what was happening in the middle of the supper. As for the old comte, his eyes gradually became strangely fixed.

Now, no one could any longer doubt that a company as colored and diaphanous as church windows was mingled with that of the supper. Everyone could see the Merovingian individuals distinctly. But even the little girl did not feel very frightened because, alive or dead, everyone becomes a specter in the moonlight. And in her shrill voice she addressed the first and most apparent of the visitors.

"You're King Dagobert, aren't you?" she interrogated.

The phantom made a sign that undoubtedly meant *yes*. Then the child clapped her hands. But young Ernheim interrupted her joy.

"It's not Dagobert," he said, pedantically. "It can only be Clotaire II.[1] You know very well that it's his palace whose ruins are in this forest and . . ."

---

1 Clotaire or Chlothar II (584-629) was Dagobert's father and predecessor as king of the Franks; His own kingdom was Neustria, which included the modern Normandy and the subsequent royal forest of Brothonne.

But the shrill voice cut him off.

"Isn't it so, revenant, that you're King Dagobert?"

The transparent monarch laughed silently. He only seemed to understand half the words. He lowered his crowned head into his unkempt beard. Then he formulated: "Perhaps. You know, we probably don't pronounce words in the same fashion."

His hoarse voice was so cavernous that they truly did not hear the timbre; and young Ernheim remarked: "He's definitely a Merovingian king, in any case; his golden crown can be distinguished now, and the colors of his robe. The other individuals are no less well-conserved. We're doubtless over the ruins of the palace where the mosaic was found recently that is now in the museum of Rouen."

"Oh, those ruins!" cried Patricia. "They're the traces of *ragot*.[1] Come on, Sire, try to be a little clearer. Although we all seem to be sitting outside, are we in your palace, yes or no?"

The king made an affirmative sign. Perhaps he did not like to talk too much. However, his archaic voice pronounced: "I no longer had anything left but that mosaic . . . but these wild boars . . ."

The rest being lost in the royal hair, Patricia let her lorgnette fall and murmured: "What a bore . . ." And without taking any more interest in King Dagobert's court, she stood up and went to sit down again further away, near those who had chosen to be in shadow.

But the little girl was hanging on to the old comte's arm, and she begged him: "Speak to him yourself, Monsieur, will you?"

And the comte, turning toward the king with a very elegant gesture, commenced: "Sire, since the hazards of moonlight have brought us together, suffer that I say to Your Majesty that I have

---

1 This word had several meanings by 1906; Patricia presumably means "gossip" or "rumor," but prior to the era of modern slang a *ragot* was a young wild boar, which explains the phantom king's subsequent reference.

desired to meet you for a very long time, for I love the things of olden times and . . ."

But he stopped of his own accord, for the phantom king, suddenly animated, had just extended a great solemn arm, and his giant barbaric beard was already stirred by the words he was about to pronounce. And through the translucent sleeve of his violet and red robe the branches of the nearby beeches could be seen, agitating gently in the moonlight.

He said: "The olden times! Yes, I see now. You're the aerial beings of the dear old times for which we, contemporaries of this cold seventh century, have so much regret. If you could comprehend the nights I have spent searching for you through the branches! And now you have come to appear to me in my own palace! I knew that it was necessary not to despair. When I was only a child, my nurse sang me your past history while rocking me to sleep on moonlit evenings; and I am doing justice very late to the poor old woman; she did not lie. You are Merlin, the enchanter of Broceliande. These are Viviane and the other fays, with their fallen wings, those long pink, green, blue or white wings that one can see fluttering around them when they fly, and which, at present, envelop them like simple veils. And over there is the enchanted chariot, the one I believed that I recognized many a time on these forest nights when the beeches are haunted. It has now closed its great bee's eyes, but I can make it out. So, then, there really are spirits! You, revenants from the earliest centuries, cannot know what love we have for the ancient ages that were yours. For in our epoch the bees, magnified, do not move in those buzzing chariots. Alas, alas, our time is so distant from yours. The marvelous is no more. The fays are dead . . ."

He was speaking so loudly now that even those in the shadow had started listening; and the princesse, scandalized, bounded to her feet.

"Old man." she cried, with anguish, "have you finished treating us as revenants?"

And her furious little hand pinched Monsieur Ernheim's arm hard enough to draw blood, in order to see whether the young billionaire was alive or dead.

Now, facing the old comte, the king from more than a thousand years ago shook his head delightedly.

"The fays . . . the fays," he said, gazing at Patricia. "O Enchanter, I implore you, let them not disappear immediately! Remain with us for a while! Or rather, take me away. My companions can stay here. Take me, O Merlin, in the chariot of my nurse's songs . . ."

His excitement was such that the comte, in his turn, put his hand to his forehead to assure himself that he was really flesh and bone. And, his fingers having encountered the cold glass of his goggles, he began to shiver; for neither he nor his companions, in truth, knew where they were going.

Patricia however, still had the strength to say: "Don't take this old dead man. He's quite capable of dying of fear. You can see that he's feeling ill." And she repeated, without knowing why: "That he's feeling ill . . . that he's feeling ill . . ."

How, again, were they all back in the auto and on the road? The machine, without headlights, was traveling at a hundred and twenty an hour. Only the crown of the age-old king was illuminating the road. He was sitting, impalpably, next to the old comte, who was bent over the steering wheel, but his bearded person did not seem to be embarrassing the little girl, who, not being able to take any more marvels, was asleep on her old friend's shoulder.

In the back, inert, the others were allowing themselves to be carried away without saying anything. Only young Ernheim, fascinated by the king's crown, was repeating in Patricia's ear:

"What a piece for my collection! Do you think he'd sell it to me? What if I could steal it instead, while he wasn't paying attention?"

And as they emerged from the forest, suddenly, an exclamation from Patricia woke all somnolences with a start.

"But it's the moon!"

"What?" cried all the voices.

"The crown," Patricia continued. "The crown!"

And looking, frightened, they all asked at the same time: "Where's the king?"

The child woke up, and also said: "Where's the king?"

But it was necessary to agree that he had evaporated completely, and that no trace of him remained. And Patricia cried triumphantly: "I told you so! He's vanished!"

Then, in the din of the auto, which was climbing a hill, in a voice that was slightly thick, she sang in the face of young Ernheim, the bewildered collector and billionaire, who was searching desperately for a crown in the moon:

It's King Dagobert
Who has put our brains in reverse.

FUNEREAL MATERNITY
(*Le Journal*, 6 November 1906)

A former beauty raised herself up from between the cushions where she was coddling her forty-eight years, rang, and had herself dressed for her fortnightly excursion to the cemetery. Tall and dark in the heavy fabrics, her head plumed, she still seemed pretty to those who perceived her, against the window of the coupé, her face pale with maternity and make-up, where dreamy blue eyes, aggravated by a pathetic bruising, gazed. The bunches of dear flowers that she was taking were heaped up around her. The horses trotted nervously through the Auteuil mud.

At the cemetery, she advanced alone, laden with her flowers, toward the customary tomb, distantly situated. A slightly moist good weather reigned over the last roses, the named marbles and the wreaths of glass. The box-trees, innocently, spread the cheerful odor of gardening through the solemnity of death.

At a bend, a yellow leaf necessary to that autumnal scene, trailing somewhere, attached itself in passing and accompanied the pedestrian, mingled with the somber flow of her skirt.

She walked slowly, as if carrying with precaution, through the little pathways, the wounded femininity of mature women. Her head bowed, more dolorous in sensing herself so similar to the after-season, she ruminated her mourning with the same movement with which one bites a bitter stem.

It was not, in reality, that she thought very much about her widowhood, or even about the few amours that, important in their time, had perhaps traversed her past. But she repeated obstinately that her youth had known eight times the malaise and delight of those who are pregnant, and eight times her hope had only ended in a minuscule unfinished cadaver, the poor fruit of her entrails, unskillful in bearing their treasure all the way.

With what a stubborn soul, and what stubborn flesh she had expended her share of human force in that disappointing effort! And now, the age of conception was no more. She had progressed toward old age, wearier and more exhausted than true mothers, but unaccompanied, all alone, in the shame and despair of sterility. Everything, including her mourning, including the flowers she was carrying, was for her nothing but emptiness and irony. She had tried hard to be her own dupe, but she knew only too well what a funereal sham the tomb toward which she was walking represented. She knew that the eight poor stillborns buried under a single stone were not worth, all together, the unique true remains of a child; she knew that the tomb had no name, and could not have one, because it was only the sepulcher of her dream, a sort of trickery aimed at destiny.

Thus, the need that almost all women have to give birth had remained in her like an unsatisfied sensuality. And because that great animal desire, which also tortures beasts, raising the pacific plumage of hens in May to brood, had seized its prey so forcefully, she had tried, with all the violence of her thwarted instinct, to hang on to something. Having been unable to know maternal joy, she had invented maternal grief. She had forged a dead child with the inviable flesh, the sad flesh of her abortions . . .

She walked more slowly still. Then the tomb appeared to her. And there was, even so, a surge of tenderness, as on seeing again the little face of a baby.

Having concluded the vague prayer with which she always honored the thick marble, she disposed the flowers she had brought thereon, elegantly, with the neat gestures of a milliner. It was an intense momentary distraction for her. Then, when she had stepped back in order to judge the effect, she understood that, abruptly, her soul was falling back to its habitual bleak place, and she felt mortally unoccupied.

What to do? What to do? What to do? interrogated her entire anguished being. And in despair, she started turning round, like a wounded beast who wants to end it all. However, by the habitude of mundane discipline, she started walking again, quickly and correctly, straight ahead. Her staring eyes gazed at the tombs without seeing them. She spelled out the names without comprehending them. Her pace was almost rapid.

Suddenly, she was surrounded by another aspect of the cemetery, a landscape that she did not recognize. Astonished, she returned to herself. She was in the paupers' area.

She divined that immediately, without knowing why; and it provoked a beneficent beating of the heart. A thousand reflections suddenly furnished her mind. It was like a handful of grain thrown under a mill that was rotating in a void.

So there was a poor quarter even in the cemetery? Even death had its hierarchy. She had never thought of that before. A guardian went past. She interrogated him. He explained the difference. A concession in perpetuity for the rich, a temporary plot for the poor. After five years of eternity, the common ditch.

"And the children?" her obsession formulated, almost involuntarily.

"For the children, it's the same," he responded, with an amused laugh. "Only they have a special area."

At what a precipitate pace she headed now toward that special quarter suddenly revealed to her. When she commenced to perceive from afar the accumulation of frail iron tombs and white pearls she stopped, afflicted. So that was the dormitory of puerile death! All those little beds, all those humble funerary cradles that she distinguished, huddled together, were the austere crèche from which not one cry of childish rage, not one twitter, not one burst of laughter, ever rose?

Carried away by the whirlwind of her sensations, quivering, she remained there, without budging, without daring to approach any closer. And now, the quite natural presence of a woman of the people, whom she distinguished in the midst of those things, upset her. Standing before one of those short white tombs, the woman, seen from afar, seemed to be weeping.

In consequence of what irreflective movement were those two contrasted creatures beside one another? The plumed head of one brushed the hair of the other, poorly protected by one of those headscarves with which poor women cover their ears, knotted in an ugly fashion under the chin.

Very simply, a conversation was engaged.

"A little girl or a little boy?" asked the lady, in a muffled voice.

"A little girl," replied the poor mother, with a sob.

And, having looked at one another, they exchanged an intense gaze, the afflicted gaze of women deprived of their child, the incurable gaze, the magnificently unconscious gaze arriving from the depths of feminine entrails, where the rancor persists forever of someone who can no longer pardon life, because their reason for being has been suppressed.

Large tears rolled from the eyes of the young woman of the people. They inundated a face without freshness; for poverty, in passing over the twenty-five years of the poor, gives them in advance the dead cheeks of old age.

And the lady in black, pale with maturity and make-up, gazed with a sort of terror at that arid young face, that little thirteen-franc tomb, and the meager bouquet of violets preciously deposited on the earth beneath a unique wreath of white pearls hung on the iron cross; and she understood that the bouquet was a luxury and that the wreath represented a treasure, with its pink cardboard angel flying under a bulbous window between two blue banners.

Meanwhile, the young woman devoid of a hat, through her tears, continued to recount her chagrin with abundance and monotony. Avidly interrogated, she then spoke in detail about her dead daughter, the color of her eyes, her curly hair and the little words that she was already saying.

"A child all brought up," she repeated, with a redoubling of tears, "who has cost me so much money!"

And the rich woman, in her ignorance of matters of poverty, was extremely astonished by the positive aspect of the dolor of the poor, in which the material loss always enters by half into regret, even at the very edge of a child's tomb. The abstraction of her own woe, all silence and profundity resembled so scantly the true mourning that she had before her eyes, which appeared so brutally and so vulgarly alive in its energetic reality.

In the end, relieved by having spoken and wept so much, the other fell silent, and, still inflated by sighs, commenced examining her interlocutor with some interest. Then a glimmer passed through her eyes, something already familiar, almost complicit. She said: "You've lost one too?"

The plumed head had turned away abruptly. Ashamed, her voice strangled by the emotion of the lie, the lady replied in a low voice: "Yes."

They remained face to face for a moment, looking at one another; and the mystery of their unequal souls dramatized the brief silence.

Then the lady breathed out, running in advance, as if pursued by the terror of saying anything more.

"Listen . . . wait for me here for a moment, will you?"

The mild weather of the after-season reigned alone over things. The woman of the people, surprised and docile, waited patiently in front of the iron cross, the wreath and the two-sou bouquet of violets placed over the little dead girl. And now, from the depths of the tightly-packed tombs and the autumn, she saw the woman with the beautiful plumes and the heavy black fabrics returning toward her, holding in her full arms a host of flowers of all colors, such as no one had ever seen.

The poor woman, before that, was about to open her mouth to exclaim, but before she had finished her movement the lady was upon her, tall, pale and almost terrible.

And it was in a gesture of rage that the flowers, all the large extraordinary flowers, taken from the nameless marble of the rich quarter, were thrown into the wretched arms of the poor mother, so content and so amazed that she was frightened. And the strangled voice, the ashamed voice, said at close range, into the ears poorly hidden by the poor headscarf of beggar-women: "Take them! They're all for you! For your child . . . because you alone have the right to them . . . you alone."

Then the poor woman, buried under the costly flowers, commenced a gesture in which her entire soul was expressed.

But her inexplicable benefactress, without waiting for thanks, was already drawing away with long strides. Her forehead lowered like that of a vanquished rival, sweeping the muddy pathways with the somber wave of her beautiful skirts, she drew away, humiliated, dispossessed, finished, and probably never to return.

THE NOCTURNAL DUCHESSE
(*Le Journal*, 29 November 1906)

W AS it the Les Halles quarter or the Rue Galande? That was what the three ladies scarcely cared to know. Perhaps their four or five men knew. And then, after all, was not the café waiter—who, being in the secret police, was guiding the band—taking them where it was necessary to go? Why fatigue the mind by remembering street names? They did not have eyes enough, on that clandestine November night, to get a good look at the delightful horrors of the Underworld.

The duchesse, in particular, who had a habit of analyzing everything, experienced some difficulty in classifying her successive and violent sensations. In addition, she regretted her lorgnette, which she had been prevented from taking. Not that she was myopic, but it was a very necessary thing for her to see life framed between two crystal lenses with tortoiseshell rims

However, she consoled herself by means of the amusement of trailing one of her chambermaid's skirts through the night and the back-streets and sensing a little two-franc-fifty hat, bought during the day for the circumstance, posed on her complicated coiffure. That disguise was almost the adventure. Moreover, she knew that she was pretty anyway, dressed up like a streetwalker. It was a contrast curiously favorable to her precious complexion, made of flesh already bruised and delicate make-up, and to her hair, which rendered all the gold of a chemistry full of tact, and to her dark blue dilated eyes, dramatized by a touch of kohl.

She seemed to herself to be a singular person in these sticky quarters; and she shuddered when she spoke, on hearing the sound of her own voice, that exquisitely cultivated, moving, slightly veiled, slightly halting voice, which was one of her surest seductions. She even took such pleasure in it that several times, Sir Welly had to remark to her: "Let's not talk too much. It's too 'grand dukes' tour,' you know. We'll be noticed."

The café waiter approved. And the little baronne, terrified, secretly wishing to be at home, clung to her husband a little. As for the duchesse's friend, she affected indifference. Deep down, however, they were all scared. That was what they were seeking.

When they had arrived at the first door of the cabarets and night-shelters that they were going to see, the café waiter emphasized his importance a little more. Hearts beat faster. In the wilted brains of the society band, it was the commencement of a nightmare of choice.

An entrance: a little cashier under a smoky Argand lamp. They go up, without seeing it, a crooked stairway. A composite and dirty odor commences with the first steps. At the moment of penetrating into the cabaret, the café waiter whispers explanations: the people who frequent this place are those who live in Les Halles. They sleep by day and work by night. Between two shifts they come to take a glass. But there are always secret police in the next room.

And that is filed away in the duchesse's head: *Les Halles. Nocturnal workshops. All those who come to this cabaret are at least thieves, dangerous nocturnal beasts.*

70

As soon as the door is pushed there are wooden tables and stools under poor lamps. A few young men, sitting down, give the impression of waiting for something. Someone is tapping an out-of-tune piano. One man sings, then another. The duchesse thinks: *gypsies and apaches*. And she also thinks: *The women are very ugly, bare-headed, hair not at all arranged. And then, they truly have excessively surly expressions, the women of the Underworld! But the men are good looking. I must admit that some of these assassins are rather exciting.*

One of them has noticed her right away, a little red-headed fellow with strange eyes, clad in black and coiffed in a gust of wind, like a poet. The duchesse has seen his gaze and concluded: *That Villon is lapping me up*. But they scarcely have time to take in the atmosphere before the bare-headed women, their mouths askew, start mocking: "It's the grand dukes' tour! Get away!"

A general growl responds to them.

"It's necessary to go," whispers the café waiter.

And they go back down the rickety stairway, twisting their feet in the precipitation of the exit.

The little baronne begs to go home. The men waver and consult one another. The duchesse's friend does not unclench her teeth. But the duchesse's eyes darken. It's necessary to continue the dangerous night.

They go elsewhere, and then somewhere else. Here they go up three floors, there they go down three. And the duchesse's mind is magnificently perplexed; for she has noticed, without saying anything to anyone, that the young Villon has slyly followed her through all the stairways and all the nocturnal dives. *Is it because he wants to murder me or because he loves me?* she wonders. And with a frisson in all her nerves, she hopes that it is for one or the other motive.

They have been able to sit down under low ceilings around a candle in a corner. The nauseating taste of poverty, and doubtless of crime, enters via your nostrils and mouth, going all the way to the heart. And now a hand, probably an old offender, has pinched the bottom of the baronne hard enough to draw blood. She dissimulates the grimace of the bruise and tries not to be noticed, for fear of imminent murder.

"Ha ha!" says a man without underwear. "A pretty chair-back for a mate." And, moving his stool closer to the duchesse, he leans against her tranquilly, smoking his pipe.

How delightful it is, she says to herself, *to have a murderer leaning on me!* And she anticipates with horror catching a few infamous beasts. The men are red-faced, but they shut up under the terrifying gaze of the café waiter. Then they get up. There is only one more place to visit: the night-shelter.

"Let's not go there!" says the tearful baronne.

"Oh, it's not dangerous," said the policeman waiter. "They sleep!"

They sleep. The shelter opens at six o'clock in the evening and closes at six o'clock in the morning. For two sous one can lodge there; for four sous, one has in addition a glass of water and a hunk of bread. They sleep . . .

The human beasts are piled up in the snores and vague insults of semi-conscious slumber. The first arrivals are in stalls that are immediately reminiscent of a stable. The later arrivals content themselves with leaning on tables, their heads buried in their arms, and the last to arrive sleep under the tables, between the feet of the others, who kick them while dreaming. They sleep . . .

There are open mouths and heads tipped back, which makes one think of the guillotine. From time to time, a haggard bloodshot eye opens, and looks at the duchesse without seeing her. She searches for her lorgnette with a feverish hand. She sticks out her neck in order to see better. Then, as everything is tranquil, she finally exchanges a few reflections with her friend, the baronne and the men, in a low voice. They communicate their recent impressions.

"Those horrible bare-headed women . . . those rags . . . that piano . . ."

Suddenly, the duchesse shuts up and gives the signal for the departure; she has just perceived the young Villon, motionless and red-headed in a corner, who is examining her . . .

✳

A première at the Français, a lecture at the Sorbonne, four teas, three sessions at the hairdresser's, another at the dentist's, a Sunday at Chevillard's, and an amorous rendezvous or two sufficed, in a few days, to efface from the mind of the duchesse the strong impression brought back from Les Halles or the Rue Galande. Even when she went to bed, she no longer rediscovered the frisson. Her embroidered pillows, haunted momentarily by some terror, had once again become as bleak as usual. And she had not even caught a single flea from the assassin!

That day, when she went to bed, she wanted to die. Sitting in the pink and white of her bed, amid the subtle perfume of her last toilette, surrounded by the fabrics, furniture and trinkets of her complex luxury, she wanted to stretch herself out and writhe in the despair of ennui. But she feared, by virtue of some excessively abrupt movement, making her gloves full of cream crack, or disturbing the anti-wrinkle mask, the quasi-funereal bandages of which were always wrapped around her greasy face while she slept.

She had a headache, for which she blamed her chamber-maid, who had tightened her hair too much. She looked sadly at that night-tress, so pitiful in spite of its golden color. It was the solitary hour of the quotidian ugliness, unknown even to her husband. She thought about her forty-four years, strongly marked by perpetual excesses devoid of true pleasure, about her temples, which were going gray under the dye, and about her false hair in the drawer. Then she thought about her body, a trifle used, which shower-bath attendants, masseuses and corset-makers surveyed anxiously at close range.

And she found as she went to sleep that life was truly not good.

Until what hour did her eyelids remain closed in the forgetfulness of slumber? When she woke up with a start, no glimmer of daylight had yet appeared at the windows. The flame of the night-light was still flickering in the alabaster, casting great elastic shadows in the room, which stretched and shrank in silence in the corners. And now the duchesse, having opened her eyes wide, felt herself suddenly turned to stone by terror.

All around her bed stood motionless beings who were gazing at her silently, their arms folded. A single idea traversed her mind: *Burglars!* And having sat up in her pillows, she perceived that the entire room was full of similar beings, all equally mute, with their arms folded. And the nauseating odor of poverty, and doubtless of crime, commenced in the agitated half-light to enter her nostrils and her mouth, going all the way to the heart.

She made a gesture toward the electricity, as if to ring or to switch on the light, but her arm fell back, inert, for a voice had risen, which said to her: "Don't excite yourself so much, Madame."

Although it was the first time she had heard it, she recognized that voice. It could only have emerged, precise, ironic and distinguished, from the thin mouth of the Villon of the other evening, the man who had followed her so obstinately through the detours of the shady quarters. And with an unusual rapidity, her mind deduced from that an entire clear explanation. He had continued to follow her slyly, then, all the way to her house. He had taken imprints, picked locks. Now he had come in. Now he was there, before her, with all his companions in horror, and, like so many others, she was about to be audaciously murdered in her home, in her bed.

But the ironic voice cut through the thought. Without changing his attitude in any way the red-haired man with the strange eyes went on:

"Don't worry. We're not going to do you any harm. You came to see us the other time, why should you be astonished that we're returning your visit? To each his turn! The whim took us, tonight, to come and see what the rich look like when they sleep . . ."

And without occupying himself with her any further, turning toward the scarcely-divined mass of the men and women filling the room, he commenced, in the tone of a lecturer: "This explains to you, Mesdames, why the fact of being 'bare-headed' astonishes this race so much. Note the near-baldness of that forehead. It is, moreover, a very curious subject of study. You observe, do you not, that they are masked in their beds, as they are in their autos, it is, therefore, a natural penchant to be apes for half their life. For how many hours a day do they show their true faces?"

The duchesse finally found her voice. Turning toward the electricity for a second time, she pushed one of the buttons at random, and at the same time she uttered a loud hoarse cry, which tore her throat in passing.

Brutal light inundated the walls. Then, from all sides at once, in the white and pink bedroom, stifled, guttural and terrible, the raucous timbre of males mingling with that of hoarse females, laughter began to swell, the dull rumble of which could no longer succeed in calming down. The heads tipped back and mouths gaped, which made her think of the guillotine; a haggard bloodshot eye opened from time to time. The women, more orderly, ugly and malevolent, craned their necks.

And the duchesse, her eyes widened by fear, lifted her heavily-gloved hands, alarming and ridiculous beneath her bandages, with her little pigtail of golden hair on her back. For she saw all round her, solely directed toward her face, index fingers with black fingernails, the multiplied index fingers of the Underworld, which, only shaken by that inextinguishable laughter, were pointing at her, without speaking.

THE KING IS BORED[1]
(*Le Journal*, 7 December 1906)

CONVERTED into a laboratory, the poor little room on the fifth floor overlooking the courtyard was cluttered with flasks, burners, alembics and all the apparatus of chemists, which has retained, even in our epoch, the ensorcelled air of the Middle Ages.

In the midst of such objects, the young and austere face of the scientist would still have aggravated the atmosphere of the room if his little seventeen-year-old sister, a dressmaker working in the next room, had not frequently slipped with the skill of a she-cat into the midst of all that science to display the fugitive radiance of her golden hair, her bold eyes and her pert face of a healthy errand-girl.

She knew, however, that it was necessary not to touch anything, and not to talk too much. That is why, in spite of

---

1 The phrase "Le roi s'embête" [the king is bored] featured in a well-known anecdote regarding the late start of a performance of an eagerly anticipated play by the Republican Romantic George Sand in the revolutionary year of 1848 at the Théâtre de la République, the prologue of which was known to conclude with words explaining the work's title: *Le Roi attend!* [the King is waiting] by proclaiming that "le Roi, c'est le People!" [the King is the People], sarcastically countering Louis XIV's famous declaration that: "L'État, c'est moi!" [The state is me]. After repeating that assertion of the people's monarchy, a child in the audience is said to have added, half an hour later: "Citoyens comédiens, le roi s'embête!" [Citizen actors, the king is bored].

having a strong desire to pull his leg a little, she was even better behaved that day than usual, sitting in a remote corner, hardly daring to breathe; for she knew that the scientist, at that precise moment, was reaching the goal of all his efforts.

Metchnikoff has conceived the prolongation of human life; he was in the process of discovering something even more audacious. He was going to resuscitate the ancient dead.

It would scarcely be fitting to develop here the theory of his discovery. Be content to know that in the narrow laboratory, a frightful detonation suddenly made the little sister jump, with the shrill little cry of little girls when a bottle of champagne is uncorked. And then, from the depths of the complicated furnace where a thousand products with difficult names were simmering, an intense vapor was exhaled, which, having rapidly taken form before the tremulous young couple, proved to be the person of an extremely singular human being.

The experiment had succeeded, therefore. However, as there are always improvements to bring to discoveries, the young scientist who had just enabled a dead man to be reborn, by means of his mysterious manipulations, was absolutely unaware of the epoch, even approximately, in which the dead man had lived. So, in his initial surprise, face to face with his own work, he remained very embarrassed, not knowing what to say or do.

Who is he? he wondered, with anguish. *He's only costumed with a residue of vapor, and I have no indication that could inform me as to whether he's a contemporary of Ramses, Marcus Aurelius or Napoléon.*

He had no sooner finished listing those names than the individual started to speak, in very good French.

"Who are you, Monsieur?" he said, haughtily.

He had taken a step forward. In the light from the window they could see the profile of his absolutely bald head, where, before a thick jowl, red and clean-shaven, there was the exaggerated curve of a hooked nose. And yet, the bearing of that head was so arrogant that even the little sister had no desire to laugh on looking at him. She simply said by way of protestation, placing her fists on her hips: "That's marvelous. This one doesn't wait to be asked questions!"

To which the personage declared, with solemnity: "Pardon me, Madame. I should have waited." In the room there was a shriek even more sensational than the detonation. The scientist, very pale, clapped his hands, without succeeding in uttering a word. Finally, he was able to articulate, in a voice choked with emotion: "Do you know who this is, Mimi? It's Louis XIV!"

But Mimi was scarcely troubled. "Well, Father XIV," she mocked, in her most suburban voice, "you can say that you have a nice wig."

The king put his hand swiftly to his cranium. "Alas, no," he replied, suddenly mild. "I perceive, on the contrary, that I have left my wig in eternity . . ."

Having made that observation, he moved away as far as possible from the light, with his head bowed, his belly protruding and the chagrined lip of an aged ecclesiastic being molested.

Thus, the pride of the first moments had abandoned him completely. That was a fortunate circumstance for the brother and sister, for they were able, without too much difficulty, to succeed in dressing him in a suit that was still decent, which had belonged to their father. Then, seeing him so discomfited and demoralized, they pushed politeness as far as procuring him a small, gray old gentleman's wig with a short fringe in front.

"He looks just like an American," said Mimi, complaisantly, when the costume was complete.

And without further delay, all three of them went down the staircases and outside. For the young scientist was counting, in all justice, if not on making a fortune with his discovery, at least recovering the extremely costly expenses of his experiments, for which he had sacrificed his small personal fortune and his sister's poor dowry.

Although the king expected anything, in returning to earth, he was already astonished by the clothes he wore. However, feeling the warmth of his little gray wig under a bowler hat, he had recovered some insolence. His head had straightened and his leg advanced advantageously, in spite of the trousers, as if he were posing in silk stockings for Hyacinthe Rigaud's portrait.[1]

At first, the city did not appear to him to be very different from the Paris he knew. They were in the Notre-Dame quarter, and from the little Rue Zacharie and the Rue Chat-du-Pêche he could not see anything truly gripping. He even thought that he recognized a few silhouettes of old women in discolored rags, those who trot along without epoch and without age in the old quarters, with a little basket or a formless shopping-bag on their arm. At any rate, not a single auto or tram had yet been revealed to him.

They arrived thus at the omnibus office. While the scientist occupied himself in getting tickets, Mimi tried to distract the king. She was exhibiting in his company the politeness of a provincial relative. Stopping before a few posters she asked him innocently: "Can you read?"

He directed a solar glare at her, without even taking the trouble to respond. He began to absorb himself in the posters. In spite of his mute pride, he had a desire to ask for explanation, for he said, anxiously: "These printed things are evidently edicts promulgated by my successor. But what kind of drunkard can a tire be that drinks obstacles? What is that species of game that possesses an incandescent beak? What new kind of torture is practiced in the Palais du Cycle? What can a 'match' signify? A 'handicap'? And what is a motor? And above all, above all what in the world does 'fifty large artistic cylinders' mean? The French language has changed a great deal!"

---

1 Hyacinthe Rigaud's portrait of Louis XIV in coronation robes was commissioned by the king in 1701 and hung at Versailles; by 1906 it was displayed in the Louvre, where it can still be seen.

Suddenly, a frisson ran down the royal spine, for he had just read: *Louis XVI furniture*. He started thinking. So, he had not been the penultimate Louis of the dynasty. That impressed him more than the rest.

"Louis XVI . . . Louis XVI . . ." he murmured, unawares. But he was interrupted by a little nudge on the elbow. Mimi was there, laughing in his face.

"That's a slap in the gob for you, eh, Father XIV?"[1]

Immediately, he became pale and red with anger, for he thought of certain details of his health.

At that moment, the scientist returned. Pushed, bustled and bewildered, the king found himself engulfed in the omnibus without knowing how. And the racket of the windows in his ears was already preparing him for the inferno of railways stations, autos, autobuses, taxis, luminous advertisements, cinematographs, shop windows, foreign passers-by, disconcerting women, the howls of newsvendors into which he was about to be precipitated on arriving in the brilliant quarters.

However, the first attempt of the scientist to interest science in his discovery was sterile. A second attempt also failed, as did a third. The Sun King, an habitué of salons, cabinets and assembly rooms, still ended up leaving the scientist akin to some chronic genius systematically refused by all newspapers and periodicals. There was the famous conspiracy of silence. He and his sister having become the dismissed guides of the outmoded sire, they gradually began to take umbrage. Father XIV, moreover, was not very sympathetic. When the initial alarm had

---

1 The colloquial phrase *en bouche un coin*, which I have rendered quasi-literally as "a slap in the gob"—although employers of contemporary English slang might have preferred "one in the eye"—was employed in France as a contemptuous signification of astonishment or amazement.

passed he had recovered his arrogance completely. He allowed himself to be served and escorted from morning till evening without unclenching his teeth. Having learned that France was a Republic, following some unfortunate little accidents for his family, he had further emphasized his disapproving silence. His inferior lip advanced further and further at the spectacle of the twentieth century, seeming to say before all modern democracy as before simple Teniers: "Take away these apes."[1]

One day, the scientist had an idea. *Since science doesn't want to occupy itself with my discovery,* he thought, *in spite of all the true documents I can bring to the groping of history. I'll try to interest society.* Having examined his idea he finished up with this absolutely exact conclusion: *There's only one possible milieu for my enterprise. I'll go to see Comte Robert de Montesquiou.*[2]

Robert de Montesquiou knew the scientist, as he knew every interesting person in Paris. That is why, a short time later, the negotiations having been concluded, the Pavillon de Muses was in rumor as in the days of the finest receptions. It was the beginning of summer; in the famous Vasque de la Montespan, the most precious ornament of the comtal garden, a perfumed bath florid with roses awaited the king. It was one of those ingenious and charming finds that we owe to the only seigneur of letters who subsists in France since the death of the magnificent Villiers. About a hundred select persons composed a sufficient court for the *petit lever*—or, rather, the *petit bain*—of the king. In order for the surprise to be even more remarkable, how-

---

1 A well-known anecdote related that Louis XIV, when presented with a painting of peasants by the Flemish master David Teniers the younger, ordered that the "*magots*" [apes, or ugly people] be taken away.

2 Robert de Montesquiou (1855-1921) had long been the most notorious dandy and snob in Paris when the story was first published. As previously mentioned, he had included a tribute to Lucie Delarue-Mardrus' poetry and pulchritude in "Deux Muses" in *Professionelles beautés* (1905), which also includes an essay on her husband's translation of *Les Milles et une nuits*. Montesquiou's collection of sonnets, *Les Perles rouges*, was published in 1899.

ever, and to bear fruit more surely, it was decided that the king should initially be confounded, a simple American silhouette, among the guests, not one of whom would know his identity. After tea, a little music and a few recitations of sonnets judiciously extracted from the tragic *Les Perles rouges*, they would pass into the garden "the hands of which would take charge of showing the way," as Montesquiou said, in his voice almost as clarionesque as that of Renown.

Daylight arrived. In a frock-coat, necessarily opal green, Comte Robert did the honors. His head high and his beautiful Apollonian forehead rivaling in commanding presence that of the king, who, recognizing among the ladies certain types of his aristocratic past, held his head so straight above the modern collar that one feared at every moment seeing his divine right divined by an audience of alert atavisms.

It was then that, Madame de Rohan[1] having recited something, he could not help asking the scientist: "Are these truly my Précieuses?"

For he rediscovered very justly in his opal-clad host the ultimate great-nephew of the beribboned marquises by whom the bureaux of wit were ornamented.

He was begged to be silent. In any case, his impression faded quickly because around him the language of the ladies reminded him of his initial astonishment before the posters; and he continued to repeat: "The French language has changed a great deal," until, the general conversation being established persistently on the "states of the soul," he suddenly got up ostentatiously, stamping his foot, and cried in a powerful and impatient voice: "States of the soul! States of the soul! The State is me!"

---

1 The English actress and mandolin-player who employed the stage name Daphne de Rohan was at the height of her meteoric carer in 1906; she was not a member of the famous French aristocratic family whose surname she had borrowed.

Comte Robert and the scientist had rushed forward to stop him. Too late. An entire discourse followed, in which he exhaled his superb rancor in such a tone that the young duchesses, scandalized, cried in chorus with exquisite voices: "There's a funny gigolo!"

And the red-faced and furious gentlemen all departed together.

"But it's a hoax!"

A great disturbance followed. The *petit bain* had failed. And the scientist, having found himself outside, without knowing how, with His difficult Majesty, suddenly lost all hope. Exasperated and angry, he finally made a decision.

"After all," he said to him, "go exhibit yourself. I don't want to know anything any more."

His wig on sideways and his lip disdainful, the Sun wandered, abandoned, through Paris. After a short time, having followed a fatal slope, he found himself, quite naturally, established as a cab driver. That is the end of all the best families. Furthermore, the boiled leather hat went rather well with his type. The hooked nose learned to lower and redden in squalls; the royal back rounded out under the overcoat. In spite of his memory still shining with gilded carriages, he snored in his vehicle while it was stationary, like a simple former notary, picked his old nag up when it fell on muddy days, without agitation, abused clients who gave him a good tip, was able to answer to ladies in a hurry with a peremptory: "I'm on my break," and look down at everyone from the height of his grandeur on the great days when it did not please him to "charge." He had a little flag and a meter that he manipulated shrewdly to maximize his profit. But all the same, remembering the time when he was the sovereign of France, he would rather have chosen a French counter for his vehicle . . .[1]

---

1 The taximeter for calculating fares based on a combination of time and distance travelled was invented by the German Friedrich Bruhn in 1891; its

Thus his afterlife destiny would doubtless have finished, but for a circumstance that was decidedly extraordinary.

There is no need to state the names of the king and queen who came in great pomp to render us a visit, in the wake of so many others.[1] They were not the enchained sovereigns, yellow, brown or black, that the Republic made to figure in its great triumphs. A serious gala had therefore to be prepared for them, including a reception at Versailles. And the head of protocol, alarmed, riffled feverishly through the treatises and manuals of the history of France, fearing to lose his footing in etiquette, in the sight and knowledge of all Europe, scrupulously informed by the newspapers.

At that moment, the scientist and his sister thought of finally taking advantage of their ancient discovery. Having set out on campaign, they ended up discovering their king while he was having lunch, blue with congestion, in a coachmen's rendezvous at the corner of some blind boulevard. Their steps, this time, in view of the difficulty of the circumstances, succeeded at the first attempt. Appointed as chief of protocol the next day, the coachman Louis, dying of pride, clad in garments from the best museums, beribboned and plumed, in grand curls, received in the Hall of Mirrors, with his calf forward and his entire century in his eyes, the royal guests of the Republic, fearful with admiration.

You can imagine the ceremony, and how the town of Versailles, resuscitated in the historic overflow of its great waters and the magic of a royal autumn, launched over the astonished world the splendor of one of its most beautiful days of old.

---

eventual employment in Parisian autocabs caused some ill-feeling because the French still remembered the humiliation of the Franco-Prussian War.

1 The reception at Versailles is fictitious, but the idea of an important state visit undoubtedly reflects the fact that Edward VII and Queen Alexandra visited Paris in 1906, amid much publicity, in a symbolization of the *entente cordiale*.

Everyone, inclined instinctively to the ground, the foreign king and his queen as well as the French people, would willingly have kissed the extended fingertips of the man who "had he not had the dread of Hell, would have had himself worshiped."

But no one, in the disorder of the excitement, was able to hear, at the top of the steps that overlooked the park and the waters, the secret murmur of the monarch's mouth. Instructed by the adventure of his modern life, the Sun King said clandestinely, for himself alone, in the shadow of his rolled wig, under his grand sunlit plumes and before the rumor of respectful and delighted crowds:

"Well, my colonists, there's no error. I believe that it's me, this time, who has given you a slap in the gob!"

CHRISTMAS STORY
(*Le Journal*, 25 December 1906)

DOES not the golden night before Christmas, shining from all the windows, overflow outside, through the streets of towns and country roads? In spite of dead beliefs, is there not something in the Occidental air on that marvelous anniversary that envelops the world for twenty-four hours with an atmosphere of legend? People force themselves toward joy, from brand new bambinos putting their shoes in the fireplace to dismal party-goers getting ready, with an unaccustomed enthusiasm, for a joyous midnight feast. Perhaps it is the soul of the Christmas bells that spreads out; perhaps it is the Druidic spirit of mistletoe, or something unknown that falls, at the hour of the three masses, from the height of great cathedrals and little bells, and also the snowy sky from which the flakes descend like flowers.

It is a unique room, narrow and frozen, in a poor quarter of Paris. Nothing joyful is in preparation; no sign of Christmas shines there. A turned-down lamp illuminates the three items of furniture poorly. There is a cradle next to the bed and next to the cradle the young mother, who, with a movement innate in women, is rocking her new-born with her foot while singing some ancient song.

Abandoned with her child.

There are thousands like her in the world because that misery of women is as natural as the insouciance of man. The man has taken his pleasure and has gone on to something else. The woman has had her pleasure too, but she is attached forever to the work of her flesh. For it is a necessary injustice that dangerous feminine loins only obtain their share of sensuality in order to enable the redoubtable tree of human generations to grow.

It is easy to imagine the ordinary history of that young woman, a schoolteacher or lady's companion, doubtless an orphan, led by the vicissitudes of existence to that condition, which was not made for her cultivated mind, her bright brunette beauty or her big blue eyes, which the interior storm of a passionate soul frequently darkens.

Because of the primal law that pushes young couples to unite, that room now contains the result of an amorous season: a young woman, pathetic and alone, and a healthy little boy asleep in his wicker nest.

Without a situation, now that she had more than her own existence to sustain, she was only living on some old savings and a little humiliating charity. She had known the cruel offices of administrative beneficence, the maternity halls and the stern lady patronesses who protect the misery of girl-mothers with a disapproving gaze. All that charity was there, represented by that new cradle, by the promise of putting the baby out to a nurse and finding a place for the mother, and also by the warm and ugly layette that is given to young paupers in order that they be consecrated, as soon as their swaddling clothes, to the sadness of a positive life devoid of ornament.

And the young woman gazed, while singing her minor ritornelle, at the vile knitted blue bootees hanging at the end of the cradle, which were only waiting for the baby to wake to enclose two minuscule feet in their mesh again. Then, having suddenly remembered that it is the twenty-fourth of December, she stopped rocking and singing, and started to meditate, with immense eyes.

She thought: *This is the night on which, when I was a child, I put my beautiful little shoe in the fireplace of our home. I didn't know that a day would come for me when Christmas, for me, would have this lamentable face. I'm cold; I'm ill; and above all, my heart is so swollen that it seems that it's going to burst out of my breast. And here before me are my son's blue bootees, and today is the first Christmas of his existence . . . yes, tonight is the night of gifts . . . what can they expect, then, those two little empty bootees? I don't even have a one-sou rattle to put inside . . .*

She leaned her head against the cradle. The dark torsade of her hair covered the white nape of her neck. Her eyes closed, she reflected in her dolor, and large tears passed through her lowered eyelids, rolling straight from her cheeks to her knees. For her imagination, sharpened by the eve of Christmas, was building around those blue bootees an improbable and desolate romance.

"Little bootee, little bootee, which is opening in vain for the toy that isn't coming, you are to become the footwear, as long as a thumb, of the first steps, and then the mischievous clog of the schoolboy, and then idle shoe of the dreaming adolescent, and finally the sad shoe of the man. And I'm very much afraid that you will never know the good presents of life. But when the tiny pink feet that can now both fit into the palm of my hand have become the great feet of some poor fellow, then, threadbare sole, you will drag yourself along the roads of existence in the very ancient and ever-renewed tracks of the unfortunates who walk upon the earth with no other goal but to die in pain somewhere, one day, as soon as possible . . ."

And she repeated, opening her eyes more immensely:

"As soon as possible."

Her tears had stopped. An idea that she dared not fathom was born in her, so terrible that her vertebrae shuddered at it.

She looked at her sleeping baby. Thus, while the grown-ups were living their obscure and wretched lives, he was asleep, he did not know yet . . .

For a long time she stopped thinking, not wanting to go any further. Then her thought was formulated, timidly and fearfully:

And why must he know? Why learn to live? Why not stop at the beginning, instead of waiting for the perpetual evil passes, at the end of which there is never anything but the banal decease of a poor man? Why not continue eternally the entirely rosy sleep of the new-born? Why not die right away, in order to remain a little child forever?

The great stormy eyes darkened further and further. And abruptly, she got up and began pacing back and forth with long strides. A strange joy animated her gradually.

"Little bootees," she said, suddenly, almost loudly, "I'm going to give you a fine Christmas gift anyway, a magnificent gift, the finest of tonight's gifts!"

She smiled.

"It will be a very familiar story, an everyday news item: The dramas of poverty. A mother who kills herself with her baby."

How long, fallen back in her place, her head bowed, did she remain in her silent agony, her teeth clenched and her eyes staring? When she raised her head again, everything within her was consummated. Upright and cold, she advanced toward the cradle.

Now, said her thought, *now little child of Christmas, nothing can defend you any longer against the heroic gesture of my hands . . . yes, heroic. For your neck burning with slumber will not be much thicker under my fingers than that of a bird . . . and yet it's you, it's you that is going to be difficult to kill. Oh, how difficult you're going to be! For me, who is so big, death will be, on the contrary, very easy . . . Here I am, my son! To save you from my beautiful present, you see, it would be necessary, this minute, for an angel to descend next to your cradle!*

She was leaning over brutally; and as her hands were already creeping, and her gaze was coming closer, her heart suddenly stopped beating. For the baby, having woken up a moment before, his pupils dilated upon the invisible, made exactly that little grimace habitual to new-borns, which is known as "laughing at the angels." And his eyes, still devoid of gaze, gave the impression of contemplating that which, much later, people in the process of dying seem to see again.

In truth, the smile of that doll was something more formidable, on that night swarming with legends, than if someone from Elsewhere had suddenly surged forth and cried: "Don't touch him!"

Then the young woman understood, with horror, that the angel she had evoked, the Angel of Destiny, had indeed descended next to the cradle in order to interpose himself. She understood that there is a mystery as great as death in the eyes of new-borns. She understood that one ought not to bear ignorant hands to the throbbing heart of such a creature, because life is, in spite of everything, divine, and it does not belong to anyone to assault divinity.

That is why, her heart finally broken, sobbing, she let her head, the hair of which ought to have gone white in a matter of hours, fall over the cradle. And, with her cheek against the puerile mouth that was now searching for the nipple, already having taken refuge beside her son as if on the shoulder of a tiny friend, she started to speak to him, through the torrent of her tears, rocking him convulsively.

"Oh, my son, oh, my poor darling, your mother, who has nothing, has made you a gift all the same for the first night of Christmas. In your little blue bootees I wanted to give you the present of death. And now, for the second time, it's life that I've given you . . ."

And as admirable hope, which is sufficient in itself to repair the woe of living, for those who are suffering, took hold of her again, in spite of everything, she lifted the child in her arms with a swift gesture and, opening her blouse to feed him, she added, almost laughing, confident and saved, as if she were murmuring a marvelous secret in his fragile ear:

"And then, perhaps you, my son, will be fortunate . . . ?"

BLUEBEARD'S WARDROBE
(*Le Journal*, 22 January 1907)

AS she did every night, Princesse Mina found herself alone at home at the end of her fatiguing day of an adored young woman. No one knew that hour of her life when she finally gave herself a rendezvous with herself, after having royally thrown as fodder to society so many gazes, attitudes and speeches, so many laughs and sighs, expressed by her twenty-five years, her violet eyes, and her light and copious dark golden hair, pompously elongated all the way to her knees.

Now she concentrated again. Her heart beat rapidly with the great joy of long-awaited meetings. Around her were the customary furniture, fabrics, flowers and perfumes. With an almost timid gesture, she opened the white lacquered wardrobe of her immense dressing-room and gazed at the compact crowd of her suspended dresses. Then she gave them a little nod of the head, as if to persons. And suddenly, the entire empty house seemed marvelously populated.

Might one not have thought, in fact, that the array of dresses was a long line of women? Different and yet similar women, since each of them represented a moment in the existence of the beautiful Mina. Or rather, was it not the young woman herself, suddenly multiplied as if by a play for mirrors, who filled the house?

She murmured: "Princesse, I salute you."

Then she sat down facing the wardrobe and her magnificent eyes studied it complaisantly.

The dresses were suspended from the same single metal bar by forty coat-hangers in the form of shoulders. There were short ones and long ones, simple ones and complicated ones. Either they were separated in two, one part fitting the torso and the other the legs, or they went straight from top to bottom. Like the different stones in a necklace, they combined their contrasted colors. Blues could be distinguished next to reds, fresh-leaf greens next to faded-lead yellows. Thus the autumn of muted velvets rubbed shoulders with the spring of muslins, like frivolous damsel-flies.

In spite of the accumulation of those multicolored prisoners, however, a few personalities found the means, in the narrow space of the wardrobe, to stand out. Certain costumes suddenly floated before Mina's eyes like a blue patch of morning sky, others like evening twilight. One of them, narrow and violet, resembled a bishop. One, which was brittle and silver, shone with the cold splendor of a frosted window; another, which was cloth of gold, stood upright in its corner with the pride of ancient monarchs. There were some, made of superimposed tulles, which danced motionlessly in their places better than almas, and there were some whose amorously embroidered and diversified fabrics changed color without budging, like the tails of peacocks in the sunlight.

All of them, she had ornamented for fêtes or intimate hours. Public dresses, private dresses; and their ribbons and sashes, irresistible tentacles, had seized desires in passing.

Thus, each of them, for one day at least, had fulfilled the role of idol in the multiple ceremonies of life. And now they were reposing; the tender places of Mina's loins and breasts remained, in spite of everything, carefully reserved in fabrics, whatever dress she was wearing. In the same way, short or long, each one tapered toward the bottom, foamy and noisy in imitation of a wave, in order that the eternal feminine siren should always find herself in her element. And was it not because all of them had thus contained the warmth and odor of a person and the pathetic beating of a heart, that a residue of breath persisted in them, almost making them young women?

Mina thought that, without Mina, none of those dresses could have any significance. They were only beautiful because they had heightened her beauty for a moment. They were only the sheaths of her fugitive youth, in its numerous manners of being. Sooner or later, they would have been narrower or broader, different. Like coffins, they had been made to measure, to the measure of Mina's twenty-five years . . .

She philosophized for some time on such matters, strangely; and that was a new and dangerous pleasure for her. But that night, her imagination was even more intense. She got up, took one of the dresses at random, and threw it on the divan. It was a narrow dress in gray-green velvet. She looked at that almost human thing, empty of her, inert in the cushions like a body without a soul, and she thought:

If that recumbent dress is suddenly as funereal as a cadaver, it's because it is presently full of nothing. However, it has only ever been animated slightly, by myself alone; for a young woman varies so much in accordance with the dress she wears. On the days when I dressed in it, I was like this and like that, but I did not have the same soul as the times I put on that long white tunic or that errand-girl skirt with its quasi-masculine jacket.

Leaning on the back of her chair, her chin in her palm, she dreamed for a long time in confrontation with the dead dress. And it was at the moment of finally going to sleep that her meditation found these few phrases:

Yes, each of my dresses is, when I wear it, one of my fashions of being. It represents one of my hypocrisies or verities, a quality or a fault. But not having enough of my qualities or my faults, true or affected, it constitutes, given the other dress, a gross imposture in its isolation. For it is no more exact that I am always a gray-green velvet woman than a woman who is always sad, for example, or always cheerful. All fixity is a lie. Now, each of my dresses, being fixed, is a lie. So, that wardrobe is full of lies.

She went to sleep that night on that syllogism. But the next day, having, after a long day of youth, having found herself again before the wardrobe, she resumed her reflections more bitterly at the point where they had been interrupted.

If my wardrobe is full of lies, she continued, *by virtue of the fact that I only wear the dresses one after another, it follows that I ought, in order to be true, to wear all my dresses at once.*

She cast a long glance over the forty coat-hangers and sighed:

"The truth is a difficult thing."

Then she reflected more profoundly once she was in bed, for the instinct of obstinacy is vivacious in women. Since she had begun to seek the truth, she wanted to carry her enterprise through to the end.

That is why, a few days later, she reached this conclusion:

Since it's impossible for me, in order to be true, to put on all my dresses at once, I shall at least destroy the causes of the lie, my forty dresses. The first act of the seeker of truth is an exterminating gesture. Throwers of bombs are a modern example, and also the men of the Revolution who preceded their institutions with a reaping of heads.

She smiled at that phrase, for her robes resembled closely enough, in the shadow of the wardrobe, the bodies of guillotined women.

Bluebeard's wardrobe, she thought. *You're going to die too, Mesdames, because you have lied.*

She had extended her hands without even looking. She felt that she possessed the firm soul of an administrator of justice.

The dress that she took from the shadow was one of those masterpieces of nuance and arrangement that make a costume into a veritable great flower. And now the little hands, clutching the fabric and the adornments, sacked them with the passion of an assassin. For, occupied thus in annihilating wealth, the symbol of a daily lie, Mina, the lofty princesse, at that solitary and nocturnal moment, bore within her the rancor of the world.

Die! cried her thought, *die, red dress, because you are not the blue one! And die also, blue one, whom I am killing with two criminal hands, die, simply because you are not the red one!*

And thus, from color to color, from the fresh-leaf green to the faded-leaf yellow, from the bishop's violet to the peacock's tail, to the golden morning, and the evening twilight, to the path of morning sky, all the admirable and fallacious dresses, alternately representing the numerous but unitary person of Mina, princesse and philosopher, died in a single night.

Quivering, the irritated beauty gazed at her work. Heaps of debris strewed the carpet, unfurling like a wave across the room. Mina trampled over an inexpressible medley. But Bluebeard's wardrobe was empty.

What a relief, she thought, wiping her forehead.

Suddenly, her staring eyes and devouring fantasy invented something else.

"I've understood!" she exclaimed, out loud.

But she reserved for the following day the execution of her new idea.

However, the project was only realized after several days. One morning, in fact, Princesse Mina, triumphant and carnivalesque, descended into the street wearing a new dress made of the debris of the other forty.

Suddenly inspired before the remains of her destruction, she had said to herself:

Now, from my revolutionary act, enlightenment has emerged. Now that everything is cast down, it's up to me, the destroyer, to re-sew. I'm going to make myself a unique dress with the scattered elements of all my dresses, and thus find the solution to the problem that I proposed to myself and which seemed inextricable: to wear, in order to be true, all my dresses at once.

One can picture the spectacle of the busy street where Mina appeared, clad in her new philosophy, in the form of a long simarre made of fragments of cloth of all colors and all fabrics, painfully torn apart and stitched together.

The entire city, on seeing it, seems to utter a single cry of amazement and hilarity. A black-clad assembly surrounds her multicolored person. A hundred thousand index fingers point at her. And from all those breasts, lifted up by universal laughter, a single word emerges, repeated from one horizon to the other:

"Harlequin! Harlequin!"

Mina has become livid under the unanimous insult. She raises herself up on her toes, rolls the dark amethyst of her stormy eyes. She tries to speak; but in the midst of the general howl her wan voice of an emotional young woman is lost. And no one hears her cry, as loudly as she can:

"Don't you see that they are my forty dresses in one, all my personalities at once in the sunlight, without a single one being forgotten in the shadow of the wardrobe? It's the robe of justice! It's the robe of equality!"

The crowd becomes excited. The sniggering jeers almost become a threat. At present, Mina runs away as fast as her legs can carry her, mocked and pursued. Her heart of a hunted animal leaps madly in her breast. She just has time to precipitate herself into her house and shut the doors behind her. Then she falls, almost fainting, into the first cushions she comes across, her two fists on her breast, where the breath is wheezing like the bellows of a forge. For a long time she remains almost unconscious among the same cushions. She ends the day thus, in a poor condition, and only recovers slightly with the descent of dusk.

Mina is a nocturnal dreamer. Obscurity brings light into her soul, and gradually brings out the significance of such a violent adventure. When she goes to bed at dawn, still fully dressed in her baroque garment, she has almost discovered the meaning of what has happened to her. It is thus that the events to which one has been subjected cease to be troubling when one has, so to speak, found their formula: a difficult but necessary mathematics.

Mina therefore woke up the next day saying: *Evidently, it's me who was wrong and not the crowd. One cannot reconstitute oneself newly with old elements.*

Having thus rid herself of the annoyances of the day before, she continued: *It's necessary, in order to be true, to find something absolutely new. I don't want any more old verities. They're worn out, like the lies. What I want is a virgin verity. Or, rather, I want the Truth.*

She got up in her dress striped with a thousand colors and went to stand in front of the mirrors. Slowly, she unfastened the dress. All abruptness was annulled in her. Grave and reflective, she picked up the dress she had just taken off and tore it apart, with the mild gesture one uses to stifle a woman.

"The entire past is dead," she said, "but what will be born of the new?"

And as if the response to that question had suddenly burst forth, she suddenly saw herself in her mirrors emerging naked from the last dress, torn to pieces, like a human Aphrodite surging from a multicolored sea.

Then she clapped her hands, animated by a great excitement.

"The Truth! The Truth!" she cried, passionately, her arms extended toward the mirrors.

And with an instinctive, irrational gesture, she undid her hair with a single thrust, and threw away all the combs and tortoiseshell that had retained it.

Her quivering hair enveloped her. She shook her head, and a wave of reflections ran down her back. Her smooth, mat, upright body with its two florid breasts seemed, amid that ardent fleece, to be bracing itself in the heart of a furnace. And as she moved slowly through her house before going out, the sway of her hips, cadenced by the primitive march of her bare feet, resembled the grace of panthers. Thus, free of the cage of clothing, the beautiful female animal advanced in her nonchalant and native glory.

I shall go now, Princesse Mina thought, *to confront the hypocritical crowd, the clothed crowd with the veritable truth. And because they are all as naked as me beneath their fabrics, they will doubtless understand. For to be naked under clothes is to possess the truth beneath lies. If they jeered at my Harlequin dress the other day, were they not right? Certainly, there was a great lesson in their laughter; but I didn't understand right away, so difficult is it to divine immediately the enigma that events propose to us for our own good.*

When she was in the street, a tranquil Eve trailing behind her the comet of her golden hair, she stopped, after a few paces, in the middle of the invincible crowd that had immediately gathered.

A silence of amazement and scandal reigned.

She said: "I am Truth. Once, it emerged from a well. Personally, I am emerging today from the profundity of my thought. People were right, recently, to laugh at my dress. My only true robe is this. It is my primal nudity, like yours, which has been buried for centuries under the fabric of civilization."

She had taken her hair in her hands and extended it in the sunlight to the right and the left. She sensed the four elements quivering therein, and she spread the ingenious tide of ramified trees in the open air, the splendid waves that were freely displayed in the wind that scatters as it passes over the earth, the savage fire that launches forth. And already the birds, from the rooftops, were flying toward her, mistaking her for a great swaying plant. Bolder than the rest, a pigeon simply came to alight on her head and coo, as on the statues in gardens.

But the clamor of the crowd, retained for a moment, suddenly burst forth, with a formidable amplitude, repeating:

"Cover it up! Cover it up!"

And thousands of human arms, remembering the gesture of lapidation, searched the pavement for undiscoverable stones, in order to massacre the intolerable nudity.

The birds had fled. The pigeon flew away, frightened. The police arrived.

And the crowd, escorting the magnificent creature who was being brutally dragged to the police station, vociferated behind her, in a growling indignation and vehement anger:

"She's stark naked . . . ! Stark naked . . . ! Stark naked . . . ! To prison . . . ! To prison . . . !"

THE IMPOSSIBLE EYES
(*Le Journal*, 3 February 1907)

YVON had once been a strange little boy who liked dolls. He wept every evening before going to sleep in order to have one beside him on his pillow. Every night his mother heard him cry out, got up and approached, knowing in advance what was happening. Yvon, awake, had retreated into the gap between the bed and the wall, his teeth chattering; he pointed his finger at his toy, the glass eyes of which were gleaming like gold in the semi-darkness of the night-light, and said: "My doll is looking at me!"

Puberty had arrived to efface those puerile things. Imbued with the superiority of grown-ups, nascent in him, he had shrugged his shoulders at such memories of childhood. Now, as he became a man, he began to take account of the fact that his former soul of a little boy had been the truest of his soul. In fact, the eyes of mistresses, which have always fascinated the masculine will, had a singular attraction for him, which increased every day. As he once had before the little person of wax or cardboard with the fixed eyes, he experienced a sentiment for the feminine gaze in which amour and fear were mingled.

What was that gaze asking of him? He wore himself out in vain seeking the meaning of that anxiety. More and more, like someone risking himself on the rim of a dangerous well, his mind prowled cautiously around feminine eyes, without being able to stop—with the result that his girl-friends said: "He's a sly individual; he never looks you in the face."

His torment increased. At length he imagined that the varied irises of his lovers might, in accordance with their color, have a respective taste. Was not his anxiety then a sort of mental greed, a thirst to know the taste of the gaze?

He had wanted to drink, one after another, many precious mouthfuls. He thought of certain slightly faded blue eyes whose savor was evidently that of slightly sugared water. He thought of eyes tending toward green, which were saltier than drops of sea-water. There were some of yellow-brown that were as piquant as vinegar, and others, darker, heavy and too velvety, that were as sticky as syrup.

Thus the eyes, the luminous place in the human face, were only for him a secret beverage.

Having found such an explanation, he felt relieved at first, but he did not take long to agree with himself that no gaze had, in reality, the taste that he wanted. From then on, he understood that, like many others, he was simply a seeker of the impossible.

The taste that he desired was something as simple, clear and profound as a spring. He wanted eyes like the water that one takes in the palm of the hand at the foot of certain oak trees, the water, diaphanous blood of the earth, that is only perfumed by the odors of the soil and roots traversed, the ivy and ferns that are steeped therein; the docile water in which reflections of dawns and dusks lie; the formless and colorless water possessing all the colors mirrored within it . . .

Yes, he desired that natural water, those natural eyes. He wanted to drink therein the aspects of divine life. He wanted, in approaching them, to perceive in their utmost depths his dream of verity, like a naked naiad. He wanted to slake every thirst there, to drown his soul delectably there. And he also wanted the spring that he sought, the gaze that he pictured in

102

thought, to be something reserved for him alone. He required that the miraculous eyes of a woman, awaited without believing in them, would never have beheld anyone but him.

Several years passed over his dream. In the meantime, his memory registered many beautiful eyes, which he added to those he already knew, as if he were adding colored stones to an invisible necklace.

Now, an evening came, which seemed similar to others, an anodyne evening of an outing in the city. It was a matter of some drawing room comedy, followed by a supper. The true comedy, as always, was that, unrehearsed, of the social gathering in which everyone exhibited his best smile, reserving internally the secret bite of irony. Amid the general shoulder-rubbing of black suits and dresses, Yvon felt his veridical personality assimilated to others. He was no longer anything but a figure in the banal number.

He watched the play of the actors, applauded, saluted here and there, chatted like the others, resigned in advance to his role as a monsieur at a soirée.

And then, as he took his place at supper, side by side with young people that he scarcely knew, or not at all, having lifted his head, he saw, facing him, his dream. Wide open, the impossible eyes were there. It was a slightly pale young woman, slim and pretty, with neatly-coiffed brown hair. But how could Yvon have distinguished those few details? Breathless, immobilized as before the head that metamorphoses into stone, he only contemplated the two immense eyes the color of water, simple and profound, like the springs one encounters at the foot of certain oak trees.

And with a frisson that made him go terribly pale, he perceived that, strangely fixed, they were looking at absolutely no one.

She was, however, chatting to her neighbors; she even laughed from time to time. But it seemed that her irises, in turning toward her interlocutors, missed their target every time and fixed themselves elsewhere, looking toward something invisible and marvelous.

"My dream . . . my dream . . ." Yvon stammered. And only the ordinary human indifference that surrounded him prevented him from being noticed.

At one moment, however, the young woman having fallen silent, looked straight ahead. Then her two extraordinary pupils were planted directly in Yvon's eyes, and it was as if two blades traversed him.

Swiftly, he put his hand to his heart, retaining the shock of joy and anguish. Then he opened his mouth to speak, to clamor toward the eyes that were staring at him. And finally, simply, having recovered a little consciousness, he made them a sign, a small thin sign that signified all of his soul . . .

But already, the clear gaze had turned away.

When they got up from table, there was a noisy dispersal through the drawing rooms. People were laughing, smoking, attacking pianos. In the midst of that chaos, Yvon clutched nervously at the arm of a young man he knew.

"Introduce me . . ." he stammered.

The other looked at him, alarmed. Yvon was astonished that he did not know, immediately, that it was a matter, at that moment, of his very destiny.

He explained, specifying the person to whom he wanted to speak, but in terms such that the young man, supposing that he was suddenly amorous, started to laugh.

"Don't get carried away so quickly," he said. "She's nothing but a doll, that little woman."

Yvon shuddered at that word, and an inexplicable anger shook him.

"Her, a doll?" he growled, making the gesture of someone about to kill. Intoxicated by indignation, he added: "With those eyes?"

Then the young man, adopting a more mysterious expression of amazement, said: "How do you not know, then?"

And, lowering his voice further, he drew Yvon aside.

"Above all, never give the impression that you suspect. It's a tacit agreement between all those who know her. You've seen that she speaks, laughs and amuses herself like an ordinary person? Well, she's making a semblance! Isn't it a beautiful example of coquetry, in spite of everything, and the cunning of women? Think that people and places are described to her minutely in advance, in order that she never has the appearance . . . !"

And as Yvon continued not to comprehend, he leaned over and whispered, imperceptibly: "She's blind."

Yvon did not have time to exclaim, for the pretty cripple passed close to them at that moment on the arm of a friend and the young man commenced complaisantly: "Dear Madame, permit me to introduce my comrade, who is . . ."

He did not finish. The two clear eyes, by chance, were plunged into Yvon's for a second time. And the unfortunate, tottering, discomposed and crazy, rediscovering the cry of his predestined childhood, started howling with all his might, and recoiled in the midst of the terrified crowd:

"My doll is looking at me . . . ! My doll is looking at me . . . !"

THE LAST COIN
(*Le Journal*, 21 February 1907)

A S she sat down at the roulette table, Princesse Patricia could not retain the yawn that the amusements of life normally provoked in her.

Almost nothing succeeded in distracting the blasé beauty. But in particular, she did not like games—cards, tennis or any others—which are regulated, cold things, from which there is no point in hoping for anything unexpected; that explains why, through the numerous casinos and other gaming houses visited in the course of her society tourism, she only ever deigned to throw five or six louis on to the baize, over the shoulders of the players, simply in order not to have passed through without risking a little money.

But that afternoon, as she experienced a peremptory need to interest herself in something, it seemed that she might end up being impassioned like the others by the circuits executed by the capricious ball among its two colors and its terrible numbers.

An excursion by auto had brought her there that same morning with her husband and two couples of friends. They had found known landscapes there and familiar snobbery. They had taken out of their traveling trunks two or three costumes adapted to the location and put on the necessary hats. Then, at about five o'clock they had quite naturally swelled the international assembly that, with the ardor of ants conquering a sugar lump, surrounded the roulette and trente-et-quarante tables from morning until evening,

As soon as they entered the halls, the little company had dispersed in accordance with individual tastes. Now, alone in the midst of the foreign crowd, slightly ashamed of being seated in that place for the first time in her life, the princess, having distractedly placed two gold coins in front of her, was parading her lorgnette over the circle of faces surrounding her, with ennui.

For some time she had been inclined to dangerous meditations on the youth that was passing, and she did not know why the ancient saying of one of her grandmothers kept coming back to her incessantly: "The entire history of a woman is contained in the five reflections that she provokes in passing: 'She'll be very pretty; She's very pretty; She's always very pretty; She's still very pretty; She must have been very pretty.' Afterwards, there's annihilation."

She wondered with anguish whether her lovers, when they said in loud voices that she was always beautiful were not thinking silently: "Still beautiful." And besides, was there not already a threat of the final annihilation in that "always beautiful," which contained a sort of astonishment?

In the midst of the indifferent assembly leaning toward the game, her dramatic eyes were darkened by all that interior distress. And while she incessantly replaced, automatically, with two gold coins, those that were raked away from her, she sensed that her heart, always a little constricted, was contracting more and more harshly.

With a particular care, she began to study the women sitting at the table; above all, she plunged her gaze into the side of the neck, which seemed to purr insolently with indubitable youth, or where dolorous maturity, like a malevolently clawed hand, was so rapidly commencing to rip up the underside of the feminine chin.

And her thought said: *That one is already touched . . . that one is entirely intact . . . as for those others, they have another three years at the most . . .*

Thus the lorgnette made its circular examination. Passing over the men, it framed by turns the young and old women, the beauties and the nonentities; it lingered on the princesse's peers, the beauties full of authority whose precious heads, adroitly made up, were coiffed by large plumes, which all fell back in the same direction with audacity and nonchalance all the way to the shoulders. It took an interest in femininities devoid of grace or arrangement, faces denuded of age, and those, too blonde or too dark, of foreigners. And now Patricia, with an extreme astonishment, perceived that on all those unequal faces, an identical expression had been established, like a kind of leveling. The game petrified them. One might truly have thought that the Gorgon's head, bristling with snakes, was blossoming in all its horror in the center of the bowl where the croupier released the ball.

The men emerged from time to time from their great absorption, in order to look at their neighbors or the passers-by who brushed them. But the women, the very young who possessed insolent immaculate necks as well as the beauties swaying arrogant plumes, were all stiff, with their teeth clenched; and their eyes, if they chanced to raise them, looked around distractedly, without any longer seeing anything or understanding anything. Obstinately focused by the feminine temperament, gripped by the same trance, they had lost all consciousness. Even the coquettes no longer knew anything of hours at the looking-glass, make-up and the fabrics that weighed upon their shoulders. Roulette accomplished that miracle; for the first time in their lives they forgot, in public, that they were pretty.

Suddenly, however, Patricia, jostled slightly, turned round haughtily to look her careless neighbor up and down. And she saw, occupied in piling up a few hundred-sou coins, an extraordinary old woman whom she had not noticed before, perhaps because she was too close to her.

A sort of plush toque in the form of a bowl covered her almost to the eyebrows. Fringes of silk and fake rose petals hung down from it; and her rare and bristling red hair descended in disorder along her dirty face, hollow and ravaged by the scars of old age, where the distended mouth moved, muttering, over large loose teeth. Patricia devoured with her eyes the ridiculous and tragic detail of that feminine misery. She saw the rag wound around the old neck, the calico of which the clenched hands with swollen veins parted, the large earrings that collided with one another over the breast, the blue glassware of which was finishing tearing the soft ears. She gazed above it at the worn-out eyes, eyes framed by wrinkles and swellings, but which still gleamed in a sinister fashion, over the handful of piled-up money. And with a frisson that chilled her to the depths of her soul, the beautiful princess thought that she had before her the final annihilation of which her grandmother had once spoken.

Bitterly, the old woman began to jabber. She had just lost her money at a single stroke and was arguing in a vehement and hoarse voice with her neighbor to the right, who accused her of having stolen five francs. Her neck was trembling with anger, her yellow teeth menacing. That did not last long. The adjudicator, shrugging his back-clad shoulders, passed on, in order no longer to hear the shrieking of the old thief; in any case, the cry of "No more bets!" had reclaimed all attention. And Patricia, hypnotized by the frightful old woman, wondered what it was necessary to do to enter into conversation with her.

As she was racking her brains, one of her cavaliers came to inform her that they were going back to the hotel, having just enough time to dress for dinner and a première that was taking place that evening. But he saw by the gaze that the princesse launched at him, shaking her head negatively, that it was futile to insist on taking her away. And, drawing away in order to rejoin the others, the gentleman wondered what new amour, incredible gambling debt or unusually broken bank would be the result of that obstinacy.

After a certain time, the hour for dinner already having passed, the old lady, after having terminated the calculations on a piece of paper, where some personal martingale was doubtless inscribed, got up from the roulette table and, frowning reflectively, a walking caricature, drew away, without perceiving that she was being followed.

Through unexpected streets, there were many small steps, in a darkness punctuated by yellow and red lights, until Patricia, astonished by the adventure, found herself installed in a tram that was heading for the next town, directly opposite the gambler and almost alone with her.

But it was only when two or three other passengers had descended along the route that the princesse, her heart beating rapidly, decided to start a conversation.

Should she talk about the weather or the discomfort of trams? The old woman was looking at her suspiciously with sunken eyes. Then, recognizing her former neighbor, as if she suddenly understood everything, she laughed hoarsely, and in the racket of the tram, which shook them both face to face, she leaned forward and said: "I've seen you. You play like an innocent; it's obvious that you've never gambled. But you've done well to take it up."

And as Patricia, intimidated, not knowing what to say, smiled without replying, the old woman continued volubly, her hoarse and malevolent voice dominating the noise of the tram: "Yes, you'd do well to devote yourself to it now. It's the sole consolation when one commences . . ." Then having lifted a stiff finger, she ran it, with diabolical gentleness, over the slack skin of her terrible septuagenarian neck.

Patricia had a momentary start of fear.

110

"What do you mean, Madame?" she said.

She had placed her elbows on her knees, and, with her head in her hands, approaching avidly, she gazed at the old woman.

The other darted a gaze of sinister malice at her. "You understand very well, little lady. You have glasses on you with which to see, haven't you? Oh, I don't say that it leaps to the eyes yet, but it will come so quickly, so quickly now, and every morning you'll think: 'And to think that that faded thing is now my most beautiful, and that it's going to sink further every day!' I don't know who you are, but I know full well what I've been . . . anyway, that isn't important. It's sufficient to know that *the anxiety* has come."

Patricia wondered whether the old clothes-merchant whose equivocal gaze enveloped her might, by chance, be a fortune-teller. Quivering, she looked at her. And, perhaps for the first time in her life, in the depths of the unexpected tram that was carrying her away while shaking her, she felt something weighing upon her like a domination.

"When I tell you," the old woman went on, "that it's the only thing that can console those of the race to which you and I belong, you can believe me! I know something about it. Look, you're going to think that I'm lying, but listen to me carefully: one no longer even thinks about money. If you knew where I lodge! If you knew how I live outside that gaming table! Yes, I'm there from morning till evening. I have martingales or I bet 'like a drunken woman,' it doesn't matter. And when I have no more money, I steal, as I did this evening. And truly, in that fashion, I no longer perceive myself at all . . . nothing, you understand!"

She pawed her chin again and added: "Of course, the day when I can no longer play, the day when I've truly lost my last coin, it'll be necessary to kill myself, because I'll have finished life. Yes, Madame, the universe, for me is contained in a hunded-sou coin."

She shrugged her shoulders.

"Anyway, me, that's of no interest; but only say whether you heard the little sound of the money shifting, which clicks in the silence of the crowd through the immense halls? Eh? It would make a din, that crowd, if it weren't gathered in that place! Oh, it's a good place, a gaming house. Have you noticed that it's the only place on earth where socialites give the impression of being interested in something? And it's there that faces are sincere! Nothing but sincere faces! A sincere humanity! That's because life is intense there, life is direct. And then, too, it's the house of equality. No one any longer has a race, an age, or even a sex. Do I astonish you? It's only because I speak quite well when I happen to remember my past. The others don't know what to say, that's all. But at every table you'll find at least one old woman like me, who calculates and mutters and steals. Oh, they aren't part of the classic band of those who enrich themselves or hang on to the end of their evening. No, those are the pure, the true players. And I assure you that they wouldn't exchange that for youth. For, you see, alongside that, there's so long to live."

Patricia, stunned, kept silent in her corner. As the old woman talked, she recalled the petrified women of a little while ago, the drama of the roulette played mutely over the multiple face of the crowd. And she sensed that the great soul of the game had been revealed to her, like a pathetic circle of the human inferno. She understood how, for the inveterate, life is no longer possible after that existence of a hundred thousand atmospheres around the green baize. All the long hazard of life concentrated in the blink of an eye: the slow balance of destiny tipping a thousand times in an hour; entire years elapsing in a single evening—how could one forget that to return to vegetate in the ennui of time, in the idleness of events? After having drunk the pure alcohol of the game, how could one recover a taste for the insipid water of ordinary passions? What amour, what ambition, what literature was worth that precipitation of all the phases of the soul around a ball hesitating between two numbers, or a card falling on top of another?

No, she thought, *the old woman certainly isn't lying. She's happy, happier than me, happier than the young ones. She's right, there's no longer anything, for her, but the concern of losing or winning, which makes life throb in confrontation with the game. Even that formula has been surpassed. There's more than that. There's the breathlessness of being before a mystery: Chance. That's why what changes the faces of true players into stone is, in sum, a pure abstraction, a sort of damned asceticism!*

An abrupt halt of the tram awoke her from her meditation. The old woman stood up in order to get off. Then the princesse, with a spontaneous, unanalyzable impulse, made a great movement toward her. But having moved her lips in order to say something, she could not articulate a word, and fell back into her corner, impotent.

Seeing that, the old woman, in her haste to get out, inclined her hideous plush-coiffed head slightly, and darted a little glance of scornful farewell at Patricia. And doubtless she was thinking in her mysterious and ferocious unknown irony: *That poor slut can't have understood anything of my speech. All the same, I'll have vexed her!*

When, later that night, the princesse's husband and her friends came back from the theater, they found her in her room, collapsed in an armchair, with a mirror in her hand. But none of them was able to read, in her pale and desperate face, the dilemma that occupied her soul:

Would it be better, she was thinking, *when the moment comes, for me to commit suicide, like so many others, or to become an old gambler . . . like so many others?*

THE HAUNTED WATER
(*Le Journal*, 3 March 1907)

LITTLE JEANNE, with a large school-bag under her arm, was passing over the Pont du Carrousel one winter evening and could not help slowing down in order to look at a surprising spectacle: the lights of Paris reflected in the water.

Her heart beat faster. It was the first time that she had found herself there, at that belated hour; for it was only since she had been ten years old that her mother, a milliner, sometimes charged her with little commissions on her way home from school.

This evening, therefore, hasty and a little fearful, she was hurrying to the address she had been given, in order to get back quickly before complete nightfall. And now, suddenly, the twilight over the water stopped her. She had been instructed not to idle on the way; but a ten-year-old schoolgirl cannot have the seriousness of a true apprentice. In any case, little Jeanne was such a particular child, albeit docile and mild. As soon as early childhood it had been perceived that she was "not like the others." And although she went meekly to school and was marvelously healthy, her relatives only watched with a sort of muted anxiety the frail person with the overly large eyes living and developing in their midst, who did not talk or play, and whose confidence no one had succeeded in capturing.

How was it imaginable, for example, that the ordinary sight of the Seine and its reflections, known to everyone, could strike her to the extent of making her forget the time? No one in Paris would have had the idea of leaning over the balustrades of bridges and quivering, as in the theater, simply because the slow rhythm of the black Seine was lengthened or shortened by the yellow, red and green streaks that the various lights of the city and the navigation allowed to fall into the nocturnal waters.

Nevertheless, after a moment, recaptured by the eminence of reality, the child started running in order to make up the lost time. But it was to come back very late, the commission completed, and to lean over again in the same place, devouring with her eyes, insatiably, the illuminated water that hypnotized her.

A first idler, noticing the absorbed girl, stopped behind her in order to look at whatever she was looking at; and, as he could not see anything that could excite curiosity, he began craning his neck, advancing and retreating, more and more intrigued. On seeing that, other passers-by also stopped and looked in their turn. Women having been added to the men, coachmen having stood up on their seats and baker's boys having slipped through the packed ranks, within a minute there was a compact crowd on the bridge, which, behind Jeanne, began to whisper commentaries of all kinds.

Meanwhile, finally extracted from her reverie, the child ended up turning round. Then she saw around her, with a frisson of fear, three hundred faces occupied in examining her. And it was with the gesture of a little hunted animal that she recoiled when the first passer-by, in the middle of the crowd of others, began to interrogate her.

Bewildered by surprise and timidity, she blushed, lowering her head and twisting her fingers. Then she ended up stammering, nearly weeping: "I was looking at how beautiful it is on the water . . ."

Then the crowd was shaken by a great burst of laughter. And immediately, scornful and disappointed, the people dispersed, shrugging their shoulders and saying: "If it were a corpse or a barge run aground, one could understand! But stopping to look in the water . . . !"

And the majority among them concluded, with rancor: "She's crazy!"

Then the circulation, momentarily disturbed, was reestablished. Liberated from the troop that surrounded her, the poor little girl, white with emotion, went home without saying a word. But a neighbor had preceded her, who, at the moment when she came in, was recounting the incident to her mother. Scolded, punished, and even having received a few slaps, little Jeanne wept all night. And henceforth, there was a refrain in the house every time she was charged with an errand: "Above all, don't do anything foolish outside!"

Her mother, struck by that adventure and full of resentment, said to her almost twice a day: "Instead of having ideas that aren't like other people's, you'd do better to bring me good notes from school, like little Anna or little Marie . . ."

The result was that the timid culprit, perfectly convinced that she had been wrong, since the grown-ups affirmed it, strove in her ten-year-old heart to resemble her comrades and not to look at the water again when she passed over the bridge at twilight.

However, her instinct being stronger than her, after a time she could not help raising her eyes slightly as she crossed the river, and then looking. And always, when night was falling, the same phantasmagoria fluttered before her eyes.

It was, for her, something so marvelous, the multicolored fire that danced indefatigably in the water, that she wondered with amazement why everyone didn't stop to contemplate it for hours. And she began to observe the faces of those who passed over the bridge in order to assure herself that they did not notice anything. But not once, even at the most beautiful moments, did a single person give the slightest glance to the fluvial splendor. Noses lowered, eyes bleak, they passed by. A few were chatting and laughing. None of them, whatever class they belonged to, accorded a second of admiration to that fête of the somber water stabbed by gleams, to that magnificent adventure of every evening.

And little Jeanne ended up saying to herself: *I can certainly see things that other people don't see; that's why they call me crazy.*

One evening, attracted irresistibly, and fearing the idle and sniggering crowd that, by virtue of a simple impulse of imbecility, flocked and mocked without knowing why, the child had the idea of going down very close to the water, on the bank, where the shadow is propitious to those who dream.

She went, in spite of the cold, to sit down in a corner, on a step, and her little imagination toiled.

It seemed to her, from the height of the step, that she understood better the significance of the obscure water inhabited by glimmers of three colors. The tales of fays that she had sometimes read passed through her mind. Did not the forms of the reflections resemble persons? And when a river-boat passed, trailing behind it a tress of light, it appeared to her that a troop of fishy beings, lively and scintillating, swam insistently around the hull of the boat like a shoal of luminous eels.

She went home that day quivering with a secret and inexplicable joy. And every time she had occasion to cross the bridge, she went down to the same place to sit down for a moment at the bottom of the same staircase, in order to gaze at her dear Seine living by night.

Now, it happened that a flood made the river rise so high under its bridges that the circulation of the boats was interrupted. Those were fine evenings for little Jeanne. The water covered half the ordinary staircase, as if it had made an effort to get closer to its fragile friend. And the reflections were so clear, now that nothing was any longer stirring the Seine, that the little girl expected incessantly to see faces appearing through the liquid shadows. She was soon convinced that, decidedly, all those beings of light standing in the middle of the little waves, whose tails were beating feebly, were nothing other than water fays of a sort, invisible to others.

That thought became even firmer in her mind when she observed, under the arches of bridges, in the depths of the river, colonnettes of fire that loomed up, so close to one another that one might have taken them for the pipes of a fulgurant organ. Were not those fleeting architectures of light the palace of those marine ladies, the fresh-water sirens that little Jeanne loved?

Her immense eyes detailed things one by one. She did not take long to remark, at the foot of a large brown barge moored a few paces away from her, a reflection of a particular kind. Isolated and green, it moved slightly in place, stretching its body of a precious serpent as if it were trying to make signs. It was so close that one might have thought that it was about to emerge from the water in order to crawl up the steps and coil seductively around the schoolgirl's feet.

And Jeanne began talking to the friendly water spirit in a low voice.

"You're Melusine, aren't you?" she breathed.

But there was no response except for the slight jiggling of the eddies, by virtue of which the mobile and indecisive green lady at the foot of the silent barge zigzagged like durable lightning. Without a doubt she was saying in her mysterious language:

"Come with me! I'll take you to my castle of reflections. You'll also know my sisters. Some are translucent and as red as fish in bowls, and others all golden. There are also some as green as me. Can't you distinguish any from here? There's an entire shoal lingering under the Auteuil-Austerlitz pontoon. If you come with us you'll learn to live submerged; you'll also be a beautiful evening mirage, shifting, mute and retractile. And when the circulation is reestablished, more rapid than river trout, you'll cleave through the water with us, in pursuit of the slender boats full of people who don't see us."

And as, sometimes, for amusement, boys threw stones from the bridge into the Seine, little Jeanne saw her fresh-water sirens flee and disappear with the thousand scaly gleams of a frightened fish-pond.

And she said to herself: *It's necessary to refrain from scaring them . . .*

That is why, on the evening when she decided that it was time to respond to their signs, she took all the precautions in order not to trouble the somber water around her.

She had taken advantage of a slightly longer errand with which she had been charged to return late over the bridge. Then she had descended to her usual place.

Undoubtedly, in the house, her mother was already anxious, not having seen her daughter return; but with the insolent laughter of a child, she was amused with all her heart in thinking of the pleasure she would soon have in joining the sirens' round-dances in their palace and fluttering in the dark water with the whimsy of a will-o'-the-wisp.

She looked around slyly to see whether anyone might notice her.

It's necessary that I pay attention, she said to herself, *for people would surely believe that I'll drown and they'd immediately come to prevent me from going with the ladies.*

Then, as everything was black around her and no one could distinguish her, she went down one step gently, and then two . . .

The icy water circled her legs. Her teeth chattered.

When I'm entirely in the water, she reasoned, *I won't be cold at all any longer.* And with a little mute laugh: *Since I'll be fire, like the others!*

119

Then, feeling the glacial circle reach her waist, with a single movement, she let herself go, her arms extended, hands forward, ready to seize, through the muddy and obscure water, the sirens invisible to ordinary eyes, and who, for so many evenings, had been waiting for her, each in her place, doubtless because she was a dreamy little girl without speech . . .

✳

It was not until two days later that the body of the drowned child was found, under the large brown barge.

Thus the green siren had attracted her, in accordance with her magical promise. And those who, filing through the Morgue, felt sorry for the poor little item of wreckage, stiff between two banal cadavers, did not know that her heavily lowered eyelids had closed upon a joyous and dancing paradise of flame and water.

That is why none of them had the idea of looking, in the evening, in the direction of the illuminated Seine. Perhaps they would have perceived there, mingled with the fascinating reflections, the little fiery soul of the child poet. But people do not look at anything, or, if they look, they do not see anything—which comes to the same thing.

And all of them, on going home, astonished and tearful, repeated: "Such a young child!"

While the next day's newspapers concluded, unanimously: "The causes of the suicide are unknown."

THE ROMANCE OF A PARMA VIOLET
(*Le Journal*, 10 March 1907)

A Parma violet, similar to all the others, was born in Provence, on the side of a hill, in one of the industrial fields that supply the factories of Grasse with perfume. Its little spring companions lived like her, blooming in the sunlight. Their pleasant odor was their conversation. They combined dainty greetings with it when there was a slight breeze. Upright, their heads in the sky, in the manner of human beings, they were each protected by an oval green leaf, and that gave them the appearance of carrying umbrellas, like ladies.

In her minuscule floral brain, my violet was proud every morning to sense, on her somber head, a bright hat of dew. She stiffened then, in order not to drop the burden of that large precious drop, which shone in the sunlight of the Midi like a diamond of at least half a carat. But a breath of wind passed, the violet saluted, and the diamond fell; and every morning, that was a disappointment for the fragile ambitious flower—for she did not have exactly the same character as her comrades.

Perhaps that came from the fact that she was very deep-set in her leaves and alone on her plane. In fact, her mother, having given birth to her seeds, had perished violently, only leaving on earth a single daughter, who, by chance, had germinated and flowered, but completely isolated. So she did not always take part in the pleasures of youth. Better sheltered by her leaves,

121

she danced with more reserve than the others on the days of the mistral; and at the times marked for the visitations of butterflies, she only accorded rare rendezvous. That is why she was not yet betrothed.

She therefore left her sisters, crumpled and docile, fixed to their stems, to submit to the comings and goings of infidel insects, those winged violets. But if she did not flirt much with the important bumble bees with the loud voices or the tightly-corseted wasps, she had been able, without seeming to be doing anything, to conquer the amity of an already-aged cricket full of beautiful and secret qualities.

That cricket was almost a stranger for the host of other violets. He was rather forbidding in appearance, as very knowledgeable individuals often are. That physical disfavor notwithstanding, however, one discovered, in frequenting him that in his narrow body, as dry as a wisp of straw, the great soul of the sunlit countryside dwelt in its entirety.

In addition, he knew so many things! He had inhabited the vast hearths of humans, before which families sat, and also the burning ovens where their daily bread was baked—with the consequence that, a little creature lost in the immensity of the Provençal fields, his natural chatter made philosophical speeches to the violet on certain days.

"The destiny of a flower," he often declared, "might be something more than life and death in the sun. It's possible, for her, to dream of a marvelous afterlife in which she acquires an almost human form. I don't want to reveal any more to you, but doubtless you, a pretty violet twice as reflective than the others, who knows that a drop of water on your head has the weight of a fleeting gem, will know that afterlife one day, of which I cannot say any more, not wanting to betray the secrets of humans."

And the violet, during the long hours of the day, inclined her complicated little vegetal figure, and dreamed indefinitely.

Now, a day came when a troop of women of the people, sent by one of the factories, penetrated into the field and, in a few hours, collected all the Parma violets, without a single exception; and the poor things, abruptly torn from their soil, thrown pell-mell into baskets, exchanged fearful reflections. Many fainted in the catastrophe. Others said: "This is the hour of death, then. We are, however, all still young. Alas, alas!"—for those frail individuals of two or three centimeters loved life as much as the great creatures of God.

My violet did not say anything, but she thought: *I've finally been removed from the stem that held me prisoner. I'm free and detached now, like a beautiful blue fly. It's doubtless the afterlife that is commencing. Adieu my natal hill! Adieu my cricket, my dear cricket! It's your indefatigable speech that has taught me that all is not finished on the day of death . . .*

Is it necessary to recount all the phases through which the thousands of collected comrades passed once they had entered into the frightening and dark dwelling where the slow history of flowers that become perfumes is continued and concluded?

They unfurled, like an immense embalmed wave, through naked chambers; they passed through the busy hands of workers, fell into further baskets, and finally, still alive and moistened by the southern dawn, they found themselves, in compact masses, in the midst of the whistles and trepidations of steam. They were disposed in an apparatus of unusual form, which, thus flowered, figured for a moment an imposing cone of violet freshness.

At that moment, the pensive pupil of the cricket said to herself: *This, then, is the promised afterlife! How splendid our solidarity is! We have all realized this beauty!*

She had not finished her thought when suddenly, by virtue of some trigger mechanism, the cone laden with flowers plunged at a stroke into the inferno of a vat of boiling oil.

An indescribable instant! When the apparatus emerged from the vat again, all that remained around the giant cone was a formless, colorless, odorless mass. From every flower the oil had extracted her perfume like a little soul. So absolutely empty were the imperceptible cadavers that they were promptly thrown into a corner, good for the sewer.

Meanwhile, the soul of the violet, in the midst of such a terrible metaphysics, continued to live and reflect; for through the horror of the vats, pipes and alembics, she—and she alone—retained the consciousness of the vast original field.

It is impossible to repeat in detail the thousand peripeties of the nascent essence. Only know that one morning, it was, for the original field, the hour of the final resurrection. And that resurrection, after the varied martyrdom of the factory, burst forth in the spring sunshine under the aspect of a bottle of authentic triple extract.

Thus it was given to an entire hill of violets to add a rich phial to the various accessories that shine, ludicrous, costly and charming, in the cupboards of coquettish men and beautiful Parisiennes.

And now, reawakened, assimilated to one another even more closely than in the days of their vegetal life, the little companions of old, liberated from their tiny bodies, resumed chatting to one another in that liquid form, glad to recognize one another and to find one another again, although truly too narrowly confined.

The memories that they evoked, memories of the time when the butterflies loved them, were so much more intense than that primitive life had been, that their conversation, in the form of perfume, traversed the glass of the bottle and spread throughout the cupboard.

However, my violet did not speak, having retained her native soul intact. Thus transformed she sensed herself, a precious drop, similar to the hat of dew that had once coiffed her. And she was still waiting, fervent but without impatience, because, throughout the infernal adventure, she had not forgotten what her cricket had said.

One day, a hand took hold of the bottle in the cupboard. A beautiful young lady removed its various envelopes and opened it. And the collective spirit of the violets, like a magnificent butterfly of old, invisible and lighter, began to fly hither and yon in the room, so present, in spite of being unseen, that the young lady uttered a little cry.

Ecstatically, she said: "What a beautiful essence!"

And having inclined the bottle preciously over her handkerchief, a large drop spread over the fine linen and steeped it with a moist circle. That drop was none other than the pensive violet to whom a marvelous afterlife had been promised.

This is certainly happiness, thought the violet.

But she did not feel particularly happy. Thread by thread she spread over the white handkerchief. The beautiful young woman had plunged it into a muff where her little hands also held it, sagely joined. She traveled. Subsequently, the violet saw new things: a drawing room where many ladies, as complicated and as delicate as flowers, saluted to right and left, while a few rare messieurs, as black-clad and agile as insects, came and went from one to another.

And the poor little thing thought: *Why did my friend the cricket not tell me that the life of humans is exactly similar to that of a field of violets?*

Suddenly, the hands of the beautiful young woman, occupied with a cup of tea, dropped the handkerchief and the drop of odor that inhabited it, without perceiving it.

Then another hand, that of a young man, picked up the handkerchief with precaution and hid it swiftly in the pocket of a waistcoat. Through the obscurity of that pocket, the great beats of a heart were perceptible.

When evening came, alone and shut in his own room, the young man took out the handkerchief gently, and began respiring it and kissing it, with frissons that resembled sobs; and his halting voice murmured his thoughts, saying:

"O perfume, perfume of the woman I love! O drop of violet! Here you are, like a phantom full of grace, under my mouth. When I respire you, O perfume of the woman I love, you remind me of her gaze, her voice and her gesture, more than that, of all that is unexpressed in her very dear person . . . I love you, O drop of violet, pearl that contains, like the sea, all my desire! O perfume, breath of her kiss, O you who render the beloved person to me, for a second, I love you, real presence, drop of violet, soul and flesh of the adored!"

Then the timid violet, spread over the fine linen of the handkerchief, finally understood the mystery of the ancient words. And, saluting from the depths of absence her friend the cricket, she felt that the hour of her happiness had come, since Amour, as to a human being, had given to her, a humble little flower, an immortal soul.

THE DREAM OF A KABYLE EVENING
(*Le Journal*, 17 March 1907)

A little in advance of her little Franco-Arab caravan, upright on her mule, her eyes dilated by fatigue, Princesse Patricia was still drawing closer to the goal of her journey. Since the morning, for a long time, they had been climbing forested roads through zeen oaks and flowers. Bouquets of irises, pansies, forget-me-nots and violets were suspended from the harnesses, and Patricia had even ornamented the gray head of her mount with a mauve and white crown.

Pretty in her short skirt and tailored chemisette, under her large Italian felt hat, she felt simplified, almost happy. Her soul, for a peaceful moment was sleeping within her like a troubled individual in repose. She was not thinking about anything, satisfied that her gaze, as she went higher, was engulfing so much beauty.

An African landscape: inhabited valleys, clumps of oleanders, around streams charged with pebbles . . . everywhere, in the paths, disorderly springs flowing around the hooves of the mules; everywhere, expansive blooms pressing against one another under the branches, like natural flower-beds. In the low country, in the hothouse warmth of the underwood, they had encountered bands of monkeys; now, they were going toward the snow. They were climbing. There were temperate mountains fringed with oaks, cut by green clearings, where the long fresh grass had a fallacious air of durability. The maritime Thababor mountains cut out their jagged silhouettes against a sky already softened by the imminent dusk. And beyond the valleys, peaks and rivers, infinitely distant and blue, was the sea, the supreme horizon.

A sudden caprice, such as she sometimes manifested, had brought Patricia to Algeria, which she already knew. But without wanting to linger seeing again the colonial capitals and the landscapes of habitual tourism, she had decided to undertake this little new expedition in Kabylia, over little frequented trails. A rich francophile Arab had offered to guide the journey during dinner at a luxurious villa in Algiers and the whimsical beauty had accepted, in spite of the timid protestations of her entourage.

Now, faithful and resigned, she was followed, on mule and horseback, by her husband, the rich Arab and a few friends brought from France. Five indigenous horsemen closed the march.

The goal of the journey was a little highly-placed spring, which the Arabs called "the Spring of the Seven Stones," because they said that it was impossible, so glacial was it, to pick up seven stones in succession with the hand. They were to sleep at hazard at forest stations and kabyle habitations, but a Spahi, sent in advance by the sub-prefect of the region, had received orders to have meals and receptions prepared by guards and indigenes.

Patricia, therefore, slightly in advance of the others, was actively pushing her mule. She was happy in the illusion she had of being alone in the landscape; and now, at an abrupt turning in the path, in a grassy clearing, she perceived a little white-clad pastor sitting under a tree, who was guarding a few goats.

That was not a new spectacle for her, but as the child seemed to her, at a distance, to be sitting in a posture even nobler than that of others, she steered her mule in his direction, and stopped a few paces away.

The child, motionless in his place, watched her coming as if she had not been introduced. Then, Patricia searched in her bosom for her silver lorgnette and, aiming it at the impassive little shepherd, she stifled a cry of admiration.

He might have been ten years old. He was draped in the white and red robes of Arab pastors, his legs bare, his waist circled by a cord, his head enveloped in wool and linen, and he advanced a perfect little foot in the grass, as dry and brown as that of a mummy. But Patricia scarcely noticed those details, gripped as she was entirely by the pastor's face, occupied by his three blue tattoos, the heavy silver earrings that quivered in his right ear, and his violet mouth, split and succulent, rounder than a Muscat grape; and above all, she was fascinated by the consternating beauty of two immense, improbable eyes that opened in the dark face.

Between their heavy bistre eyelids charged with shiny black lashes, those eyes were so bright, of such an unexpected blue, that their color could truly only be compared with the large oblong opal that the princesse always wore on her left hand.

And Patricia, quivering on her mule, extended her neck toward the inconceivable eyes that were fixed on her without blinking, like two green stars, above somber Muslim cheeks.

Her heart was beating forcefully. Her teeth were clenched. She understood, face to face with the exotic little boy, that she had suddenly arrived at the goal of all her voyages, all her anxious courses through life.

What she had awaited in vain in human gazes, she found before her at a bend in an African path, at the back of a grassy clearing, in March, and her overturned soul could scarcely conceive such a miracle. For was not the gaze of the large pale irises of the coppery child that of Cleopatra, Adonis and Circe? Was it not the sacred that one sought in the display-cases of museums where millenary faces reposed? Was it not all that one demands of art, music, the sky and the sea? Was it not the Ineffable?

And the princesse, her hands joined toward the motionless little masculine idol, dedicated to him at that silent moment all her being, what might be called her spiritual flesh and her physical soul; and she felt that she would never again be able to live without those fascinating eyes.

The abrupt arrival of her caravan, which caught up with her, extracted her from her dream. They were astonished to find her halted; they pointed out to her that the day was already declining, and that it was necessary to hasten to complete the stage before nightfall.

But she, pathetic and stubborn, cut off all the overlapping speech around her with a gesture. "It's here that we're stopping," she declared. "I've arrived."

The Frenchmen looked at one another, amazed, trying to take account of it, but resigned in advance to everything. The indigenous horsemen, passive and lordly, dismounted without even trying to understand, by virtue of the habitude of fatality. Only the rich Frenchified Arab, Si Ahmed ben Ali, raised a loud laugh of protestation. Then, having perceived the little shepherd still sitting in his place, he made an angry movement toward him, shouting at him in Arabic to go away quickly, with his goats.

And the child, bounding to his feet, his face distressed, was already fleeing as fast as his legs could carry him when Patricia uttered a cry. Leaping from her mule, she ran after the barefoot child in order to bring him back by force, in spite of him howling and weeping with terror.

And, pale with scandal, she exhaled: "What, Si Ahmed! You're chasing him away?" Then, mutedly: "Him . . . ? This god . . . ?"

And Si Ahmed, short and stout, square in his jacket, started to laugh so loudly that the veins of his forehead swelled as if to burst around his Turkish fez.

The Frenchmen, however, had nearly understood. They had known their princesse for a long time. One of them took Si Ahmed to one side, for they all feared for him some eruption on the part of the willful and disconcerting young woman.

In the meantime without any longer looking at anyone, she applied herself to domesticating the frightened child by means of coaxing.

"Si Ahmed," she said, imperiously, "come here. Translate what I say. Tell him that he is a god, that I love him, that his eyes are too beautiful to be human, that . . ."

And without waiting for a response, clasping the child to her with a maternal gesture, she started murmuring things to him with all her soul. And her thought said:

Little siren, would you like to come with me to my country? I shall take you away with the same precaution as if you were precious antique glassware. And when we've arrived at my home, in my city, I shall care for you, unique object, as if you were living in a mysterious display case, unknown to everyone. For I shall shut you away and keep you for myself alone, amid incense and flowers, because I would be tortured by jealousy if others could also look at you. I shall ornament you with golden robes and tiaras, O adorable little pontiff. I shall put myself on my knees before the green turquoises of your eyes, before the blue emeralds of your eyes, and for hours and hours, I shall weep with joy at the feet of the sacred person; I shall sink into your gaze, which is like the star called Wormwood in the Apocalypse, I shall admire you until death!

The Frenchmen gazed covertly, without saying anything, at Patricia, ecstasized before her find. Dusk had finally arrived. The visible summits were flamboyant, illuminated by violent colors. The sea darkened. The shadow rose from the depths of the valleys, like a silent tide, toward the heights; and the forest flowers of the underwood manifested their presence by means of more evident perfumes.

Si Ahmed, no longer able to retain his hilarity, suddenly cried in the silence: "Truly, Princesse, I'm astonished that a little wretch like that can interest you! He's ignorant, that child! He has no idea of civilization. He doesn't understand anything. He doesn't know anything."

"He knows that he's beautiful," growled Patricia.

"Him? Let's make a wager—that he doesn't even know the color of his own eyes."

"Shut up!" said Patricia, wildly—for that thought plunged her into an abyss of stupefaction.

Then, having turned with a distressed face toward the child, she took him to sit down further away from the others, holding him by the shoulders like a prey, devouring the fabulous eyes with her gaze—which, in the increasingly emphatic twilight, were now contemplating her without tears or fear, completely reassured, almost brazen.

Their double gleam was like two circles of daylight in the gloom. One might have thought that the blue moonlight of African nights was about to filter through their somber lashes . . .

And in spite of the rapidly invading night, Patricia saw that those eyes, scanning at her from top to toe so insistently, had so much intensity that she felt herself blushing and paling under the gaze of her divinity.

Suddenly, the opal irises lit up in the half-light, as if charged with animal phosphorus. The violet mouth opened slightly. A few guttural words emerged with a little hoarse laugh.

"He spoke to me!" exclaimed the princesse, in a stifled voice; and as if she were calling for help, she said: "Si Ahmed! Si Ahmed! Come here! Tel me what he said."

And, the child having repeated his phrase, the princesse, her head bowed, waited, trembling, as if destiny were being pronounced in the commencing night by the taut mouth, as round and succulent as a muscat grape.

Then Si Ahmed translated, calmly: "He's asking whether you'd like to give him shoes like yours, and also what it is that you have around your neck—which is to say, your false collar."

Patricia had stood up very straight. The Frenchmen saw her groping her way toward them. They all stood up.

"We're leaving," she said, in a somber voice.

"Where are we going?" her husband asked, timidly.

She murmured: "We're returning to France, to Paris, else-where . . . let's go! Let's go!"

Such anguish punctuated her voice that they all kept silent, impressed.

They mounted up. The heads of the beasts were turned toward the descent. It was a flight, a retreat half way, a return toward the cities, the abandonment of the Spring of Seven Stones, glacial and highly placed the goal of the journey.

But why would Patricia have continued her route, having just drunk from the translucent and bitter springs of the child's eyes, which had seduced her?

On the point of disappearing around the bend in the path, however, Si Ahmed saw her make a gesture. She removed from her finger the large and magnificent ring in which the oblong opal shone between diamonds. Then she made a little sign to the child. Doubtless, as a souvenir, she wanted to throw him from a height the ring that resembled his gaze . . .

But Si Ahmed stopped her arm.

"Don't do that, Princesse," he said, "if you don't want the child to be murdered tomorrow in a corner of the wood."

A flash passed through the darkened eyes of the princesse; but she recovered quickly.

"Rather give him twenty sous," said Si Ahmed.

Then, the child having put out his hand, the silver coin glinted in his obscure palm. And a laugh of joy and amazement, hoarse and puerile, burst forth in the shadow, followed by numerous harsh syllables, by which the raucous little god summoned all the benedictions of the heavens upon his benefactress, the Nazarene.

But she, intoxicated and wounded, her teeth clenched, her head bowed, drew away into the night at the pace of her mule, engaged in the steep path. And she had clasped her hand over her complex Occidental heart, for she felt, mortally plunged therein, the two blue darts, the two ironic arrows, of the gaze of the child who resembled the divinity, but who was not the divinity.

THE GIRL WITH THE COCK
(*Le Journal*, 31 March 1907)

WHAT charming old friend, a shrewd connoisseur of the hearts of children, had sent little Catherine the Easter gift that she was busy unwrapping that morning, sitting in her narrow bed?

The pretty little girl is seen, red with emotion in her white pillows, shifting her delicate hands around the pieces of paper that protect the large sugar egg, of the contents of which she is as yet unaware.

Around her, the room is bright and tidy, ornamented with puerile images and neat furniture, in the special style of the nurseries in which children raised in the English style grow up so pleasantly. Her mother, her big sisters and her governess look on, smiling. The windows, splashed with early spring sunshine, frame within their troubled panes the park, already green, profound, leafy and cultivated, where the lilacs are beginning to sway gently in the temperate air of Saint-Germain-en-Laye. The birds are singing, the sky is blue, the weather fine.

The last piece of paper having been removed, little Catherine, with great emotion, opens the Easter egg, white, pink, and swollen, the sugar of which seems between her fingers to be a marvelous honey. And now, instead of the anticipated bonbons, falling in a cascade on to the sheets, she sees, crouching in the oval prison, a living chick, yellow and round, like a ball of plush. It has a minuscule and black eye, which is gazing fearfully in profile, a hooked beak that is chirping, thin clawed feet that are clenched. And its tiny heart is beating forcefully, through the fragile thorax, which a slight tightening of the fingers could crush at a stroke.

Little Catherine has uttered a cry. With an almost fearful precaution, she has taken the baby bird in her two hands and pressed it against her tremulous mouth. The witnesses laugh at her pleasure.

"Maman, Maman," she says, "is it really for me?"

And there are surprises, enchantments and exclamations. The child can scarcely calm her joy sufficiently to allow herself to be washed, dressed and coiffed. Finally ready, she goes down into the park, avid to carry her little treasure to some corner of the grass, to be alone with her Easter gift, with the living thing that belongs to her. And her ten-year-old breast is swollen with the sentiment of the possession and the responsibility, inflated too with the muted joy of spring, the happiness of being a little girl on vacation, released into a beautiful April garden, clutching in her warm and respectful hands a living being that will be the intense amusement of her hours of liberty.

✳

Children make unexpected finds. Anxious to emerge with honor from her role as a mother, having placed her chick in the greenhouse, Catherine imagined, in order to replace the brooding of a warm natural hen, installing in a corner a large feather duster stolen from the servants' parlor. The chick, still as fragile as an egg, immediately took refuge there of its own accord. And as she was afraid of seeing her adoptive son perish, the little girl took care, every morning, to pour a little red wine into the paste of bread crumbs, with the result that from day to day, the little creature of yellow plush grew visibly, ornamenting itself with commencing plumage, parading its gangling and comical body of a healthy little chick in the grass, or wherever it was taken.

His neck, already arrogant, straightened. A few curved pinions appeared in his tail. A dainty crest, like a dentellate cotyledon, began to emerge from his head. And it was thus that it was perceived, very rapidly, that the Easter chick was nothing other than a cockerel.

The first enthusiasm having passed, it seemed that the little girl ought, in accordance with the extreme versatility of children, to lose interest in her ward and simply abandon him among the poultry of the henhouse. But what pullet, throughout the world, could resemble that one?

Quickly habituated to his mistress, he became her inseparable friend. Enterprising and brazen, he leapt on to the table at lunch, pecking the plates, stealing butter from the butter-dish and pillaging fruits. He also caught flies on the wall and pecked with a vigorous thrust of the beak all the shiny objects that caught his eye. When Catherine came back from school, he advanced quickly toward her in the alleyway, and then followed on her heels across the garden like a short shadow. And she ran, laughing, turning her head in order to see her cockerel pursuing her. He hastened the strides of his stiff little feet, his neck extended and his crest on fire.

Now he had become strong and tall on his legs; and, doubtless because of the wine on which he had been nourished, he was aggressive and dangerous to strangers, upon whom he precipitated himself, bristling with malevolence. People were afraid of that combative bird, ever ready to leap at their eyes. And because of that, Catherine probably loved him a little more, because for her alone he showed himself to be tractable, and as gentle as a tame turtle-dove.

Often, at play time, she placed him on her narrow little girl's shoulder or her extended wrist, in the manner of pages of old carrying a falcon. Or she placed him against her chest, over her striped smock, buckling her schoolgirl's leather belt over the hot body of the bird. Then there were gallops through the branches, shrill cries to the four corners of the summer, embalmed with the odor of mown lawns. The warm garden twisted its branches in an intact sky, the multicolored blooms in the flower-bed were splendid in the sunlight. Outside the shrunken pathways there were corners of shadow that were almost forest-like.

It was there that the little girl, panting, intoxicated and gone wild, let herself fall down with fatigue after running, her bright floating hair clinging to her temples, her large fresh eyes laughing and her teeth sparkling in the green gloom, with all the gaiety of her ten-year-old soul, freely exalted amid the vegetal richness.

Then the great blue, green and golden cock raised himself up on his feet, already armed with nascent spurs, shook his feathers of flame and, with a great effort, as if he were accomplishing a mysterious duty, crowed as if to render his soul. And the fleshy coral of his crest expanded, like a dazzling flower, in the filtered and dancing light of the branches.

"Bayard! Bayard!" cried the little girl. "Shut up! Go to sleep!"

He knew his name. He understood. Crouched in a corner, he lowered his crested head over his elegance of changing reflections, and his bewitching eye, darted in profile at the little girl, glinted in the shadow like a droplet of fire, full of the ancient enigma that similarly illuminated the augural and hypnotized eyes of the sacred fowl of Rome.

But the happy days of complete confidence passed. An anxiety began to spread through the blood of little Catherine. She quit the nursery. She was growing up. Her elbows became sharp, her movements awkward. She lost her appetite for mad gallops and panting games in the grass. At a slower pace she now roamed the pathways, her soul troubled, anxious about something unknown. And behind her, faithful and dependent,

Bayard, the great dangerous cock, marched with a military step, more important, it seemed, redder and more peremptory than the usher at high mass.

Catherine still loved him. She took him on her knees in moments of solitude when, sitting on some old stone bench, she let the joy or sadness of the seasons penetrate her, motionless, living and passive being, like a plant. A pink flower from a chestnut tree, a sprig of linden, a dead leaf or a first snowflake fell in silence on to her differently combed hair; then she bowed her head and voiced her ennui quietly.

"What's wrong with me, Bayard?" she murmured. "What's wrong with me?"

And the cock, by virtue of acquired habit, climbed on to the customary shoulder and clung on there with all the strength of his hooked claws, to such an extent that Catherine's family said to her, from morning until evening: "It's ridiculous, at your age, still to be playing with that cock, like a little girl. People will make fun of you. When are you going to rid us of that nasty beast?"

And the little girl sometimes wept silently, because of the growing animosity toward her favorite; and she looked at him when, standing up with one leg in the air and his breast forward, he seemed to be giving her an advice of defiance and audacity against all the malcontents.

One afternoon, mounted on the gardener's cart, her cock crouching on her shoes, the somber girl felt more cheerful, more like her ten-year-old self of old. Once again, four years having passed, it was the eve of Easter. And the April air, along the rustic route that goes toward Mareil and Fourqueux, already had the scent of a bouquet. They were going to the establishment of some horticulturalist, where the gardener hoped to find cuttings. Catherine thought about the sugar Easter egg from which her great friend Bayard had emerged one morning. She started to laugh at that memory. She was decidedly cheerful. The excursion amused her. She also rejoiced in delivering a whole parcel of garments to a poor family in Mareil in whom her parents took an interest. She had been given sole charge of the task, and because of that she felt invested with a certain importance.

They arrived. Followed by her cock, Catherine, leaving the gardener to his cuttings, headed for the wretched dwelling of her protégés.

As soon as she crossed the threshold, her heart was gripped frightfully.

"Oh, my poor demoiselle!" the mother was already weeping.

And there was a concert of lamentations, an assault of unhappy gazes, which greeted the poor visitor pitilessly. She was informed of all the worries, the rent to pay, sickness, the lack of work, foreclosure, hunger . . .

Defenseless against that flood of human suffering, which assailed her overly narrow shoulders, the child felt very small, intimidated, ashamed, as if abandoned in the midst of a strange, mutedly hostile clan. She blushed, displayed her large packet of clothing, and regretted not having any money.

And suddenly, a bloody phrase fell upon her heart like an adroitly delivered thrust: "And to think that we have nothing to eat, and that tomorrow is Easter Day!"

A kind of tremor ran through the girl before the mystery of Coincidence.

"Easter . . . Easter . . ." she thought. "And these people are dying of hunger. And my family reproach me for my games . . . Yes, yes, it's a warning! I'm no longer a child . . . I ought no longer . . . I ought no longer . . ."

She had become very pale. She bent down toward her great friend Bayard and, effortfully, held out the docile and confident

140

beast to the poor people who were harassing her pity, and she said, almost in spite of herself, stammering with anguish: "Since you have nothing for Easter, here . . . by eating him boiled, he won't be too tough . . ."

And without saying *au revoir*, without turning her head, recklessly, as if she were being pursued, she ran away, her palms over her ears and her eyes closed, because she knew that behind her, vindictive and brilliant, her great cock was struggling in murderous hands, and that his raucous voice was already calling for help; she knew how, his crimson crest congested by anger, dolor and fear, the cock would be swelling his magnificence with changing reflections, bristling his golden neck, the throat that a sacrilegious knife was about to cut.

But she did not turn round and she did not retrace her steps, for she understood, confusedly and desperately, that she had just delivered to death, in the person of the familiar beast, her tranquil candor, her games, her garden and her gaiety; because in the life of young beings, an hour always comes when childhood has to die, sacrificed, between the cruel and sad hands of grown-ups.

THE LADY IN THE GROTTO
(*Le Journal*, 9 April 1907)

THERE is doubtless no need to specify in what corner of Algeria or Tunisia, as a result of the explosion of a mine by workmen building a road, a subterranean grotto was discovered, extended under the colonial earth, previously unsuspected by human gazes. The only thing that it is important to know is the fashion in which Ali, the temporary domestic of Lord and Lady Fitzhalls, ran to his masters' villa in order to inform them of the discovery.

Had Ali understood, in his deep Arab brain, that the little lady took pleasure in local things, and was eager for any novelty and for everything picturesque? Had his sure primitive instinct informed him that she would love to be the first to gaze at the marvel so unexpectedly brought to light?

He ran along the sea road, near to which that morning's calm and rounded waves unfurled. He climbed the abrupt road that led to the villa. His heart was beating rapidly when he knocked on the door.

The little lady, pink and blonde, illuminated by two beautiful bright blue eyes in which her poetic soul burst forth, woke up at the noise he made. Rapidly dressed, she went down to enquire about the event.

She had only been living for two months in that fortunate corner of Africa, to which some concern for her husband's health had brought her, and, being healthy and enterprising, she had already seen a great deal under the guidance of the naïve, wily and faithful Ali, who took her to the significant places in the village and the surrounding area.

When he had explained everything in a guttural French that was very difficult to follow, the lady went with him, and they both headed toward the work-site, he glad to serve his employer and she palpitating with excitement at the idea of what she was about to see.

There was a great movement in the work-yard when she appeared there. Among the indigenous, Italian and French workers she bore the authority of her frail and fresh Nordic beauty and also her wealth, quickly evaluated in the locale by the tips distributed on arrival.

With polite precautions she was taken, torch in hand, toward the treasure that the hazard of a stick of dynamite had just abruptly revealed to modern eyes after thousands of centuries in which the rock and the water, far from any human gaze, had accomplished their magnificent and secret work in subterranean silence.

Trembling with emotion, Lady Fitzhalls, sustained by the workers, descended into the dark hole of the grotto. Torches and lanterns were flickering in the black hole. The lady's eyes blinked. When her gaze had adapted somewhat, she distinguished the forms that surrounded her; and without being able to take another step forward, she put her hands to her breast and retained the sharp cry of her admiration.

Can you imagine what the sensation might be of entering alive into a great lily, of being the first creature to stand in the midst of complicated stalactites and stalagmites, on which no human eyes have previously opened, of feeling that yours is the initial gaze visiting the millennia-old palace of obscurity?

The little lady looked around and did not feel too infimal to support the burden of such a divine adventure. Her imagination could not invent anything more extraordinary than the reality that pressed around her in serried ranks of specters, the multiform offspring of the darkness. It would have been necessary to accumulate all cults and ideas to be able to express what she divined through the eternal midnight of the grotto.

Pale riches were accumulated in the blackness, riches that had not existed before the lady was there, since no conscious presence had yet confronted them. She saw distances that wound around and diversified like a series of cathedrals the color of snow, at the end of which the blue daylight from outside was reflected with the glint of a precious stone. Above her head there were millions of inverted stone candles that seemed to be weeping wax. In the shadow of coverts, great unfinished white elephants extended their immense ears; petrified linen was hanging; pearl flowers blossomed; the wings of swans opened; wan giant hands reached out. All the doves of the New Testament were designed, all the Catholic virgins, next to ecstatic white Buddhas, all the great organs of the mass lined up their various livid pipes: seraphic allusion, damp alabaster, and sculpted shadow; it seemed that an incommensurable white coral had ramified the pallid vegetation of a nocturnal ocean.

The torch shifts. Other naves appear, other larvae surge forth. And at the tips of all the stalactites, elephants' ears, candles, flowers and wings, the drop of germinative water is always suspended, the patient tear whose infinitely slow work has forged that buried pantheon or pandemonium, in which all the symbols and all the myths of human thought are entangled.

The lady listens. All the way to the depths of the most tortuous naves, the dripping of the stone is incessant and thin. The stalagmites glisten. Little lakes rounded out in places are swarming with living fish, blind like those of catacombs, since eyes would have been useless to them in the darkness.

The lady gradually pulls herself together at the first faint of astonishment. At present, she is running around, brushing things, shuddering at the folds of virgin chaos, one by one.

Immaculate conception! says her thought. *I am the first to see and touch it! This is the grotto of the fays, the abode of the blind sirens; the blind treasure of the night is here!*

As she leans between two baroque columns, she discovers, by advancing her head, an unexpected excavation. She ventures into it. And she is soon hidden in the utmost hollow of the tormented stone, with the sensation of entering into an immense seashell. On arriving in the depths she stops, because she has just encountered water. She raises her lantern and looks.

A natural basin is there, profound, the obscure water of which glitters from time to time with a frisson of fishy scales.

"Sirens! Sirens!" murmurs the lady.

And her little Anglo-Saxon soul, nourished on tales and poetry, extends entirely toward the imaginary inhabitants and her soft voice whispers incantations to them.

"I am a woman like you, I am a woman of the sea, like you, on my proud isle, looming over the waves like a great ship. I understand you. I love you. Don't be alarmed by my presence. My blue eyes are like two salty drops of the Ocean. Come, hidden sirens, blind sirens. I will lend you the gaze of my eyes in order to explain to you what your anxious hands touch in the darkness. And perhaps you will understand the sun; and perhaps, gradually, your closed eyelids will be unsealed to daylight and allow your pupils to be seen, which have never been contemplated, more profound and enigmatic than the marine gulf in which you originated, O captives! I have come to deliver you, my sisters. Emerge from the surface, rise toward my guiding voice!"

※

They had some difficulty in persuading her to go home. And henceforth, her days were spent in the grotto, where, penetrating to the hidden pool that she had discovered, watching for scales, she murmured ancient verses and sang refrains from Scotland and Ireland, in order to attract the young oceanic women.

Not that she really believed in their existence—but that poetic game was an instinct of her soul, moistened by the mists of the north where so many melancholy fays are born.

It was thus until her husband, feeling better or becoming bored, decided that it was necessary for her to quit her Africa and her grotto and return to her native Europe.

Time passed, events succeeded one another. There was life, with everything it brought with it to the beach of days, from the depths of the unknown abysses of destiny.

After many years, Lady Fitzhalls came back, alone and gray-haired, toward the country of her dream, toward the unforgettable grotto of her youth. Doubtless she had lived with the latent memory of the sirens, and carefully cultivated in her heart the hope of returning to them one day.

The British soul can be constant and respectful thus, and poetic to the end, like that of an adolescent girl.

The blue eyes of Lady Fitzhalls, still blue in the bruising of her aged face, reopened again, therefore, one morning in April, upon the landscape of old. But without wanting to look at anything around her, or giving herself the time for an emotion on rediscovering the beloved soil, she marched at a nervous pace, very pale and almost fatal, toward the past grotto, toward the mysterious abode of which her gaze, before any other, had violated the milky splendor.

She did not want to stop at the sad surprises of the entrance, which was now defended by two guardians and a turnstile. She paid, with a curt gesture, the five sous demanded, and passed through.

Electric light, the globes of which were suspended like gross stars, illuminated the snowy churches to the depths of their secrecy; and one saw, in that raw light, the profanations accomplished by the thousands of tourists who, for years, had passed through there: chipped elephants' ears, stone linen defaced by signatures, broken wings. Everyone, in coming here, had left behind some personal insult.

The lady's heart was horribly constricted, but she lowered her eyes, not wanting to notice anything, in haste to go straight to the place that might not have been discovered by the crowd, toward the pool of the eyeless sirens, who had been waiting for such a long time, hidden and fearful in their stone spiral, for the first human soul to return, the one who was able to recite ancient verses to them and sing refrains from Scotland and Ireland.

When she was before the hollow of the dark water, she stopped, her heart suddenly joyful—for, in fact, no light illuminated the cavity known to her alone, the unique corner of the grotto that had remained faithful to her.

But as she groped, already murmuring the words, toward her scaly submerged friends, a little Arab porter, posted in a corner, approached with an acetylene flashlight, and with a habitual, mechanical movement, directed the light toward the depths of the excavation—with the consequence that, dilating her eyes in order to perceive some marine daughter, Lady Fitzhalls, with a hoarse cry, saw before her this inscription in black letters, engraved in the haunted rock itself, the miraculous rock of her youth:

Splendid Hotel.
Magnificent view over the sea.
Modern comfort. Electricity. Elevator.

THE AMOROUS WARDROBE
(*Le Journal*, 21 April 1907)

AN old provincial house, standing in the middle of its garden. It had once contained many people. All of its windows had been full of faces, young or puerile. At present, silent, it only respired by virtue of the presence of three inhabitants, an aged monsieur, an aged lady and an aged maidservant. It was an existence devoid of interest, for the life of old people in the provinces is almost always cold, meager and eccentric.

That is why the house possessed corners that no one any longer knew, from attics whose key had been lost to abandoned sheds. Among others, it possessed a room on the ground floor that had once had the function of a lumber room, and which was now decaying slowly in mildew, dust and obscurity. Cobwebs had ended up veiling its window completely with the crepe of forgetfulness, and even the mice no longer went there because there was nothing to nibble.

Among the rejected objects and all the deformed things accumulated in that dark room, in a corner almost opposite the window, there was a wardrobe, a good wardrobe of sturdy substance and charmless style, the tarnished and stained mirror of which was shaky in its Louis-Philippe ornamentation. One of its feet was lame at the bottom and almost all its decorations were chipped. Perhaps it could still have been serviceable, for it was made of durable wood, but, forgotten in that hovel and disaffected, it was dying of inutility—for objects are a little like domestic animals that perish of chagrin when they no longer have a master.

Its damaged silvering, however, still remembered having reflected the lives of several families, with everything the quotidian brings of petty dramas and petty comedies. The sole witness of things forever dead, that wardrobe, in the profound heart of its mirror, afflicted by abandonment, felt the multiple secrets of its past fading away a little more every day. And nothing new came to revivify it, since, in the guise of reflection, it only repeated, from dawn to dusk, a dark and monotonous midnight similar to annihilation.

Thus, the seasons passed around it and the years went by, devoid of form and color.

Every time that April returned, however, the sad wardrobe, from the depths of its darkness, felt incomprehensible frissons passing through its ligneous body; and in the silence of its prison, it started to creak involuntarily. At times, it was even seized by a tremor so forceful that it was like a great muted blow, which, suddenly shaking its immobility, almost caused it to stumble on its lame leg. And every time that phenomenon occurred, it knew thereby that over things and people, in houses and gardens, everywhere except the moldy redoubts of old dwellings, it was spring.

One day in April, as it was stretched thus and filled the shadow with the noise of its laboring wood, an event occurred in the room where nothing had happened for forty years: the door opened and a young woman came in

Was she a niece on vacation, who had come, by a hazard of destiny, to spend Easter with her old uncle and aunt? Had she, while ferreting here and there, found in the severe and dusty house where she was becoming bored some key or hook, and had natural curiosity impelled her to go into that locked room?

She was probably not pretty, and the lines of her face and body doubtless allowed it to be anticipated that she was marked by the family seal, destined to continue insignificant generations, and her blood would flow, prejudiced, deceptive and mean, to be charged with all the stupidity, bleakness and unconscious crimes of societies. But she was fifteen years old, and to be fifteen is, in spite of everything, to possess some beauty.

Over the supreme freshness of that age, at which childhood and youth seem, for a single instant, to meet and embrace, does not a furtive breath of poetry and comprehension always pass? There is an anxiety, a melancholy, something inexplicable, which even troubles the petty anodyne hearts of banal adolescents. There are tears for no reason when night falls. There is an unreflective curiosity that, without knowing why, opens old locked doors in passing.

She had quit some "lady's work" in order to wander through the house alone. She did not know what she wanted. She went into the obscure room hesitantly and looked around. And her slightly red girlish hands, with an impulsive, almost involuntary movement, strove to open the rusty and black window on which the cobwebs hung.

She employed a more violent effort. There was a rattle of shaken panes, a screech of paralyzed hinges, and the two battens were wide open. A flood of light entered like a violent inundation. And the first thing that the young woman saw, in the deteriorated mirror of the wardrobe, was her reflection standing before her, pale and seemingly distant, like a phantom of herself.

Quickly, she took out her handkerchief and began wiping the mirror, carefully; for feminine instinct impelled her to clarify her image. In spite of her cares, however, nothing remained of her in the wounded silvering, ravaged by time and damp, but a vague mirage, a kind of faded pastel in which blots and holes persisted.

And yet, it was with complaisance that she advanced, tilting her head to one side, arranging her hair, turning one way and the other. Then, having recoiled slightly, and finally becoming still, she suddenly smiled. Then, all of spring spread into the room.

✳

The outside is reflected. Branches sway in the mirror; clouds pass by within it; the distances therein are blue and violet; the sigh of the month of April is exhaled there entirely.

And the young woman understands something, confusedly. A lyrical frisson runs through her. An unknown emotion overtakes her. April and her fifteen years are identified in a single shudder. Standing in the dust, among the discarded objects and deformed things, before the lame and creaking wardrobe, she is, for a moment of her existence, a poet.

She raises her arms and shakes an exalted face.

"Bonjour, spring!" she exclaims, involuntarily.

But she stops quickly, blushing, because she believes that life is in the lady's needlework that she has just quit, and not in the mysterious impulse that suddenly seems to her to be stupid.

And she goes out, ashamed, and closes the door behind her, but forgetting to close the window.

✳

The shadow, disturbed by the daylight, has taken refuge in little corners. The mirror of the wardrobe continues to reflect the garden. And it is a landscape more beautiful than nature, troubled and glaucous, that the old Louis-Philippe frame concentrates within its chipped decorations. A bird flies into the room and is deceived by it. In flying toward the fictitious trees, the trees that it has never seen before, it bumps into the glass and is astonished. The wardrobe creaks. The bird has alighted on it, at the very top, and the little song that it commences is full of precipitate questions.

"What is this garden similar to mine, although differently orientated and so pale? Why can't I enter it with my wings? And what is that creaking I can hear, similar to that of the big oak tree in the lawn?"

And the starts of the laboring wood are full of sage and slow responses.

"I remember now," says the forgotten wardrobe. "O bird, if you have alighted on me and are singing for me, and if I creak without knowing why when April returns, it's because I was once a beautiful tree in the sunlight, and I have not forgotten, in spite of my metamorphosis, that green sap once flowed in my vegetal veins and the very heart of the earth beat in my profound heartwood."

And the bird sings, and the wood recalls, and the mirror, like a fountain, replicates the garden heavy with lilac. And already, one of the real branches outside is directing its effort toward the window, through which, at length, it enters the room, to mingle its veritable ramifications there with the fallacious ones in the mirror.

Then the creaking of the wardrobe is augmented, for its ancient soul is perhaps still attempting the gesture of budding, in the surge of universal amour that is stimulating the triumphant renewal of everything.

And the young woman has departed, forgetting the open window, departed to live her banal life until the end; she will never know that, because of a smile of her fifteen-year-old mouth and a poetic instant of her fifteen-year-old soul, she has left behind her, in the room whose door has been closed again forever, an entire miracle of spring.

THE BLACK COURTESAN
AND THE WHITE FATHER

(*Le Journal,* 28 April 1907)

THE rapid African dusk was already darkening the halls of the museum of Carthage when the young white Father, the guardian of Punic antiquities, got ready to return to the convent. His day was terminated. He cast a distracted glance toward the windows.

Outside, the Fathers' garden, calm, with walls encrusted with fragments of statues and steles, swayed the blooms in its flower-beds. The fields of April barley that covered the site of Carthage quivered lightly in the direction of the sea, and the silence of the past and the evening reigned over the green mountain. On the horizon, the Mountain with Two Horns projected a dark blue reflection into the water.

The Father was a little tired, from having escorted visitors from one display case to another all afternoon, repeating the same phrases before the same objects, making the same jokes about the same comical masks of clay or plaster. An hour earlier, however, he had found a new quip concerning the death's head of the black courtesan who was showing intact teeth in a special glass case.

He thought about that with some satisfaction. His keys rattled in his belt. He took another few steps around in order to make sure that everything was in order.

In places, gold jewelry shone within the showcases, with a singular petty gleam, before being extinguished in the night. The roundness of urns was vaguely emphasized in the corners, amid the jars of Carthagnian make-up, Tanagra statuettes, pieces of iridescent glass and lamps with three beaks: all the meager and curious treasure of museums.

The Father headed for the door; but suddenly, passing before the head that he had mocked so cleverly, he perceived a slight unusual noise: a kind of dry creaking behind the glass. He stopped, surprised, and craned his neck. Then he shivered, because it seemed to him, face-to-face with the head, that it was looking at him fixedly from the depths of the three round holes in its macabre face.

The hour of dusk is an hour when it seems that one ought to understand something of the eternal mystery of the world. Perhaps the shadow in the midst of which one commences no longer to be able to distinguish the things of ordinary life reveals a little of the secret of the invisible.

The Father, immobilized in his place, understood in that way that the silence was speaking to him through the frightful mouth of the death's-head. Livid and trembling, his hands clutching his white robe, he listened.

Without speech, the head of the courtesan said:

"You are a holy father, full of science, and I am only a prostitute; but I am dead, and the dead, whoever they are, know more than the living, for they are the ancestors of the living. Now, one owes respect to ancestors. Why did you permit yourself to laugh, a little while ago, at my face? I'm grimacing, you say? In truth, if I wanted to grimace, your hair would stand on end under your red African skullcap, your eyes would bulge from their orbits, your teeth would chatter, and you would never again cross any threshold but that of a lunatic asylum."

The silence shut up momentarily. Then the menacing voice became sad, soft and dignified.

"It's a great cowardice when the strong mock those who are defenseless. Oh, what laughter all those living uttered when you insulted the little that remains of me, this poor fleshless face, dispossessed and mute! When I was also a living being in the sunlight, I was happy and rich, for I sold my beautiful dark flesh, which was flavorsome and shiny, very dearly to my lovers. I had stars that you others no longer suspect, and the most precious of the golden jewelry that you have stolen from our tombs. And since my early youth I had been given urns full of silver coins in order that my sepulcher would be magnificent and durable. Now, many civilizations have passed over our tombs, while respecting them. You alone have dared to put your hands on the sacred city of the dead; you alone have had the sad courage of hyenas and vultures.

"No matter! That is the right of the strongest, and if the seizure of that booty has hardly cost the heroism of your legions, it is a conquest nevertheless. I am therefore resigned to the slavery into which I have fallen. I accept without astonishment no longer being anything but an object, less important than a sigillary ring, remaining a prisoner in this narrow dungeon of crude glass, I who have drunk in the depths of my palace from Tyrian cups more costly than precious stones. But the thing that surprises me, O priest, is your laughter; for the dead know everything, and I know that religion nourishes the idea of eternity."

The young white Father had lowered his forehead deeply. The gravest voice of silence continued:

"Tell me, why do you teach your children to take off their hats when a funeral procession passes in the street? Why do you sanitize the dead? If you are going to mock the face of a skeleton, why do you talk about eternity? Yes, I know . . . you say: 'They're only old bones, and no longer have any importance. They've been in the ground for centuries.' But if you believe in eternity, why do you talk about centuries? What are thousands of centuries compared with eternity? There are no 'fresh dead' in the way that there are 'fresh eggs.' The dead no longer die. As soon as the most banal, the most vulgar and the most despicable living being is six feet underground, your instinct impels you to consider him as something sacred; if you believe in the sanctity of the dead, why do you not tell yourselves that their wisdom is augmented with the centuries of death, and that those who are no more than dust know much more than a recent cadaver buried with so much emotion and ceremony?"

Night had fallen completely. Nothing could any longer be distinguished but a form, a reflection, a labeled disorder of glass cases. Only a few stars were scintillating in the windows.

More confidentially, more intimately, the voice concluded: "No! It's necessary not to laugh at the dead. It's necessary to be in intelligence with them, as if they were your contemporaries. That is the charity they expect from the living. In any case, we are all contemporaries. Listen! Listen, O unreflective young man, you who sit down in church to hear the lessons of preachers: you permit yourself to laugh at my death's-head, but you have an exactly similar one under the skin of your face! But I'll shut up now. The fallen night is as dark as my body of pleasure once was. It seems, this evening, that my former beauty has been spread throughout the universe, that it is enveloping beings and things with its somber softness. That is why, no doubt, you comprehend so well the words that I am murmuring . . .

"Understand then, O young priest, since you are trembling before me like a culpable child, since an anguish full of repentance is in your heart, understand my supplication! Speak! Don't leave me any longer under this humiliating glass, among these urns, these jewels and these jars of make-up. Take my head, at which you laughed without knowing, and return it to the earth that is good for the dead. Return it to the germinative earth, to the warm living earth that is the destiny of the dead!"

The mouth of silence had shut up. Nothing was whispering any longer in the shadow. Slowly, the white Father extended his groping hands in front of him . . .

＊

The next day, there was a great emotion in the convent, for, on inspecting the halls of Punic antiquities in the morning, one display case was discovered in which the glass had been broken and from which the precious head of the black courtesan had been stolen.

Everyone was supposing, commenting, and discussing. All the newspapers in the region, and even those of Paris, talked about the event. It was the conversational topic of the day in the drawing rooms of Tunis for several weeks.

But who in the world could have suspected the clandestine nocturnal ceremony in the course of which the young white Father, alone at midnight in the garden of the convent, had accomplished the pious funeral of the ancient head, the intact and fleshless head of the black courtesan?

Similarly, no one ever explained why the young priest, previously without secrets, had planted in the corner of a preciously-labored flower-bed a beautiful rose-bush with very dark red roses, known as "mourning roses," which he seemed to salute with a little sign when the wind from the sea, inclining a somber and sumptuous flower like the body of a black courtesan, caused it to render politely a salute full of intelligence, mystery and gratitude.

THE METAMORPHOSED
(*Le Journal*, 5 May 1907)

ALL three seated in the little drawing room under the lamp, young and charming, they composed a calm evening "at home." Louise, the little wife, was embroidering. Jean, her husband, was smoking, and Pierre, the delightful friend who sometimes came to see them after dinner, was recounting some pretty story in order to make them laugh or reflect pleasantly.

Around the simplicity of those three beings, their invisible existence floated like a pathetic phantom, unknown to each of them. Their interior thought, present and silent, mingled its secret complication with the apparent spirals of the moving blue smoke of the cigarette.

Louise, the embroiderer with the sage eyelashes, who was not saying anything, was perhaps listening to the voice speaking within her, louder than that of the storyteller, of the natural soul, the inexpressible soul that palpitates, ever in expectation, in the electric and mysterious body of women. The friend Pierre, a patient, vindictive and glacial character, was perhaps nourishing some hidden project of vengeance with regard to Jean, his comrade, who had probably, at a moment in their camaraderie, without being aware of it, inflicted an unpardonable wound on him by some act of felony. And he, Jean, crafty, cowardly and unhealthily superstitious by nature, a pale and suggestible fellow whose anxious and charming mildness doubtless allowed his mind to labor, had been afflicted for a long time by the insidious words of his inseparable Pierre.

For Pierre saw Jean every day at the office of the insurance company in which they were both occupied; and every day, in a diabolically detached tone, he cultivated him in a given direction, with a view to a long-prepared result, which he was certain of obtaining.

Louise, an ignorant little victim, did not know that she was the constant object of the thoughts of the two men. She had married without any penchant the unexpected fiancé who had been wished upon her, a poor foundling raised by charity and without tenderness in the home of two aged adoptive parents who had treated her more like a servant. Only the habitude she had of never going out, her silence, and her extremely bright eyes, large and fixed, had decided Jean to marry her without a dowry and without a name, although he would have observed immediately in her, through her natural seductiveness, certain abrupt and incomprehensible movements of anger, as there often are in weak individuals.

Now, there was happiness for him, because he considered his wife as an object belonging to him, and that sentiment of property replaced grand amour in him. Was grand amour, in any case, truly anything else?

So she was embroidering, that evening, without knowing anything, and her beautiful eyelashes were posed over her fresh cheeks. However, from time to time, by virtue of an involuntary movement, she raised her eyelids and planted her colorless gaze in the void, as if, unconsciously, she were contemplating the form of her destiny there.

Every time her eyes were raised like that, something akin to a shudder passed through the calm room, for then, the friend, Pierre, said to himself: *He's watching her eyes; I can see him.*

And the husband, Jean, thought: *How right Pierre was when he recommended that I observe her eyes! Everything that he pointed out to me is perfectly exact.*

159

And, feverishly biting the amber of his cigarette-holder, he continued his meditation:

Yes, certainly, her pupils are strangely retractile, and there's no doubt that they change color in accordance with the hours and sentiments. And then, what are they looking out for thus, from time to time, in the corners? I haven't yet been able to see whether they're phosphorescent in the dark, but I'll surely perceive it some night.

He had placed his cheek in his clenched hand.

I didn't attach any significance to that cosseting at first, that love of the warmth of cushions, the indolence that is transformed, at the moment when one least expects it, into a disconcerting nervousness. How she played, the other day, with that ball, as if she were rolling on the divan, how overexcited she was! And those brief and violent revolts without a cause! Here, on my hand, is the fresh mark of yesterday's fingernails. And yet, I'd only teased her slightly . . .

His thought continued:

I wanted to scorn her because she's ignorant, but her intuition is stronger than all my logic. She doesn't know anything, but she divines everything. Because of that, I was able to believe at first that that stranger with the large eyes was the white relative of archangels. But isn't it the same obscure soul that sleeps in the mysterious eyes of animals that has made her so terrestrial and so ideal?

And the conclusion that he dared not formulate tortured him once again:

No! There's no reason in her little brain. Reason is human. In her there's nothing but instinct, that sort of formless and sure intelligence that allows animals never to be mistaken . . .

Then every day's question came back to him, imperiously:

What is that creature? A foundling . . . no one in the world will ever be able to tell me where she comes from . . .

He darted a covert troubled glance around him. Pierre finished his story. Louise had stopped embroidering, the needle in mid-air.

160

"Did you like that story?" said Pierre, in an affectionate voice. "Well, I know an even prettier one to tell you. It's a fable. Doubtless you don't know it."

And, having allowed a brief silence to fall, he articulated slowly, looking his friend in the whites of his eyes: "*The Apologue of the Cat Metamorphosed into a Woman.*"

When Jean returned home, now, he took care to open the doors silently, and stealthily. He introduced himself into the drawing room, where his wife was normally to be found, as if he wanted to surprise something.

Astonished, she raised her eyes abruptly and gazed at her strange husband, mute and pale, suddenly standing before her. But for her, there were so many inexplicable things in life that she did not even seek to understand that new attitude.

Jean generally found her stretched out in the cushions, beside the beautiful gray and white angora of which Pierre had recently made her a gift, and which she had quickly taken in great affection.

That fragile comrade of her solitude distracted her; it was, in the empty house, a discreet and harmonious presence, slightly sacred, something like a living household god, part of the furniture and the warmth. Louise's idle palms loved to encounter the warmth of the animal, bushy at the wild ears, the little muzzle as cool as a rosebud, the immense Asiatic eyes whose distant gaze was never importunate. The tiny bestial heart that beat next to hers was less strange to her than those of humans, whose words and actions had never been able to touch her buried being, consecrated since infancy to the destiny of living without saying anything. And also, the need for maternity that is innate in women, as imperious as that of eating and drinking, incited her to care for her favorite with enveloping gestures, the same ones that little girls have for their dolls and animals have for their offspring, and which are for them a natural movement, like respiration.

One day, entering unexpectedly in that fashion, Jean did not find her in the drawing room; and, searching for her through the apartment, he ended up finding her on the balcony, her gaze turned toward the roof and her hands in the air.

He pounced upon her with wild eyes.

"What are you doing here?" he stammered, trembling. "Are you going to run the gutters now, by any chance?"

She uttered a little laugh. She said that she was calling the cat, which had run away—but she quickly fell silent, frightened, so dangerous did her husband's depression seem to her.

It did not burst forth yet, that day, but his irascibility increased. Louise fled his hostile eyes, which intimidated her. She suffered for a long time without showing anything, devoured by a dull anguish, always sensing injustice and anger prowling around her poor little defenseless person. Then, one evening, suddenly, as Jean was smoking without looking at her, grimly sitting in a corner, she started to sob loudly because her heart could no longer retain the chagrin that had been swelling within her for too long.

Then Jean turned round, and she saw that his pale face was distressed by a morbid violence. He shouted at her in a voice trembling with rage and fear:

"Miaow! Miaow! I know full well what you are now."

And the poor woman, in the distress into which that unmerited harshness plunged her, fell in a surge of child-like despair upon the beautiful cat that was stretched out beside her, and, passionately seeking refuge with the only creature that loved her a little, she began clutching the angora against her, burying her little streaming face in the white and gray coat, repeating between two suffocations:

"Oh, my beautiful cat, you're my only friend! You love me! You understand me don't you? Don't you?"

Her head was thus hidden in her folded arm, among the cushions, against the favorite animal, which was purring next to her cheek, when Jean rushed to the divan, seized the frightened cat by the skin of its back, its fur bristling, its claws unsheathed and its eyes dilated. Before Louise could make a gesture, he ran to the balcony, and then, with a single effort, he hurled the animal into the void and the night.

He closed the window again. Standing in a corner, his wife, livid, her head forward, was getting ready to launch herself at him. And in that brief moment preceding their hand-to-hand struggle, he saw in the insensate eyes that were staring at him, a blue and yellow gleam ignite: the phosphoric animal gleam that sets the ensorcelled eyes of cats ablaze, which, in spite of his patient observation, he had never yet been able to glimpse, in the hour of descending obscurity, in gardens and apartments.

It was only a few days after the disappearance of his friend that Pierre came to ring his doorbell. Louise opened the door. Perhaps he knew everything, but he had it recounted to him, with a magnificently feigned stupor and chagrin: the savage scene after which Jean had disappeared, running madly through the night, never to return.

He expressed compassion, before retiring, with words of pity that were almost sincere for the abandoned woman, whose destiny henceforth mattered little to him, his work being consummated. He was liberated.

Nevertheless, it was only ten years later that he knew the veritable accomplishment of his difficult task. Doubtless he had almost forgotten that episode of his life on the day when, having grown old, now the calm and gentle father of a family, sitting in his study, he found the following letter in his morning correspondence, dated from some city in Africa or the Americas.

Pierre,

Why didn't you tell me that she wasn't the only one?

I've been traveling the world for ten years and I've come here to die of fear or horror. My revolver is here in front of me, placed on the table.

Listen carefully: I've known them all, European, black, yellow, ugly and beautiful. Well, they are all metamorphosed.

I've said it, I've proclaimed it to the other men around me, and they thought I was mad. I've been locked up several times.

Yes, I've been treated like a madman because I wanted to save my brothers, the males. And now I'm dying, hating you, because, without you, my eyes would never have been opened, because I would have been happy, like the others, with the disguised animal that every woman is, with the animality that makes a semblance of being humanity, and which respires alongside us, the men, foreign and dangerous, without our ever perceiving it, in spite of the eternal malaise we feel in confrontation with her, sensing that she is not our true companion.

But adieu. I curse you, and I'm dying.

Jean

In spite of the time that had passed, in spite of his different destiny, in spite of his changed heart, Pierre rubbed his hands together softly, with a smile that brought a little of the youth of old back to his lips. And for the few seconds that the smile lasted, all the way to the utmost depths of his being, he felt divine; for, as the proverb says: vengeance is a pleasure of the gods.

LISE AND THE CHIMERAS
(*Le Journal*, 14 May 1907)

LISE'S dressing-room: an immense room whose window is open over Notre-Dame de Paris. Lise is seen in a soft and precious indoor robe, sprawled on her divan among the cushions. In her right hand she is holding a sculpted silver mirror, and in her left a gold-framed magnifying-glass. That is her quotidian attitude.

A mild greenhouse warmth envelops the small creature like a rare and very sensitive flower. Lise is afraid of catching cold, afraid of moving, afraid of changing her habits, afraid of no longer being able to see her nicely crumpled muzzle in the mirror facing her, and, under the bushy fleece of her hair, her myopic, almost colorless eyes with fatigued eyelids and excessively long lashes.

That explains why, throughout the old patrimonial house in which four families could live comfortably, that second-floor dressing-room is the only room still alive. Lise eats there and drinks there, receives there and sleeps there. Her entire existence is spent there, that of a delicate runt in whom pompous generations are finishing dying out, having run out of blue blood—for she is the daughter of dukes and the widow of a prince, and her maternal family, which is foreign, is related to reigning kings.

Thus, she is there, respiring, a voluntary prisoner of four walls. Her personality of a dainty princess-in-the-tower is further emphasized by the things that surround her. She has gathered around her the furniture and trinkets of her predilection. Amid the superimposed cares, the special flowers, the drapes with fading colors, on shelves, on dressers, frail and costly jigsaw tables, there are innumerable series of japonaiseries, fetishes and amulets in ivory, glass, jade and enamel, always representing little stylized animals: mice, frogs, crabs, insects, lizards, five or six times smaller than nature, carved in those rich substances, with eyes of ruby, sapphire or emerald.

Lise loves them more than people. She also loves, in the cups placed here and there, hundreds of little pearls, chosen over the years and bought from numerous merchants who file through the enchanted dressing-room.

Today, in the stormy weather, Lise having opened a window—which only happens very rarely—a fragment of the cathedral appears, with its rose-window and its unequal ornaments. But Lise does not see that. Notre-Dame is something too gross for her. She prefers, if she is bored, to let her little golden slipper fall off and to gaze at her little foot. That consoles her for everything,

And then, two or three friends come to see her sometimes, who recount meager gossip to her. Or, delicately, prettily and at length, they talk about her. Perhaps they even pay court to her a little, but that does not go very far; for Lise, who is too small to look at the cathedral, is also too small to like amour.

That day, perhaps because of the storm in the air, at about six o'clock in the evening, she had an inspiration. And having run, she found herself, still on the same divan, by virtue of the cares of her first chambermaid, sitting before a light rosewood table. She had an inkwell in the form of a toad in front of her and a sheet of perfumed paper, and she was holding in her hand a goose-quill sheathed in gold, which she used to write her letters, in order to give her the writing of a giant, which it is the fashion to have if one is a contemporary young woman.

And, alone with her thought, trembling with emotion, she got ready to write on her piece of paper something capital, heroic and almost testamentary: a list of her trinkets.

She commenced, therefore, before committing such a formula to the paper, by inscribing at the head of the page her ordinary nickname, and then her complicated and ancient marital name. The quill grated. The paltry hand traced: *Lise, known as La Miette,*[1] *Princesse de . . .*

At that moment, a considerable and dull impact, like an enormous fall, was produced on the balcony, which seemed to make the old house tremble in its entirety on its foundations. The window-panes rattled, the animals of jade and enamel leapt on their shelves, the pearls tinkled in the cups. And as the tiny grand dame, her quill in mid-air, was already turning livid at the thought of an earthquake, she discerned through the open window, introducing itself into the room, crawling, something gray, long and alive, the heavy and muffled tread of which was evidently heading toward her.

Terrified, she dropped her pen, which fell on to the carpet. Her eyes blinked in bewilderment. She searched with a panicked hand for her magnifying glass but did not find it. The form was still advancing. Nailed to her divan, the princesse could not attempt any movement to call for help or flee. With a paralytic gesture, however, she finally succeeded in applying her magnifying glass to her right eye, and with the cry of a sparrow, which was strangled on its way through her throat, she saw before her, stationary and gazing at her, a terrible animal, so large that the entire window seemed obscured by it.

Was it a gigantic cat? However, the scales of a fish were glittering on its back, and it walked like a gorilla on four human hands.

---

1 i.e "the crumb."

167

Lise had not had time to recover her respiration when a second shock shook the house, and then a third, and then others.

And the infimal princesse, clutching her gold-framed magnifying glass in both hands, having darted a glance toward the outside, saw that a procession of beasts, all as large, strange and terrifying as the first, was getting ready to come in, also via the window, bracing themselves on the balustrade of Notre-Dame, from the depths of the artificial forest of stone where her myopic gaze had never ventured. She saw them from afar, like divers, presenting themselves upright and then, after having drawn their feet together, launching themselves into the void, to end up, with a feline accuracy, exactly on the balcony of the dressing-room.

The entire balcony shuddered. The interval that separated it from the cathedral was populated by cat-like bounds and the flutter of bristling wings. Now the beasts were hanging on to all the projections of the balcony. With an amazing rapidity they filled the room and started spilling all the way to the princesse's divan. An odor of wild beasts and goat spread around her, which aroused such disgust that she almost forgot her fear. And, parading her scandalized magnifying-glass here and there, she saw that some fifty apocalyptic creatures were crowded between the furniture, flowers and trinkets, so tightly packed that the color of the carpet could no longer be seen . . .

All of that satanic fauna sprawls, with phosphoric gazes, the hooves of goats and wild boar, the claws of cats and the talons of birds of prey. A little white elephant waddles; the muzzle of a bull bears a single rhinoceros horn; the beard of a goat terminates in the visage of an ape; the beaks of pelicans clack; cats with three heads huddle in corners; a kind of hippocampus with panther's claws grazes like a horse; an immense silent wingless bird is enveloped by the membrane of a vampire bat, as if it were bearing on its head and back a veil of thick and sticky crepe.

And now, in the gray and black swarm that is seething before her, Lise suddenly distinguishes two almost human beings, who are visibly fraying a passage through the others with teeth and fingernails in order to get closer to her—and that scares her even more than everything else she has seen . . .

✳

One of them succeeded in reaching her. His head bore a heavy horn and his back had little gray wings. She thought that she divined the Evil One by his claws, and above all by the stink that he spread as he moved. But, although his face might almost be anyone's, he did not speak. His black lips moved slightly, his bright goat's eyes looked to the right and the left, and then, with a sort of belch and an incomprehensible hand gesture, he stuck his tongue out at the princesse.

She tried to recoil into the depths of her cushions, horrified, holding her nose. But she thought she would die when the second individual, the least bestial of them all, after having bleated and growled two or three times, finally began to speak.

He was a kind of hairy dwarf, whose enormous head resembled those of certain old women when they are furious. Haggard yellow eyes were sunk in large cavernous orbits, the animal nose flattened against the cheeks, and a somber mouth cleft to the back teeth opened terribly before the princesse.

That mouth said:

"Do you recognize the Chimeras of Notre-Dame? Here before you is the entire jungle of the forest of stone. We come from the east, the west, the north and the south of the cathedral. We watch night and day, like good guardians. Look at us! Crimes, vices and folly are us! Monsters are us! We are, nine times multiplied, the seven enormous sins of Paris. Yes, from the mass mental alienation of the days of the Revolution to the solitary dream of the satyr watching for his petty prey, it is us who lead the eddies of crowds. We cover Paris! Night and day, under our hypnotic and perverse gaze, how can that city not be more demonic than the Great Courtesan? Look at that devil sticking out his tongue in a corner. That's what he has been doing to the city for centuries. And me! For do you also see my enormous mouth, how it opens? That is in order better to engulf, my child! I engulf, I engulf . . . I eat! Ha ha! I eat Paris, me! And look at all the others, my dear heads of cats, pigs, goats, bulls, birds of prey: my dear demons! They make such beautiful grimaces at the four cardinal points!"

Lise gazed with astonishment at the talking Chimera, perhaps beginning to be reassured, in spite of the hoarse and violent sound of his voice—for that human beast was speaking quite simply, like someone reciting great verses who does not understand them.

The Chimera, having allowed two or three grimaces to pass over his face and sketched the gesture of putting himself on all fours again, straightened up effortfully, darted an anxious glance around, and continued:

"You see, it's because our creators, the anonymous ancient artisans, bore within them the deformed and dangerous soul of the crowd, and naturally transmitted it to us. Now, if you want to know why we're before you today, imagine that this stormy weather has put electricity into our backs and that the noise of your pen on the paper irritated us. What can you be writing? Does it astonish you that we heard you? We have rather big ears, though."

At those words a kind of faunesque laughter ran around the assembly. Lise saw the forty faces frown at her in a sinister fashion. Not one moved, however.

170

The talking Chimera, nearer and eager to touch, started grimacing while bleating, executing a kind of sideways hop; then, coming back to look the princesse in the whites of her eyes, he growled: "You seem very disgusted! How you're pinching your nose between your two little fingers! Do you think we smell bad?"

Another menacing snigger ran around. The Chimera started to dance, with abrupt kicks. Then it stopped. Then it made another bound, and was finally able to articulate:

"You owe us respect, think of that! Being of the devil's party, we're half of cathedrals. There are also angels and the blessed, but they're always looking up in the air. We look down, into the streets . . . into bedrooms . . ."

His gaze was so close and so shiny that the princesse, half-asphyxiated by the fetid breath, felt a kind of flame reddening her cheeks. Already, all the other Chimeras, packed into the corners, were doubtless getting ready for a deadly pounce on the divan, when the first stroke of the evening angelus fell solemnly from the height of the cathedral through the stormy air.

Then, a great noise of calm wings, smoother than a seagull's flight, brushed the balcony. A shadow passed over the window. Then, all the beasts, with a unanimous movement, started crawling across the room, while the giant cats with three heads commenced purring obsequiously. And in the midst of that peace and sudden immobility flowing from the window, at a pace as silent as the swimming of a swan, a white angel of small stature, with short furled wings, carrying a long trumpet, came forward. His odor was so delightfully fresh and delectable that it immediately annulled the stink with which the atmosphere was charged.

"It's the Angel of the Last Judgment," whispered the speaking Chimera. "He's our shepherd, so to speak. He's always standing in our midst, on a special pedestal, ready to sound the Resurrection. Do you see what beautiful white wings he has? He's very proud of them, in spite of the fact that wings are, in sum, animal. But what is most admirable about him is his blond hair and his blue eyes, abysms of omnipotence. As soon as he approaches us, we Chimeras become emotional, wheedling and as poor as dogs."

The Angel said: "You're not greeting me? I've come to see what all my assembled livestock are doing here. I was occupied with a dream; but the angelus sounded. That brought me round. When I lowered my eyes I saw the four corners of my cathedral empty. Have these monsters mistaken you for an angel?"

Lise, immobile, did not say anything. The Angel went on:

"Do you truly believe me to be of the same species as these Chimeras because we live together alongside the towers? No, rather comprehend. I'll explain it to you. It's true that one doesn't look at a cathedral with a magnifying glass. However, you, who belong to a very thinking family, must go to mass on Sunday? So you've certainly reflected on these matters . . ."

As he spoke he raised his vehement head, where the hair seems to be borne away by an eternal gust of wind. The contralto trembled in his neck like a little tower. He stood, bright and light, before the princesse, and his eyes gazed, as innocent as those of new-borns, as profound as those of old men.

"Listen," he said, raising two fingers in the ritual gesture of a priest. "These beasts that you see before you are the crowd such as it would be if we were not there, but we, the angels, are an essence that is disengaged nevertheless from that crowd. We are thought, art, music and metaphysics. We are the ideal. Yes, from the terrifying and banal everyday crowd, an angel can rise up . . . That seems disparate to you? Look at the cathedral, though. Is it not harmonized and equilibrated in spite of its asymmetry? Represent thus a formula taken from the chaos of the human mass."

He raised his limpid eyes toward the sky.

"Oh, it could be so simple to live! But unfortunately, as soon

172

as humans have intentionally brought together three pebbles on the ground, the principle of monuments is born among them and, in consequence, the principle of complication. Never more will they be able to see the simple sunlight, except through the symbol of some colored glass. They will always need their heavens to be cut out by thinking architectures."

He agitated his arms, carried away by his discourse. He continued speaking for a long time, and gradually, his voice mutated into a kind of plainsong, analogous to that of forty Gregorian masses. And his passionate wings, opening and closing, shifted the air in large gusts, like an immense fan.

Lise, seeing that, did not cease repeating in a low voice: "Soon he's going to break something, for sure. I'm afraid for my shelves."

Her anxiety was such that the Angel ended up noticing the expression in her eyes, and he said: "My words seem to be disturbing you. You're doubtless astonished to see me judge things thus. But am I not the Angel of Judgment?"

He had a smile that seemed to illuminate the commencing dusk. Suddenly, he declared: "Now you'll understand! I'm going to sound in my trumpet the resurrections of the great crowd. I'll sound the heroisms, the mysteries, the ideas, the beauties and the dreams. I'll sound Paris, I'll sound the world!"

For the first time, Lise spoke: "Oh! No, if you please?"

And the irritated little face contracted even further while her two little palms were applied swiftly to her doll-like ears.

The Angel looked at her for a moment in silence; then he placed his finger over his mouth and, making a broad gesture, he flew through the window like a tranquil bird. Then, the entire chimerical band followed him, in bounds and flaps of wings, each according to the means of its race, returning to the four corners of Notre-Dame, facing the red and yellow sunset.

Seeing that, Lise rubbed her eyes and looked around, surprised.

Nothing, any longer. She was sitting at her table among her cushions, before her piece of paper. Had she really been dreaming? Had she gone to sleep momentarily on her little folded arm? In any case, would she ever dare to recount such a stupid nightmare to her friends?

She switched on the electric light. Shaking her frail visage, she leaned over her blank paper, obstinate and myopic. As she tried to pick up her goose-quill, however, she perceived it on the floor, in front of her, very nearly crushed by some diabolical claw or hoof.

Mute and irritated, she got up in order to call, when she saw on the carpet, near the window, which was still open, another white quill that appeared to be very similar to hers. Having picked it up, however, she observed that, instead of being a goose-quill, like the other, it was nothing but a feather fallen from the Angel of Judgment. Doubtless he had caught his wing on the frame of the window as he flew away.

Then, picking up the prodigious object, Princesse Lise, known as La Miette, returned to her table; and, rancorously, having used the end of her pen-knife to sharpen the extremity of the pinion feather fallen like a gift from the brilliant and supernatural wing, she applied her golden magnifying glass to her left eye, inclined over her perfumed paper, and wrote, angrily:

List of my trinkets.

A WOMAN IN HELL
(*Le Journal*, 13 June 1913)

WE are still far from knowing everything that exists in the simple terrestrial world, even though we are already anxious about the mores of the Moon, not to say Mars. However, it has been revealed to us, among other secret particularities of our planet, that somewhere in the open sea—no one knows in what latitude—there is an island unknown to geography that has been exclusively populated, since the earliest days of the world, by a colony of devils.

Do they constitute a reserve on which Providence can draw when it wants to provoke modern cases of possession? They must be, in any case, similar to the slightly comical but very dangerous kinds of demons that have beards and goat's horns, and spread a sulfurous odor when they move.

We can imagine very nearly the mode of existence of those satanic islanders, which are, in any case, only satanic in the human sense of the word, when they approach some strange creature, and among themselves, they are not harmful or frightening, all being of the same species.

They believe that the world ends at the limits of their marine solitude. They are utterly unaware of the existence of men and women. However, a vague tradition, a sort of informal liturgy has remained in their race since the epoch of the Old Testament. They know that events took place in remote times, in the course of which they, the devils, were plagued—and yet they have lost the magnificent name of Lucifer, and even, in addition, that of God. But the imps are nevertheless able to murmur tremulously the mysterious word "angel," which they only pronounce while lowering their voice and their eyes.

Apart from that last remembrance, life, for them, has scarcely any complications. They have an absolute monarch, who is simply the strongest and wiliest member of the colony, who lives alone in a tent made of animal skins. The rest of the people are content with burrows. They walk on four feet or two, depending on the moment. They are hairy, horned and unclothed. There are phosphoric gleams in their yellow eyes with retractile pupils. Marriage does not exist, but a free union logically contained, as in animals; and when the amorous season is over, the she-devils cradle and nurse their newborns, which have the faces of Siamese cats. But maternity, for them, is merely a normal and succinct crisis, like amour; it does not encumber their entire existence.

As for the language of the island, it is evidently rudimentary, scarcely articulate, very guttural, and manifest above all by gestures.

Now, one day, a tempest disturbed the sea. That was a relatively frequent occurrence. The somber waves arrived from the horizon and broke, white, upon the rocks. The rapid clouds dipped in the water. There was rumbling at sea, and a splendid racket on land. The assaulted cliffs trembled. The rain came down violently and obliquely; the trees all inclined in the same direction, in the midst of the disarray of their overturned foliage. Such wrath filled the world that the animals were hiding in the depths of their lairs, and also the intimidated devils. No one saw the frightful spectacle of the shipwreck that occurred at sea, a few miles from the haunted coast. And in any case, who could have divined what a ship in distress signified, since no one had ever suspected the existence of humans?

But when the storm had finally eased, the next morning, while walking along the shore ravaged by the sea, a few devil fishermen perceived, lying on the sand, a white piece of wreckage like none they had seen before. They approached and, to begin with, freed it from the sand that partly covered it.

Then they recoiled in surprise and fear, for they could not explain what they had just discovered.

Was it one of their females, since it had breasts, a face and hands? And yet, its hairless body was smooth, intact and white, like the flesh of certain fish. But what upset their minds most of all was seeing, on the head of the extraordinary creature, which was deprived of horns, a kind of gigantic mane growing, so long that it could have covered its knees, the color of which resembled none of the various known furs. Positively, it emerged like light from the head . . .

A strange frisson passed through the witnesses; and suddenly, with a precise and spontaneous movement, they all fled as fast as their legs could carry them in the direction of the king's tent.

You can imagine the tumult that filled the island in a moment. The diabolical ant-hill swarms in all directions. Soon, with the king at the head, the entire population is on the shore, marching toward the fishermen's find. They look, without daring to touch, at the hands, the feet and the face; they tremble before the long blonde hair; they are ecstasized by the whiteness of the body, doubtless dead, arrived from the secret depths of the sea.

And suddenly, with a prophetic cry, his claws clutching his hairy cheeks, the king looks at his frightened people and howls:

"I know what it is! It's an angel!"

✳

Very slowly, the woman came round. The people recoiled, palpitating, gazing at her. As soon as she opened her blue eyes, such a brightness spread over the world that the hundred thousand devils of the island fell to their knees together. The vague religiosity that remained to them from their origin doubtless dictated that impulsive movement.

She spoke. It was an agile language, incomprehensible and musical. And the entire assembly, inclined like the faithful at mass at the moment of the elevation, listened to the angel finally revealed, the sublime sexless being, beautiful, white, soft and redoubtable.

The woman said: "I'm scared! I'm scared! Oh, how scared I am! I surely died in the shipwreck and all these horned devils that surround me inform me that I'm in Hell. Here I am, then damned for eternity. If I'd known, I wouldn't have sinned so much all my life!"

However, it is necessary to say that she quickly took account of that afterlife; for, soon having seen what sort of characters she was dealing with, she set out to domesticate the entire menagerie. And every day she thought: *Is this all that Hell is . . . ?*

And because women are very adaptable, she learned to eat, drink and talk like those who surrounded her. She abstained from walking on all fours, however; and that ever-upright stance continued to fascinate the king and his subjects. And then, was the blonde comet that followed her not sufficient to reveal that the creature was of the same species as the stars? When she passed by, people dropped to their knees and turned their heads away. No one dared to speak to her. They brought her food tremulously. The king had a tent similar to his own made for her, in an absolutely isolated location elevated above the sea.

At length, definitively reassured regarding her fate, the woman ended up getting bored. The infinite respect of the perverts weighed upon her. Doubtless, she would have liked, having learned their language, to approach, converse and distract herself, but as soon as she made a move toward one of them he prostrated himself in the dust or ran away screaming in fear.

However, one evening, in the amorous season, as the woman was wandering, pensive and alone, on the crepuscular edge of a cliff not far from her tent, she saw a tall devil hiding in the bushes, who appeared to be watching her. It was an adult in quest of a mate, and he had not encountered anyone since the previous day.

What sensory madness, what animal impulse, suddenly impelled that enamored male? Bounding like a jaguar from the branches that hid him, he threw himself on the angel, on the sexless being coiffed with light, and, forgetting all liturgy, threw her down in the sand brutally. And the sun, as it disappeared into the sea, splashed the contradictory couple—the couple forever symbolic of the luminous and white seraph struggling in the grip of the somber demon—with a bloody last light.

The next day, ashamed and terrified, the unfortunate adult devil, who had not slept all night, was prowling on the edge of the same cliff, in accordance with the habit of criminals who cannot help returning to the scene of their crime. His head bowed, he calculated all the consequences of his extraordinary action. Certainly, by his fault, innumerable calamities were going to rain down upon the profanatory island.

In despair, he bit his claws, one after the other. And the phosphor of his eyes brightened, red and blue, as the shadow commenced, as if two glow-worms were lodged in his skull.

When he arrived at the location of the fatal bush, he stopped dead, sensing all the hair on his body standing on end. For the angel, upright, immaculate and naked in her starry hair, was watching him come. And the miserable devil thought: *The hour of vengeance has come! What's going to happen to me now?*

His spine low, like a culpable dog, he was already sketching a prostration when he saw, with an indescribable stupor, the angel making a sign of a significance so evident and so peremptory that he could not do otherwise, in his religious obedience, than recommence the gesture of the previous evening precisely.

You can imagine that the entire island was informed of the event in a matter of days. The height of the cliff, henceforth, saw all the adult devils in the colony file past, one after another, not to mention the old men and the adolescents. The adoration of the people for their angel, although more intimate in that fashion, was only exalted further. And the she-devils, initially jealous of such rivalry, gradually succeeded—no one knows how—in reconciling themselves to it.

The king eventually heard what was happening, and as he was invested with absolute power, he immediately declared that he intended to appropriate the angel exclusively.

For the first time, there was great discord on the island. The people wanted, at any price, to keep the angel for their collective usage, but the king intended to have her exclusively to himself. Seeing that, the woman first made the people a little speech in which she promised to remain theirs, as in the past. Then, having gone to find the king outside his tent, she swore solemnly and publicly only to belong to him alone.

"But," said the hundred thousand devils in their own language, when she came back from the tent, "what will you do, O angel, in order to keep both your promises? If the king takes you for his queen, don't you know that he will always keep you with him? And even at night, at the time for sleep, he will wrap his arms around your shoulders, in such a way that, if you try to get up to come out and find us, his great black claws will enter into your skin of their own accord and perhaps wound you mortally."

180

But she replied to them: "Leave it to me."

For she knew that a hundred thousand rogues, with their animal cunning, their sulfurous souls and all their demonic apparatus, knew less than a simple woman, since Eve, our ancestress, as soon as the first footsteps of existence, had found a way to deceive the Eternal Father himself, although he was supposed to know everything.

So, when night fell, when the satanic king commenced to snore happily next to the woman, and his great vigilant claws surrounded her shoulders tightly, gently, by means of a series of insensible movements, she slid her naked body under the edge of the tent, in such a fashion that her upper body, still imprisoned by the dangerous claws, having faithfully remained, down to the waist, in the royal bed, the rest of her person was lying outside on the warm earth, in the starry night, where the obscure devils in love with their angel were prowling.

Thus she kept her double promise.

And so profound was the admiration of the entire colony for that streak of perversity that the following day, the demons, united in extraordinary assembly, elected the angel for their sole king. Only, as they dared not attack the legitimate throne, the seraph, by virtue of a hidden agreement, became for them a secret king, more real than the other, although not nominally recognized.

So that, by virtue of having fooled everyone, the woman mistaken for an angel found herself the absolute master in Hell, without having the title—just as among humans.

THE BLACK LADY
(*Le Journal*, 30 June 1907)

GIVING the impression of being interested in the experiment, Julienne Saintange leans her beautiful head against the dark wall. She is standing in her uncle Johannez's disorderly laboratory, her blinking eyes directed toward the window, devoid of curtains, behind which the green countryside is swaying its trees in the wind.

Undoubtedly she would like to go out. She knows that, outside, there is the odor of fine weather, the taste of hay cut in the sunlight that makes her faint with pleasure every year. But she has also known, since childhood, that she is an orphan and that she owes everything to her uncle, her only family. The governess who has brought her up taught her early on to obey the slightest whims of the capricious old millionaire whose heir she will one day be.

"You'll understand," he says. "I want to prove, by means of this combination of sodammoniums and carbon oxide that ammonium is really a metal . . ."[1]

The little sorcerous eyes of the old man gaze at the series of serpentine tubes, round flasks and flames under the flasks:

---

1 A compound called a sodammonium amalgam—a compound of mercury or lead, sodium and ammonia—was described in a report to the Académie des Sciences in 1891 by a Monsieur Joannis, the resemblance of whose name to the character in the story is probably not coincidental.

all the apparatus from which the truth is going to emerge. A sort of passion makes his old, stiff hands, stained by chemicals, tremble.

He goes on: "The sodium carbonyle . . ."

But Julienne is no longer listening. Her thought is elsewhere. She sees again, under hair already graying, the delightful and bruised face of Baron de Royard. She rediscovers the shiver that shook her during the last ball when the Baron leaned toward her on the garden terrace, in the illuminated night of the Avenue du Bois, his face suddenly ravaged, and murmured to her that he loved her. Then she felt pass between them the quivering upheaval of an imminent kiss on the lips. Then the baronne arrived, innocent and untimely; she had tapped her husband on the shoulder and the enchantment had been abruptly broken.

They have not seen one another since. However, Julienne knows that she will find him again at the reentry, when she resumes the correct and dangerous social life alongside her governess, a strict adherent of protocol, but benevolent, rather suspicious, but devoid of subtlety.

Since adolescence, Julienne has been more conscious every day of her own splendor. She senses, even more than she knows, that her tall stature, when she walks, puts elegance in her manner, that the form of her cheeks is intact and warm, that her blonde hair weighs upon her head like an amassed wealth. Her passionate and severe lips, not yet brushed by anyone, repose softly over cruel teeth. A hidden willfulness is revealed in the neat line of her chin. But she divines that her supremacy reigns above all in her prodigious eyes, her enormous gilded green eyes, in the depths of which an imperious changing gaze broods.

It is only recently that she has perceived that the gaze in question sometimes makes the faces of men go pale, but she has been able to refrain from the exterior arrogance that such a power might confer on her; with the cunning modesty of young women, she does not even give the impression of perceiving that her hands are beautiful, but she bears the fatality of her beauty within her like an interior drama.

"Have you grasped it, Julienne?"

Uncle Johannez is gazing at her without benevolence. Julienne starts and pulls herself together quickly. She makes a sign that she has understood everything, frowns, and leans interestedly toward the round flask in which a bronze-hued liquid is glittering.

The uncle, who has resumed his discourse, no longer takes his eyes off her. In spite of the present austerity, she cannot help taking up the thread of her thought again. She thinks about all those who are already suffering from her beauty, those who love her and whom she does not love. Then her smile is interrupted. The forbidden face of Baron de Boyard has appeared to her again, and she understands, paling in her turn, that it is the very face of her destiny. Without resisting, she abandons herself to the imperious magnet that carries her toward that married man—her, a young woman, her, the future spouse of another. There are virginal dreams that are as culpable as the actions of an adulterous wife.

Now, with just enough time to perceive the sudden frightening, terrified profile of her Uncle Johannez and his aged hand clutching the serpentine tubes, Julienne suddenly plunges into an abyss of horror, like a diver plunging head first into a somber sea.

The sound of the explosion, which seems to make the entire manor jump, is mingled with the flare of flames and the broken glass that flies in all directions. A strong odor of ammonia has spread. Only a few seconds have passed and Julienne is no longer anything but a howling creature running through the room, her fists clenched over her face, peppered with fiery globules that are drilling into her mouth and nostrils, into the flesh of her cheeks and eyelids, and continuing to burn within, in the manner of phosphorus. Uncle Johannez, killed stone dead by a shard of glass in the eye, has fallen somewhere in a corner.

Has the governess, who was alone downstairs, run up into the room? Julienne senses that someone has precipitated toward her, that someone is trying to carry her away. A hoarse, disarticulated, infernal voice emerges from her throat. She cries: "My eyes! My cheeks! My mouth!"

And before fainting in a supreme convulsion, twisting her spared hands toward her face in fusion, she still has the courage to gasp toward the horrified gaze of the governess leaning over her: "Oh! Maman . . . Maman . . . ! Don't let anyone know! Never tell anyone! No one . . . no one . . . !"

It was not religiosity, as one might have expected, that saved Julienne Saintange from suicide. Her moral temperament was not inclined toward belief in a punishment of Heaven attaining her beauty, culpable in advance, nor toward remorse or meditation. But the strangers who, two years after the chemist's death, saw the young multimillionairess passing by, alone in her vertiginous racing car, perhaps understood that her crises of speed were only attacks of despair.

Her secret had been well kept. No one suspected that the eccentric blonde demoiselle, always dressed in black, admirably svelte in her sporting dresses, whose perfect little hands were seen clasping the steering wheel, had a monstrous face beneath her driver's mask, devoid of a nose, a mouth and cheeks, where two eyes with destroyed eyelids rolled, remaining terribly alive amid the stitches, the cauterizations and the grafts.

At those moments, was she not, in fact "like the others"? All her hidden valor had reared up against destiny. She had wanted to live in spite of the irreparable. Only the auto could still exalt the desperate woman on earth, sometimes to the extent of a savage intoxication, which was almost forgetfulness.

As soon as she had been able to quit the manor where the accident had occurred she had had herself transported to the most distant of the châteaux that she had inherited, and there, alone with her governess, the unique confidante of her misfortune, she lived in mystery and silence, invisible for her servants. Even before the governess she had acquired the habit of wearing a sort of hood made of superimposed black veils through which nothing could be distinguished of the hideousness that now occupied the place of her annihilated beauty.

Various legends on the subject of that reclusion had not failed to run round the social milieux of Paris and also the region surrounding the château. The peasants transformed everything in accordance with their own mentality. For twenty leagues around a kind of superstition enveloped the chatelaine. She was known as "the black lady." People made the sign of the cross when her auto went by, unleashed like a whirlwind over the landscape. Very few drivers had occasion to pass over those remote roads, and rural eyes were still unaccustomed to the singularities of automobilism.

One day, however, the customary screech of the horn that frightened the fields was heard in the utmost depths of houses, as if doubled by the howls of a second horn. A racing auto as terrible as Julienne's, one of the vehicles known as "dauphins", with all mechanisms, long and gray, tapering at the rear, with two bucket-seats in front and its only wing on the right, had been precipitated at a hundred and twenty an hour over the solitary roads, pursuing the black lady for several hours.

Hazard had brought the Baron de Boyard to the depths of that little frequented province. He too, for two years, had been flying at top speed over the roads of the world, ravaged by chagrin. After the troubled night of the last ball, Julienne Saintange had given him no further sign of life. He did not know what that implied. He did not know whether he had offended her. He knew the legends that Paris had already forgotten, and he suffered in silence from evasive jealousies.

Today, launched at random in his consolatory auto, he had thought he recognized the adored silhouette of the young woman as she was returning at high speed to her château. The two machines had passed one another in a flash. The great lurch of the heart felt by the baron had alerted him more rapidly than his gaze. Quickly, he had set out on campaign, collecting information. The local rumors corroborated those of Paris. It really was Julienne who was hiding in this remote province; it was really her, the nonchalant royalty who delivered herself to the furious game of the "sixty horsepower." They were her frail admirable hands that directed the throbbing beast so reliably, the overexcited beast of fire and steel, toward the conquest of the four horizons.

He had tried to introduce himself into her home, and to write to her. Everywhere, the only response was an absolute silence.

That is why, that day, maddened, ready for anything, he had begun the pursuit that was now continuing through the terrorized roads.

Evening came. The two bolides, hurled one behind the other, raised tempests of dust after them that the setting sun tinted crimson.

Foreheads lowered, teeth clenched, hands gripping the steering-wheel, Julienne and the baron, almost side by side on the road, saw scenes of terror passing by momentarily. Alerted by the insensate clamor of the horns, carters had tipped their vehicles into the ditches. There were people plunged into hedges, children hidden in their mothers' skirts, tragic arms upraised, mouths that screamed. The wind of the course, engulfed in Julienne's veils, made them flap like wings. A crepuscular bird, she felt, in the panic of the ardent pursuit, that she was skimming the ground in a reckless and sinister flight. The entire world groaned. The two diabolical machines seemed, in passing, to disembowel villages, rebounding into the solitudes, devouring like gaping maws the trees, meadows, streams and little farms spaced out in the verdure.

They were going straight ahead. Julienne no longer recognized the landscape. Then, there was complete darkness, in which the suave moon of beautiful nights was already rising. And as the bends, brutally surging forth, were almost indistinguishable in the scarcely-brushed obscurity of the blue night, Julienne finally reduced her speed and stopped.

Did she want to light her headlamps? Was she at the limit of her strength? Instantly, the baron's auto had caught up with her. Already, he was leaping out of his machine. His warm voice resonated in the sudden silence:

"Julienne!"

Hearing herself called like that, the young woman felt faint. Her heart stopped beating. She put her hands to her breast. The baron was beside her, sustaining her gently by the shoulders.

Around them was an odor of warm grass and dense bushes, the mute immobility of a summer night, ecstasized by calm and perfume. A sleeping bird, perhaps dreaming, emitted a little cry, as fresh as a drop of water.

The baron spoke. He did not know what he was saying. He spoke about his amour and his dolor. He asked questions, he made promises. Under his close breath, the mask of fabric that covered Julienne's face fluttered.

A desolate joy left her quivering against him. Her entire soul, horribly contracted for two years, extended on sensing him there, as before, tall and strong, come to protect her against the dolor of living, rediscovering the delicate odor of his moustache, hearing the timbre of his voice, which was talking once again about amour, without knowing that a human monster was hidden beneath the modern mask.

Suddenly, she felt him tipping her shoulders back. His lips brushed the nape of her neck. A frisson ran through her entire body, as if a twisted blade were plunging into her. And, uttering a hoarse cry of sensuality and horror from the depths of her entrails, she tore herself away brutally from the man she loved, running away with the instinctive gesture of pulling back her scarves, as if she wanted, in confrontation with amour and the night, to veil her poor impossible face forever.

Nonplussed, in fear of perhaps having wounded her for a second time, he remained there, his arms extended, moaning. But she, with jerky gestures, was now busy around her machine. The headlamps scintillated in the night. She climbed in again with a rapid movement, released the brake and pushed the pedals. He had not pronounced a single word.

Then the baron pulled himself together.

"You love me, you love me," he exhaled. "Tomorrow, tomorrow, I'll come back to your house and you'll receive me. You'll render me the prodigy of your eyes, your charming cheeks, your mouth! I'll hold your dear head in my hands, like a masterpiece. O Julienne! O beauty! I love you . . . I love you . . ."

The machine shuddered, and pulled away. The baron surged forward and resumed following her, involuntarily. Only Julienne's headlights illuminated the way. He was like a fascinated beast running toward the light . . .

And then, in the already moonlit night, he saw it.

They were descending a long and steep hill at the end of which, on the horizon, sharp and superimposed rocks loomed up on the edge of a dangerous bend. Julienne recognized the landscape now. She held the steering-wheel firmly between her two little palms, and, racing at maximum speed down the steep hill, she plunged straight into the rocks, as precisely as a bullet.

There was a formidable impact, the din of an exploding engine, broken glass and twisted steel—then nothing more.

The baron had uttered a hoarse exclamation. His machine stopped before the catastrophe, just in time.

Thus, by means of an exact calculation, Julienne, taking her secret into death, had smashed her head on the rocks, since it was forbidden for her ever to lift the mask from her face in order to receive on her virginal lips the first kiss of the man she loved.

189

THE MARKED TREE
(*Le Journal*, 4 August 1907)

A gesture smoothed by forty years of habitude extended old François' hands toward the blooms of his greenhouses or his flower-beds. From dawn to sunset, with the emotions of a poet and the dexterity of a milliner, he occupied himself in caring for them. He dug his old knees into the soil, or placed his old shoe on the spade, unless he lingered for some pruning around the boscage or the rose-bushes. He woke up with the daylight and went to sleep with it, like the plants. He had no parents or relatives, but his masters loved him. And in his little gardener's hut, which was reserved for him at the end of the park, he had lived happily since his youth.

Was he not the king of that hectare of land, where his cares enabled such an elegant nature to blossom? His masters only appeared there between May and October, just in time to admire the sections in the French style, the little valleys in the manner of "English parks," the year's new growths and, above all, the ingenious complications of colors and species, which made of each flowerbed something more beautiful than any lady's needlework.

Generous and rich, those masters provided without counting the expenses occasioned by such floral luxury, the cost of cuttings, grafts, seeds, repotting, the heating of hothouses, straw matting, fertilizer, water . . .

And the aged horticulturalist, master of the four seasons, led his naïve and passionate existence thus, in almost complete solitude. He felt, without being able to formulate it, that he was, in fact, a sort of debonair autocrat standing over that empire of corollas. He was the strength and intelligence of the garden. He resembled, in his omnipotence, the great beech, the guardian of the entrance gate.

Amid the affectation of so many ornamental species, whose foliage was almost as pretty as their flowers, that beech was the only tree that, by virtue of its great stature, gave the idea of domination. Certainly, the gardener did not go as far as a comparison, too difficult for his brain, but he loved that tree with a singular affection. He took care, every year, to surround it with climbing flora, clematis, nasturtiums, sweet peas and Spanish beans, whose hues he arranged with a very special coquetry. One day, he even had the childish idea of engraving his name in the bark with the tip of his knife. He did it with care and regularity. The beautiful smooth gray skin soon allowed to appear, in evident and regular letters, the simple and friendly name *François*. And it was, in truth, as if he had signed the whole garden.

So, the horticultural years followed one another, monotonously, with their exact variations, their anticipated episodes. Without taking account of the rapidity of time, the placid fellow, busy and mute, passed from one intoxication to another, and nothing disturbed his laborious and pleasant existence. During some months, his stout fingers never ceased to devote themselves to the deftness of grafting; during others there were adventures of roses. Artificial fecundations required all the flowers of certain rose-bushes to be carefully enveloped with muslin paper, in order that neighboring pollens, at the hazard of the breeze or bees, did not come to espouse those betrothed roses. The stamens removed, they waited beneath their white veils for the black fingernail of the gardener finally to bring

191

them the preciously chosen semen from which a new species would be born the following year.

At other times, it was the thrust of the magic wand of the pollination of geraniums. Then the soil, cleared of its hyacinths, violets, anemones and pansies, fragile faces of April, newly dug up, saw itself abruptly invaded by the multicolored horde of geraniums, mingled with all the summer species, emerging from the hothouses. In the midst of light meadowsweets, varied phlox, Japanese irises and gladioli with florid shafts, large begonias displayed their flowers of pink silk, the carnations sprinkled their spices in the wind, the fuchsias seemed to dance like elves, the campanulas sounded carillons for the fays, and the petunias that faded so rapidly when they were picked extended their little bowls, red, white or plumed, filled with odor.

Soft plants and vivacious plants, annuals or biennials, they presented themselves in a futile and delicate host, maintained by the cords of silver baskets at the foot of luxurious maples, lilacs, laburnums, spindle-trees and rhododendrons deflowered in May. And on the days of mowing the lawns the cut grass lying in the sunlight mingled its slightly sour petty perfume with the rich emanations of so many sugary calices.

How many times, lingering in the twilight, old François, as the day ended, gazed with the eyes of a grandfather at all the flowers that he loved like a family! As the daylight declined, their colors seemed to burst forth more vividly. And when the darkness was almost complete, the geraniums still remained, dotting the gloom like as many minuscule gleams. Then he went back inside, rubbing his hands, and the color of his dreams, during his slumber, was that of a successful flower-bed.

In October, when the labor became sinister, like a freshly-dug grave, there was the romance of the extravagantly disheveled chrysanthemums, whose mortuary odor, through the gardens, sings a silent *dies irae* until the epoch of the frost.

A short time after their planting, the masters departed. Afterwards, there was the warm and artificial life of the hothouse, its moist perfumes, its earthenware pots arranged on steps. On nights that were excessively cold, old François got up, shivering, in order to activate the fires and bring down the straw matting; and his old hands, tremulous and red, with a heroic gesture, invented for his dear plants an artificial climate, organizing, in spite of frigid Decembers, tropical nights enclosed under glass.

Thus his contented life passed.

Then, a horrible day came when destiny, which strikes all things and all beings, suddenly afflicted the property.

One of the masters, in dying, changed the situation of the family. The garden was sold with the house, and from one day to the next, brutally dismissed by the new owners, old François, stupefied and tragic, found himself far from his kingdom, all alone in a little dwelling in a nearby town. He was too old to be accepted elsewhere as a gardener or to take up on his own account some horticultural project. In any case, he did not want anything other than his garden and his hothouse. Habitude, that slow passion, had attached him to it forever. Does not the soul have roots too?

After a time, therefore, he was seen quitting the town every day, taking the road and returning to his garden. He stuck himself against the entrance gate, and gazed for hours.

The new masters must have been misers, or the young gardener they had engaged idle, for in June, the lawns, poorly tended, rose in humps and rude clumps; the bushes allowed the soil to be seen around the sparse flowers; the untrimmed shrubs extended suckers here and there. Poorly-raked shingle, broken windows in the hothouse . . .

The old man craned his neck in order to see further. His heart, frightfully constructed, made him feel ill. Rage clutched him against the grille that he could no longer go through in

193

order to save his flowers, martyred children, his entire poor vegetal harem delivered into the hands of barbarians. And, raising his head toward the beech that he had marked, and whose principal branch surpassed the grille, he gazed at it with distressed eyes.

That, at least, had not denied him. In its very heart, it continued to bear his name. Perhaps, without rendering account of it, the poor man would have liked to jump high enough to reach the ligneous arms of his friend, to sit down there and gently console himself like a sad child being rocked . . .

Several times he was chased away rudely. It displeased the people in the garden always to see that old phantom obstinately stuck to the grille. Once, the dogs were unleashed on him. The women in the town who took an interest in him said to him every day: "Don't go there any more, Père François. You'll end up being bitten and bloodied . . ."

But he did not want to listen to anyone. His nostalgia was stronger than anything. And in spite of the insults and the advice, in spite of the people and the dogs, curbed and arthritic, having become, in a few months almost lame, he continued irresistibly to frequent the grille.

One morning in August, the horizon was so black when he departed that all his neighbors begged him not to set forth.

"Don't you see what's going to come down, Père François? You'll certainly catch a chill today."

But he replied in a dull voice to all of them: "I know very well what's going to come down. It's hail. And I'm so afraid for my geraniums! The year's buds will be spoiled. It's necessary that I go to see it at close range."

The tempest caught him on the way. There was no shelter, nothing but the winding road and the evil sky, stabbed by lighting. A muted fury seemed to be accumulated in the atmosphere. Then, suddenly, it burst. It was one of those squalls of a rare violence, after which the trees, in the middle of summer, remain brown on the side from which the wind has attacked them, as if scorched by a fire.

The low sky fled eastwards at top sped. The rain could not fall, prevented by the wind, and the distances seemed visibly to be drawing closer, lugubriously.

Jostled and thrown into the ruts, rolled like a dry leaf, the old man arrived nevertheless, effortfully, at the gate. He had lost his hat and his entire body was trembling, but he was sustained by an obsession.

He clung on to the bars in order not to fall; and, overexcited by the tempest, madder than usual, he dilated his sunken old man's eyes toward the livid garden, over which series of clouds the color of ink were racing.

The noise of the panes of the hothouse, broken by wind-borne branches, dominated the roar of the elements. He saw his rhododendrons, his plumed maples, his lilacs and his laburnums all inclined in the same direction, to the point of brushing the ground with their crowns. He saw his flowers, ravaged as if by a malevolent hand, breaking one another, flying into the air, rising into the sky, whirling and descending again. He saw above him the marked beech, seized by convulsions, twisting its great arms frantically. He heard all its leaves whistling.

Hesitant, curbed, frightened, but obstinate even so, in the midst of the universal fury, he hung on to the grille more and more grimly, while above his head the beech creaked formidably. Was it lightning, or only the wind? There was a tumult, as if the column of the world had just broken; there was just time to raise his eyes, and the tree, broken in the middle, demolishing the grille in passing, fell upon the old man in a solid mass.

Did he really understand how he was dying? Did he believe that, in order to deliver him from life, the tree that bore his name was hurling itself upon him, with the entire garden?

Toward evening, amid the sudden calm of the earth, at the foot of the twisted grille, the old body was found. It was so

horribly, so fraternally mingled with the debris of the assassinated beech that no one could say, in truth, whether the spilled
blood came from the man or the tree, from the branches or
the human remains that strewed the ground in the midst of so
many crushed leaves. But those who contrived the funeral were
amazed to discover a smile on the intact face of old François.

Was it not easy for them to comprehend, however, that
because the simple and frustrated old man was no longer able
to live apart from his flowers, the mysterious heart of nature,
sometimes hidden in the breast of a beech, had been able to
show more compassion than that of human beings?

THE IMPOSSIBLE RETURN
(*Le Journal*, 18 August)

A man is returning to the château of his past. The movement of the train rocks his reverie. He thinks about the time when, while married, he loved silently the youngest daughter of Maître Farel. She had doubtless been about eighteen years old. Nothing was more beautiful than her brown eyes between dark eyebrows, which were elongated toward the temples in the Egyptian style, or more elegant than her narrow body, her petite highly-perched head, and her gestures.

He saw again in a dream the blue-tinted reflection of her fringe, her cheeks, quick to blush, her beautiful mouth and her noble hands; he heard her child-like voice. She was so easily disconcerted when she spoke! And yet the things that she said revealed such an original, profound and ardent soul . . .

He still remembered moments when he had sought to retain his gaze, in order that she would not divine the amour he had for her. Was he not married then, and was she not a young woman? An infinite respect left him tremulous before her. He was afraid of offending, with a word or a gesture, that youthful candor, more fragile than a commencing flower, which had such pretty timidities. A proximity of properties and a family friendship gave him frequent opportunities to go to the château. There were excursions in a group in the rich summer countryside, cheerful dinners and music, an entire simple intimacy and honest charm. His wife was a friend of the young woman and her sisters. Similar tastes brought together the cultivated youth in vacations. He mingled with the recreations, sometimes confounded with the brothers, brothers-in-law and cousins, and gazed covertly at the life of the feminine child, rosy with innocence and health.

Many a time, in the course of games of hide-and-seek in the park and races through the graying hay, he had seized her dear virginal hands, respired at close range the sweetness of the little body, quivering with warmth and breathlessness. At those moments she looked at him with the amused eyes of child, magnificent eyes that were ignorant of everything, while he, in his man's breast felt his mature heart, his heart informed of life, lurch abruptly and sink to the very bottom of the abyss of desire.

Dear past days! More than anything, he remembered a certain falling dusk when hazard had left him alone with her in the music room. The entire park was in the open window, with its flower-beds red with geraniums, its lawns, its deep and bushy paths, where the melancholy sunset was already trailing. The young woman, sitting at the piano, was playing without looking at her hands. Her russet eyes bordered by glistening black lashes, seemed to be gazing elsewhere, hypnotized, lost in the mystery of the music. It was some page of Chopin. A desolate romanticism filled the room, seemingly overflowing over the world. Then the lover, devoid of strength against the music and the shadow, had felt faint. Leaning on the piano, he watched the little fingers, full of stormy harmony, running over the keys, and which, with so much mastery, tormented the twilight, charging it with such desperate accents.

Perhaps she had no suspicion of the dangerous poetry that her playing was releasing into the evening. And yet, it seemed that her entire soul was vibrating at the tips of her passionate fingers: that enigmatic soul of young women of which no one knows the secret, and which they do not know themselves, a soul enclosed in the preciously sealed vase of the flesh, as yet hermetic, of which amour alone will one day reveal the true nature.

A rage to seize the disturbing musicienne against him, to tip back her head and seek the adored mouth, had tortured the man in the dim light that hid his pallor. Then, mastering himself with a supreme effort, almost sobbing, he had suddenly fled, his face buried in a bouquet of roses, with the instinct of biting, and ravaging the complex folds of the petals with his teeth.

Dear past days! Now he was returning to the château of yore, after ten years spent far away, through the multiple embassies in which his career as a diplomat and his desire to flee an insurmountable amour had dispersed his existence.

Life, during that lapse of time, had wrought many changes. He knew that the youngest demoiselle Farel had already been brilliantly married for a long time, and that she had no children. He had become a father, and then a widower. Parents had died; heritages, ruinations and sales had changed the destiny of old houses. All the young company of old, aged and scattered, was nothing more than a charming memory. But he knew from fresh news that he would find again at the château the object of his perpetual passion, since the young woman had just inherited that property and had decided to live in it during the fine months.

When he had descended at the villa he had rented for the season, not far from his former dwelling, he hastened, by means of a few rapid cares, to shake off the dust of the voyage. Then, climbing back into the carriage that had brought him from the station, he headed for the château, toward the past.

He had not informed the young woman of his arrival. He wanted to find her again unexpectedly. A lacerating and tender emotion gripped his throat. He saluted in passing the trees, the meadows, the farms and the bends in the road: all the things that had engraved their imprint in his heart forever.

What would she think of him? As he drew closer he felt a kind of fear seizing him. To confront her in this way after ten years! He dreaded that she might not even recognize him. He wondered whether he had changed greatly. Then a bittersweet smile passed through his soul. What did those things matter, since she had never loved him?

*

"Madame la Duchesse has not returned yet . . ."

Without being able to explain why, he shuddered at that statement, almost dolorously. He knew full well that she was no longer Mademoiselle Farel; but the present always wounds those who encounter it with a soul full of the past.

Without even thinking of sitting down, he was alone now in the middle of the drawing room; and, looking with amazement at the new furniture that was crowded between the same walls, he felt scandalized, as if before intruders.

He judged that he was being stupid. Was it not necessary to expect many other novelties? And suddenly, a great shudder shook him, for he had not yet thought that the person he loved might also have changed.

He was standing here, motionless, coming to terms with that sudden idea, when the door opened quietly. He turned round.

The duchesse has just come in.

He takes a step forward. The time to stammer: "Bonjour, Madame . . ." and a torrent of turbulent impressions whirls within him. Her eyes! There are her eyes, her dear red-brown Egyptian eyes. Larger? More gilded? Or is it because of the pathetic darkening of her eyelids? Oh, how bruised they are! Why is she looking at him like that? How she's looking at him!

She was so timid before! What is there in that gaze? Something imperious, almost harsh . . . Yes, that gaze has ten years more, that's all . . . Mademoiselle Farel . . . the Duchesse . . . Still elegant, but is she not taller? Between the long veils that envelop her, there are her cheeks. The dullness of those cheeks! How pale they are! And yet they seem hot . . . her mouth . . ."

The young woman has held out her hand.

"What a surprise, and what joy! I've often thought about you. You find me much changed, then!"

Her voice has become somber. Her voice is as pathetic as her eyes. He can only articulate inconsequential words. She is before him, and he cannot find her again. She looks at him intently, smiling, studying his emotion, while speaking in an assured tone, her head high. He hears, in a dream, that there is a question of the auto, a breakdown. Modern words pass. Then there are questions. She has sat down and made him sit down facing her. Each of her gestures bears the imprint of a regal autocracy. She has a fashion of saying "my house" that upsets him. And then . . . Oh, it's definitely that gaze that petrifies him, that gaze, so different in the same eyes, that gaze, full of ignorance ten years ago and which, today, simultaneously intelligent and firm, audacious, almost brazen, knows everything, dares everything . . . Yes, those eyes have quickly divined him. For several minutes, the duchesse has known pertinently that he loves her, that he has always loved her.

So, the roles are reversed. It is him, today, who is nothing but an amorous man, who is disconcerted before that individual full of experience and authority: a young woman.

He had not yet been able to reestablish the equilibrium of his sensations when he was already being introduced to the duc, the brother of the duc and neighbors arrived in tumult, wrapped in auto veils and laughing. It was, therefore, a new youth that populated the old château! Nothing any longer of what had made the charm of old—walks, games, music, reading—seemed to preoccupy these vibrant creatures, in haste to talk, in haste to go elsewhere, in haste to live. More than before the furniture that shocked him, he suffered from those strange faces. The duchesse talked to him, recalled the past, delighted to see him again. And all those polite, indifferent faces surrounded him, without anyone suspecting that today was the most poignant of his life.

He was retained to dinner. He conversed with people he did not know. Sitting to the right of the duchesse, he was astonished by her concern, by the lofty coquetry with which she enveloped him. From time to time, the Egyptian gaze, the willful gaze, posed upon him, and seemed to declare in front of everyone: "You who have loved me for such a long time, are you not my prey? I shall amuse myself in making of you whatever I want." And that was for him a sentiment of muted triumph mingled with a profound trouble. He did not know whether he wanted to weep because he was happy or because he was in despair.

That state of malaise only commenced to quit him when the hour had dispersed the entire company, in the midst of the purr of autos. The duc had already disappeared, in the English fashion. A last trepidation was lost in the depths of the park.

Alone with the duchesse, the bewildered lover finally looked her in the face. Then, his eyes imploring, he asked: "Would you play that page of Chopin for me that I loved so much one evening?"

He wanted to recapture that musical phrase; he was waiting for it like the supreme salvation of his poor soul, which, for several hours, had been sinking in an ocean of trouble.

The young woman seemed to search her memory, to remember with effort. Then she uttered a laugh that lacerated him.

"I couldn't, any longer," she said. "I never play Chopin now, you know. I only play the great classics or the latest moderns . . ."

She saw that he was suffering, and added: "I'll try, though . . ."

And when they were both alone in the music room, as before, in the dim light of a little lowered lamp, with the window open over the park, he leaned on the piano at the same angle and watched the beautiful hands running over the keys. She sought the air of old with her hesitant fingers. And it was in truth, as if, having forgotten her past soul, she was trying to recover it without being able to do so.

Suddenly, the fingers remembered. The minor song burst forth, seeming to cause a tremor all the way to the depths of the nocturnal and romantic park. A sob went up in the shadow, in the man, the lover, the man who had once, in the same place, by means of a supreme effort, retained the impulse that had thrown him toward the passionate musicienne. The last notes died away in the silence. The duchesse looked at her comrade of old. The frisson of fatality seemed to pass between them. And now, accomplishing the gesture that he had not dared before, the amorous man approached the young woman, tipped her back against him and sought her mouth. But she extended her own lips. He saw at close range the red-brown eyes, the audacious eyes. The delectable mouth bit him, prolonged madly the complex kiss that young women learn on the lips of men. He sensed the little hands bruise the strong muscles of his arms. She enveloped him with the same gesture with which she must already have drawn other lovers . . .

Then he pulled away with an almost brutal gesture. He gazed at her for a second with a wild expression; then he ran to the door and fled like a madman through the silent and black park.

He fled, never to return, because he had understood that she was no longer the woman he loved, because irreparable life had made the pure young woman of his desire into that very different being: a woman; because he bore within him an amour too grave to accept that a temporary embrace, after that of other lovers, would profane the poetry of an ineffable memory.

THE DEATH OF THE FERRET
(*Le Journal*, 1 September 1907)

It was in the time when we were six little girls, the eldest of whom was twelve years old. The imminent opening of the hunting season filled the old Norman manor, sunk in the balsamic woods, with agitation.

You can see our dining room, large and somber, with its ancient odor, encumbered with passionate attributes. There are game-bags and nets hung here and there, cartridge-belts, gaiters, water-bottles and rifles overflowing the vast table in the middle. There are open boxes from with cartridges of different colors are escaping, amusing and dangerous playthings, which are tempting but of which one is afraid; there are new leashes to couple the running dogs, a strong collar for the young griffon bitch who is making her debut this year . . .

But what one looks at most of all, heart beating, are the game-bags. The two eldest sisters are proud of touching them with expert hands. On the days when they are taken hunting, they depart at the hour when the sun rises above the damp and wan fields. Along with the three guests, the gamekeeper, and the eleven dogs, they march directly behind the father, who is slightly stooped. Sometimes, they have come back, after a long day of fatigue in the autumnal woods or crop-fields, carrying one of those game-bags over their shoulder, weighed down by a hare, or two grouse, or three rabbits. The slightly bloody mesh allowed to pass in places, triumphantly, a tuft of feathers or fur. How self-important they were, the two eldest, and how the younger ones envied them!

That day, the eve of the opening, it was not nine o'clock in the morning when they were already turning around the table in the dining room. The interest that excited the six little girls annually was augmented this time, by a capital event. After countless expeditions and difficult steps, the gamekeeper had just made the acquisition of a ferret, whose vendor had declared it marvelous when delivering it. It was the first time that use was being made in the manor of that necessary stinking beast.

They had been talking about the ferret for a fortnight. There had been long deliberations to decide where it would be lodged. They feared that it might be stolen by Quesnel, the enemy, the poacher, who set snares for the game and put out pellets for the dogs, and who, having been caught several times and prosecuted, nurtured a silent rancor against the gamekeeper and the inhabitants of the manor.

So, the six little girls are fluttering around the cynegetic preparations. Meanwhile, a hidden agenda is tormenting them. They know in exactly which rabbit cage, near the kennels, the beast of their dreams has been enclosed, the ferret that they do not know as yet, and which, they have been told, is small, thin and malevolent. A complex danger reigns around that cage, near to which their father has forbidden them to go.

To begin with, very distant, in the vagueness of the horizons, like a hateful phantom, there is the gray face of Quesnel, the mere thought of whom makes them tremble. A little closer, there are the domestics or the nurse, who come and go and might be able to surprise them if they approach the cage. Nearer still there are the dogs, whose barking might give warning. Then, attached to the forbidden door, there is the latch that it is necessary to lift, and in the shadow, there is the unknown enemy, the little wild beast, so redoubtable and precious that people dread even allowing you to approach it. All of that transforms the simple ferret into a sort of dragon, like those in fairy tales.

The six pretty demoiselles, with short garments, calves bare, with their six identical ribbons knotted to one side in their light hair, while turning around the table, open their eyes with the utmost innocence. But in each of their little brains, without their having concerted, one unique idea is palpitating. It is like the continual tolling of a bell: *I'd like to see the ferret . . . the ferret . . . the ferret . . .*

That is why, after a moment, the smallest of all, who is also the most silent, slips through the doorway without being noticed and goes out. Her character, a few years old, already established forever, is manifest on this occasion. Perhaps she is a little hypocritical, but that is because she is afraid, afraid of her sisters, who tease her, afraid of thieves, afraid of ghosts, afraid of the visible and the invisible, which threaten her fearful little being day and night, afraid of life. And yet, how determined she is, how energetically she marches straight toward what has tempted her!

Now that the dining room, the first obstacle, has been crossed, it only remains to get as far as the rabbit cage without being seen, and then pull the latch, which is a little too highly-placed. Then, it is also necessary, after all those courageous actions, to have the supreme heroism of opening the door slightly and looking at the beast. The feminine baby does not tremble. The cunning and fatal audacity of her race is already sufficient to sustain such a little woman. At a careful pace, without turning her head, she heads toward the danger.

The dogs have not barked. They are comrades full of tact. There is no poacher, nurse or domestic on the horizon. Here is the wood of the door; here is the excessively high latch. The youngest child jumps up a little in order to reach it. The latch has been tripped. Now she grips the door in her two dainty palms. She hesitates again, and then, her heart beating rapidly, opens it.

She just has time to see the disheveled straw in the shadow and the bowl of milk half-tipped over, to respire a gust of strong odor—and the enigmatic animal, doubtless lying in wait behind the door, slips into the gap, shows its wily head in which two close-set eyes are gazing, extends its slender tail, and insinuates all of its white body in order to escape, savagely, through the unexpected interstice.

A multiple terror has made the child start. With a stifled exclamation, she has shut the door again, swiftly. For an instant, the head of the ferret, pinched by that abrupt movement, appears; then it goes back in. The latch has closed again.

Having returned to the dining room, the youngest child mingles with her sisters, exactly as if she has not had an enormous adventure. She tries to laugh and cry in order that no one will notice anything. But the depths of her four-year-old soul are a little more troubled, a little more frightened than usual. Has she really wounded the ferret by trapping its neck like that? Her large eyes dilate in the uncertainty; she stops hoping, absorbed in her anxiety. Then, quickly, she resumes the attitude that ought to deceive everyone.

However, the anxiety augments so much as the day progresses that she no longer perceives what her sisters are doing. Have they not, one after another, disappeared from the dining room in order to come back equally pensive, with little bursts of laughter and forced exclamations?

In the evening, they sit down at table in the midst of an unusual silence. It is doubtless thought that the children are fatigued by their day. The parents converse without being interrupted, multiplying the boring remarks that interest grown-ups so much. Not one little girl breathes a word. Head lowered, each one is contemplating her plate, seemingly avoiding the gaze of the others, when suddenly, the gamekeeper comes in.

They see that man distressed and haggard, surging forth in the middle of dinner and stammering: "Monsieur! The ferret is dead."

At those words, the six faces of the little girls become six cherries. But who is paying attention to that?

The father has thumped the table with his fist, looking at his wife with an indignant stupor. Then, both of them, in unison, pronounce the fatal name.

"It's Quesnel!"

"I thought of that immediately," says the gamekeeper.

And there are suppositions, exclamations, an utter upheaval in the manor. A little more and they would have forgotten to put the children to bed. The nurse appears, however, also distressed, like everyone else. And it is a mute bedtime, heavy with important and hidden events.

✻

About ten o'clock in the evening, as the house had calmed down, our father was reading his newspaper by the fireside, while our mother, aided by the nurse, was finishing the final preparations for the next day's Opening, when, at the bottom of the staircase, something like a light friction was heard against the drawing room door.

Our mother opened it, surprised, and behind the door, to the general amazement, she found the smallest among us standing in a night-dress, with immense eyes and a discolored face, who, without speaking, started to look at her, and then our father.

"What's the matter?" they cried.

Was she injured or ill? Was she afraid of something?

Between her father's knees, upright and pale, the child finally spoke.

How many times had she begun to go down the stairs at a stealthy pace in her night-dress? What struggles had taken place in the depths of her tiny soul, complex but honest in spite of everything, and in which the sentiment of duty had ended up prevailing? Her heart was beating rapidly beneath her narrow infantile ribs, like that of a little bird held in the hand. And doubtless that fearful and sly child accomplished, at that moment, the greatest action of her life.

She looked at the benevolent and stupefied face of her father, which had suddenly become more redoubtable than the face of God. Then, gravely, her puerile voice articulated, quietly:

"Father, I have a secret to tell you . . ."

At that moment, the nurse and the mother turn round and retain a cry. On the threshold of the door, there is another little night-dress, another colorless child standing there without speaking.

This one is the second. She takes three steps into the drawing room, and then bursts into sobs. No one has time to interrupt her before she says: "Papa! Papa! It was me who killed the ferret. I'd been to look at it sooner in spite of your forbidding it, and I wounded its neck when I closed the door again . . . because it tried to run away . . ."

"No, it's me who did that," interjects the smallest.

And then a third voice, and then a fourth, come from the staircase:

"No, it was me!"

"No, it was me!"

"What!" says our father. He has put his palm on his hip and looks alternately at everyone. The four children also look at one another with round eyes. No one any longer understands anything. And all that is so extraordinary that the almost simultaneous entrance of the two girls who were still lacking hardly seems surprising.

One is already weeping, the other clenching her teeth; but both of them have the same secret to confess, and each of the criminals, who believed herself to be alone with her conscience, encounters the other five sisters, culpable of the same clandestine assassination. Curiosity had therefore led them, one after another, with a mathematical exactitude.

They explain. It becomes a general confession. Yes, each had acted on her own account, hiding from the others. And six times in succession, the unfortunate ferret, obstinate in trying to escape, in spite of everything, had its neck abruptly pinched by the cage door; after the sixth time, did it not have to die?

When the truth has been well established, the father judges that he owes his six daughters, the cause of such irritating damage, a severe sermon on disobedience and curiosity. The nurse has frowned her protestant face and folded her arms in front of her. The mother has sat down in order to listen. The six guilty parties, still very pale or very red, in accordance with their temperament, wait, upright, heads bowed, for what they have merited hearing.

But now, before those six little night-dresses, so contrite and so solemn, the father cannot commence his speech. A desire to laugh seizes him, and at the same time, he is very emotional. They are truly too noble, those six night-dresses, under which beat six little hearts of good family, who have combated themselves bravely on behalf of the truth.

He opens his mouth . . . and bursts out laughing. His arms are extended and his eyes are moist; for he understands very well that one alone of the kisses that he distributes to the white crowd of his daughters effaces the damage, redeeming the loss of the precious and poor ferret, six times a victim of curiosity, dead, after all, like the Chimera, for having tempted the feminine dream too strongly.

THE VIRGIN ON THE BOAT
(*Le Journal,* 10 September 1907)

TALL and thin in his damaged jersey, the cabin boy Robert is from Honfleur; visualize his bright shock of wiry hair, his gray, slightly dilated eyes, his delicate nostrils and his arms, still gauche and adolescent. In spite of his slightly distracted air, no one perceives that he is handsome. Is he not unaware of it himself?

The kids who fish for seagulls, called "mauves" in the Honfleurian language, or who throw stones at the sea between the wooden legs of the great jetty; the disheveled little girls one encounters in the narrow dead-end streets bordered by gabled houses asking passers-by for a sou; the collectors of mussels with haggard faces; the old mariners in knitted woolen bonnets, wearers of golden earrings; and all of those who spent sunlit days lying prone along the parapet of the quays contemplating the tide and the wind, had something to say to the silent youth as soon as he appeared in the port. Everyone exercised upon him the natural intelligence, so keen, that belongs to the popular Norman race. And because he did not reply either to the gibes of the old or the pursuits of the young, people were amused by his mutism and the blush that rose to his face. He was judged to be simple, almost idiotic. Perhaps he felt unhappy in the midst of laughter, like one of the captive mauves in the hands of children.

Sometimes, the foreign beauties descended from autos to have lunch at the Cheval Blanc blinked their artistic eyes at the two large windows, in the panes of which were entangled worn-out boats and old houses, in which all of the forgotten little port, steeped in the strong odors of Norwegian wood, was framed, as gray, salty and flavorsome as an old print. Then the cabin boy passed by, a fresh flower in all that grayness. And, wanting to make the pretty sailor who tempted their romantic curiosity speak, the ladies lifted up the window and called to him—on seeing which, the fishermen, witnesses of the affair, opened toothless smiles in their collars of gray beard and said: "You don't want, then, to please those ladies, Robert?"

They said that ironically, for their ignorance of what might interest cultivated gazes was definitive; but the poor boy, overwhelmed by shame, ran away and disappeared amid the jeers, to the corner of the antiquated Lieutenancy, whose unequal roofs have been reflected in the green waters of the basins since the sixteenth century.

He went there, via a detour, in order to rejoin the boats and dinghies of the inner harbor, trying to be forgotten, embarrassed by his inexplicable soul. The precious faces of the rich women who had called to him, enveloped by veils, troubled his fourteen-year-old imagination. His obscure instinct confused them involuntarily with the face of Notre-Dame-de-Grace, the ancient patron saint of matelots.

How many times, furnished with a two-sou wax candle, he had haunted the little chapel shadowed by the tall trees at the highest point of the coast! He said his prayer at length to the gilded lady, whose eyes were slightly turned up in the shadow of a white satin veil. Around her the candles, the chandeliers and the rigging of marine ex-votos were accumulated and recognizant marble plaques were multiplied. Was she not, since the cabin boy was an orphan, his mysterious mother? Incomplete sentiments tormented that uncultivated, innocent and suave being. He looked with a kind of jealousy at the infant Jesus, elegantly dressed in gold and crowned, who sat in the divine arms of the idol. How he would have liked to take that fortunate place against the breast of the Virgin! The inveterate odor of incense intoxicated him more than a glass of calvados. He quit the coast with regret, dreaming of fabricating for his Virgin some complicated little boat introduced into a bottle.

He thought about that at sea, in the declining days when the mud shone like a lacquered screen, with the colors of the sky, when the ebbing tide, gray and mild, disappeared into the pebbles, like a crab. It seemed to him then that the earth and the sea were calm forever. Doubtless, at those moments, the Virgin was flying behind the boat, like an invisible seagull, and it was also her who illuminated the water on phosphorescent nights, and it was her again who whispered through the million voices of the waves when the black tempest, rising in the western sky, commenced to insufflate its furious form into the excessively taut canvas of the sails—violent moments when the heart beats more forcefully. The comrades said then, as they took in a reef: "Look out! It's a thunderous wind that's going to pass over us!"

But no one was really afraid, because all the boats that are at sea have been baptized, like children, by the curé, with bells and sugared almonds, on the day when they emerge new from the yard. Is there not always a little crucifix nailed to the back of the cabin?

In spite of the ordinary devotion of mariners, however, more jokes were addressed to Robert every time they were in view of the Côte de Grace. The sign of the cross that he made covertly stimulated the verve of the owner and his sailor. They remarked, teasingly: "Are you making signs to your girl-friend?"

He did not always reply. He clenched his teeth and lowered his head, because there was an imprecise secret between him and the good Virgin of which it was necessary not to speak. But in a whisper, his mind said: *How I'll console myself on the first day of liberty! Oh, the fine candle that I'll burn up there!*

They were so rare, however, those days of leisurely devotion in the depths of the odd little chapel! Fishing scarcely leaves boatmen any respite, who depart with one tide to return with the other, and who often spend several nights outside without sleeping. It isn't that our métier is bad, but we endure all the squalls in order to gain a little subsistence for our numerous families. We live damp, battered and salty, constantly claimed by the maneuvers of the trawl, the tiller and the sails, incessantly menaced by the whims of the sea, a dangerous nurse who sometimes has the worst frictions of a bad mother for her children . . .

On days of dawn tides, Robert woke up amid the swarm of his little brothers and sisters in the depths of the hovel, already as briny as a boat, where their father, silent, paralyzed by rheumatisms and brutalized by alcohol, was ending his career as a fisherman on a poor bed.

The cabin boy loved going out into roseate mornings. He scarcely thought, in accordance with the saying taught in the schools of the coast, that "every man who catches a fish is drawing a silver coin from the sea," for his soul was not, like those of his comrades, eminently commercial. But his unconsciously poetic eyes admired the departure of the boats when they all took to the sea at once, brought together by the narrowness of the channel, when, their quadruple sail dilated by the wind, they resembled, thus expanded and all white with light, great flowers whose four petals were opening in the sunlight.

The boats touched one another momentarily, their sails confounded. There was something like a shoal of flying fish in the channel. They were all there, with their green, blue, red and yellow faces, with the mark "H.O." on their rude canvas, sometimes reddened with catechu, with their beautiful names, new or half-effaced by erosion, inscribed in white on the stern-post:

214

L'Étoile-de-Mer, La Surprise, Le Mutin, La Brise, Protégé-du-Ciel, La Tempête, La Sauvagine, Robins, Frère-et-Soeur, Qui-Qu'en-Grogne, La Juliette, L'Orage, Le Printemps, Sans-Souci, La Jeune-Auguste. There were also many saints' names. All of them beat wings momentarily, side by side, and then, once the jetties were crossed, there was the dispersion in the open sea, facing the little native town buried obliquely in its extravagant verdure.

In nocturnal departures, however, there was no longer anything but a somber flutter of immense night-flying moths among the red and green reflections of searchlights and beacons, a silent flight toward the obscure tide, at the end of which, the town of Le Havre, long and illuminated, sparkled like the stones of a broken necklace.

One night of the autumnal equinox, there was a sudden tempest. They were late, having just passed the Cap de la Hève when it was unleashed. And as the tilted boat fled toward Honfleur, there was the sinister tableau of that tiny thing, the sole intelligent dot in the furious immensity, that tiny thing struggling against nature entire, stubbornly against her. A cowardly struggle of the gathered elements, bounding and exasperating, it seemed, with the unique goal of dooming a wretched fishing-boat!

Hearts were constricted. They put on waxed sou'westers in haste. No one spoke any longer. The owner, clinging to the tiller, supervised the movements of the sailor and the cabin boy, obscure forms agitating in the angry shadow, scarcely illuminated by the flickering light of the beacons. Packets of sea water passed over them, brutalizing them wrathfully. The boat reared up like a horse and plunged profoundly into the foam; and the spindrift flew so high above her that one might have thought it swirls of snow in the obscure wind, as in the time of white fishing.

At the Amphar Bank, a dangerous point in the estuary, they started scraping the sand. That was doom. Now, the boat sank

215

on one side, in accordance with the movement that the fishermen call listing. Had the ballast shifted in the hold? The sails, already soaked by the tempest, were about to take on water, making the keel turn over.

The hoarse voice of the owner ordered the halyards to be cut. The sails collapsed on to the deck. Suddenly relieved, the boat straightened up again They had only kept a little jib in order to advance and get out of the sand. And suddenly, as they finally regained open water, such a fury rose from the sea and fell from the sky that the boat began to spin like a nutshell. The rudder snapped. The tiller collided with the bench and broke into pieces. In order not to be carried away by the wave, the three men had to tumble into the cabin and close the hatch on themselves.

They light a lantern as best they can; they throw themselves to their knees. It is the hour of prayer, the hour of the marvelous. It is necessary to make a vow to Notre-Dame-de-Grace, to promise her, tremulously, as if to a capricious little girl, a little boat for her chapel, a pretty toy of wood and thread, which they will go, in pilgrimage, to suspend in the incense-laden shadow, among the multiple puerile gifts brought by those who have already been saved by her at the moment of death.

Then the owner and the sailor, superstitiously, turn to Robert, the one whom they mocked, the simpleton who might, perhaps, enjoy the grace of Heaven.

It is no longer, at present, the time to tease him. A kind of crisis of fear draws them to the young man; hands clutch his garments; they implore him. One might think that they are addressing their prayers to him.

"Robert, Robert, make a vow! She'll listen to you . . . Robert, Robert . . ."

But, as if bewildered by the danger, more idiotic than usual, he does not even seem to hear them. Obstinately, with the gesture of a stubborn animal, he turns toward the hatch, as if he wants to go out. And the two sobbing voices of the men, in the gloom in which everything is rolling, where their heads are bumping, continue with a sort of heart-rending monotony: "Robert . . . Robert . . ."

A shock has thrown the two mariners into the depths of the cabin. The cabin boy, freed from their hands, has bounded; the hatch has been opened; he has gone out.

"Robert . . . !" they clamor.

They have rushed after him; their bodies engage one by one in the hatchway, heads bare; they look at one another.

The deck of the boat is almost indiscernible in the universal disaster. And yet, can they not distinguish the cabin boy, a frail silhouette in the white shadow of the surf, in the vehemence of the water? He has almost reached the mast. Suddenly, he falls to his knees. His clear adolescent voice reaches them:

"Look! Look!"

He is clinging to the mast. His other hand is pointing at something in the direction of the rudder.

At what is he pointing? Is it the red glow of Le Havre, which can be distinguished intermittently between two leaps of the tempest?

His voice continues: "Look! It's the Virgin . . ."

And the two men think: *He's mad! It's the red glow of Le Havre . . .*

But they dare not say that out loud.

The child continues, with strange inflections, as if he were smiling as he speaks:

"It's the Virgin! I can see her crown! She's at the helm! She's steering the boat!"

Tottering, he has extended his arms. Has he really imposed his hands on the tempest? At his fingertips, the wind calms down; the sea, as if gripped by fatigue, gradually falls back along the haunted boat. It is one of those lapses of the wind, such as there sometimes are in the most impetuous hurricanes.

The waves, diminished, are no longer sweeping over the boat, content to rock it forcefully. The noise has decreased.

Then the two mariners begin to weep with surprise and joy. They say that the cabin boy has saved them, that the Virgin has listened to him, that all three of them will be in port momentarily, that the current is driving them there, that they can improvise a rudder with an oar. Their voices are enthusiastic in the dark. A sinister crack of dawn, soaked by the downpour, commences at the edge of the horizon, still uplifted.

But in that faint light, in which one can discern things more clearly, the cabin boy, without turning toward the voices that are speaking to him, has resumed his hallucinated march, on his knees, toward the helm.

Petrified, the two men watch him, without saying a word. He is still advancing directly, streaming, his arms extended. Now his knees are touching the stern. Then his entire body leans over the water.

A muted cry departs from the hatchway where the owner and his sailor are grouped. They have both bounded on to the deck; they run. Too late: the cabin boy has fallen into the sea; the cabin boy has been carried away forever by the last big waves. Nothing can be done to save him.

Thus, the sea, blanched by the dawn, still crowned with signal-lights and night-beacons, has opened for the adolescent like the white satin mantle of a lady heavily coiffed with precious stones . . .

And because people, even at such a marvelous moment, only see things with their ordinary eyes, the two men, standing on their ravaged boat, facing the rising day, wring their hands toward the place where the cabin boy has disappeared. For they cannot understand why, illuminated by the exaltation of danger, he has finally thrown himself into the arms of the Virgin, where his orphan head, tormented by evasive poetry, dreamed so many times of taking the fortunate place of the divine Child.

THE HEART OF THE APPLE TREE
(*Le Journal*, 26 September 1907)

A little Norman cemetery lost in a hollow of the remote countryside, around a church no bigger than a chapel. In the shade and in the sunlight it has expanded since the fourteenth century in the manner of neglected herbage that has flourished of its own accord. And the few cared-for tombs that extend their exact stones here and there and stand their crosses up vertically, appear far less beautiful in their correctness than the sepulchers of the forgotten dead. Wreaths of ivy and pruned box, and symmetrical bouquets in porcelain vases, will never be worth as much as the decorative luxury that nature can imagine when left to its own devices.

You can see the tide of verdure that has been able to unfurl over that abandonment: virgin vines and enlaced ivy, twisted together, crawl, rise and fall back without parting company, mingled hail of sweet-peas once sown, which reproduce their little violet butterflies every year; a yew, grown to gigantic stature, seems to be the brother of the bell-tower; rose-bushes gone wild swing sprays of eglantines in the breeze; umbels as tall as people emerge from thick grass charged with buttercups, daises and mint; in places, mattresses of moss and lichen, wooden crosses planted crookedly, broken grilles and split stones; and in the middle of such vegetal and funereal extravagance, an apple tree.

Strong and gnarled, it reigns broadly over the dead. Its twisted arms extend in order to bless, trailing all the way to the ground amid the buttercups. It is unacquainted with the secateurs of spring and the beating-poles of autumn. On its respected branches it bears the four seasons by turns, without anyone coming to disturb it in the accomplishment of its monotonous destiny. The September apples, which make it buckle, remain as intact between its leaves as the pink flowers of April, for to what passer-by would the idea occur to lay hands on the property of the dead?

So, every year, tranquilly, at the hazard of the passing wind, the apple tree allows fruits to fall around it red with maturity. And the human remains that repose profoundly under the grass, with a half-fallen cross emerging from their head, ought still to tremble, it seems, under the impact of the Norman apple when, from time to time, it comes to knock on the door of their oblivion.

✳

Maurice, the son of the schoolmaster, loved to frequent that final garden, rich in silence and sunlight, in which one never encountered anyone, even though it was full of people. The child seemed gentle, reflective and cultivated from birth. Had he not come into the world in the midst of books, ink and pens? He knew that he was destined, like his father, for the métier of schoolteacher, and although his fourteen years were as fresh in his cheeks as the eglantines of the wild rose-bush, he already envisaged his life in a particular fashion, familiar with dream and meditation.

His pleasing face with the blue eyes thus appeared every day amid the free disorder of the cemetery. He liked to walk there at slow pace; he willingly learned his lessons there; often, he sat down on the old marbles of the church, simply to watch the color of the hours change in the branches of the apple tree.

In sum, that place was, for him, only a little enclosure more charming than others; he cherished its eccentricity without taking account of it, but no superstitious idea tormented his imagination. As evening fell, when the day of the after-season died bloodily between the black branches, he listened without a frisson to the crows that sometimes croaked a formless *dies irae* directly above the little cemetery. He was not afraid of the dead. Père Bouais, Mère Quesnel, and the other worthy dead who populated this corner of land truly could not make dangerous phantoms. Were they not sleeping very peacefully, those peasants laid beneath the grass, after having lived valiantly, cultivating with all their strength, like their ancestors, their native Normandy?

An evening in September came, however, when the child knew for the first time the frisson of the invisible.

Partly by virtue of distraction and partly by virtue of greed, he had stretched out his hand between two crosses in order to pick an apple and bite into it. Suddenly, he stopped in his gesture, his eyes rounded by a terrible thought. Were not those apples, which no one dared touch, partly the dead among whom the apple tree plunged its roots? Instantly, a thousand chimeras tormented the small boy's mind.

Yes, his thought finally concluded, those apples could not be anything other than the red hearts of the dead, which were returning, in another form, to warm themselves in the sunlight.

Then lowering his head, his gaze fleeing, he went out of the cemetery without looking back and returned home with his teeth clenched.

He did not tell anyone his secret, went to bed early and slept badly. The next day, without really knowing why, avoiding going into the cemetery, he went to walk alone, as was his custom, in another part of the surrounding countryside.

As he ventured, pensively, into a sunken path that he did not know, he encountered, standing in the green shade of branches through which the sunlight was pouring in large droplets, an unusual and charming being: a young demoiselle.

A veil of tender color floated around her narrow and luxurious person, in the fashion of a pair of light wings; her beautiful bright hair was sparkling under her hat; and her eyes were so large, so somber and so extraordinary that one no longer thought about looking at the rest of her petite figure. She might have been seventeen years old. She examined Maurice in passing, with a benevolent expression, as if she found the properly-dressed young peasant pretty. Nonplussed, his chest suddenly tight, he recoiled in the direction of the high bank, with a desire to scale it in order to flee.

What was happening within him? The young woman was already far away, while he remained in place, palpitating with emotion. In truth, it was the first time he had seen a creature of that sort, so marvelous and troubling. He had heard mention of the race of ladies and had looked at engravings that represented them, but he had not yet crossed the path of any real ones. His village was too far from the towns frequented by Parisians.

On the evening of that encounter he felt completely changed. His adventure among the dead was almost obliterated in his memory, so vivid did the vision of the young female passer-by remain there. And, while he persisted in keeping his secrets to himself, in the following days he fell into melancholy.

"What's the matter with you?" his sister repeated.

And his father and mother said to one another: "Maurice has a funny character. He'll certainly be a curé."

One morning, not being able to stand it any more, he decided to return to the sunken road. A passing maidservant on her way to milk the cows informed him regarding the demoiselle. She had been living on the farm, alone with her aged father, for some time. They had rented three rooms there until the end of the season, when they would return to Paris.

From then on, every day, Maurice was irresistibly drawn to wander in the direction of the farm. He did not know what he wanted. The soul of the eternal cherub was beginning to trouble his fourteen rustic years; and while the child in him was still thinking about the apparition of some fay, the godmother of Peau d'Ane, illuminating the farmhouse, the man was already prowling like a young animal around the walls behind which the woman was hiding. Feeling that he was inexplicable, he had a desire to weep all alone, lying in the grass. For the first time, his adolescent heart sank into the good and ill fortune of desire.

He did not see the young woman again until the following week, when he was wandering in search of her. As soon as she appeared at the gate of the farm, he fled as fast as he could, as if at the approach of an enemy. Then, having returned to his father's house, he sobbed until morning with the regret of not having looked at her.

Nights of poor sleep, feverish excursions, quivering stations in bushes in order to see her without being seen; the episode of the funereal apple was definitively forgotten. He could no longer reflect on anything but the slimness of a waist enclosed in a Parisian dress, two little feet preciously shod, the color of various umbrellas under which the ineffable head sheltered every day, and the perfume that sometimes remained behind the demoiselle for such a long time, as if it were caught on the thorns of the bushes.

Desire, incomprehensible desire!

I'm only the son of a schoolteacher, a poor little boy in the immense countryside. I know full well that that young woman from the depths of a land that isn't mine, from the depths of a caste that isn't mine, has nothing to do with my village destiny. And yet, because she passed along the road, I'm bearing in my breast all the anguish in the universe. What is this animal and divine enigma, then, this breath that drives beasts toward one another from the depths of distances, making nocturnal bulls bellow, dilating the crazed eyes of cats with hollow flanks, inflating the red-violet necks of pigeons, and tearing unknown and magnificent sobs from the hoarse throats of child poets?

One afternoon, there was a surprise for Maurice. The demoiselle, emerging alone from the farm, headed toward the village. Had someone talked to her about the curious little cemetery around its decrepit church? She walked slowly, under her umbrella, without suspecting that she was being followed at a distance, watched by two pretty blue eyes that amour inflamed like the eyes of wolves.

She traversed the deserted village, looked to the right and the left, and hesitated. Then, at a suddenly assured pace, she went into the cemetery.

Behind her, the boy stopped at the gate. Was he going to enter in his turn, approach his little passion, and finally speak to her? There was just time to tell her that a child was suffering for her, night and day, in the depths of the Normandy that she appeared to love. There was just time to see her at close range, to hear her voice, to respire the odor of her light garments. There was just time to beg her to stay in the locale, or, at least, to come back every year with the flowers of the beautiful season.

His hands against his breast, which was beating too forcefully, he gathered all his courage in order to dare to take a few steps forward. The young woman, insouciant and bright, looked around with a delighted expression, trying to read the names on the crosses, going around the clumps of glass and creepers that marked the former locations of graves.

Suddenly, petrified, the boy stopped in the movement that he had commenced. She had just seized one of the low branches of the apple tree, and gaily, as if she were playing with mere herbage, she shook the branch with all her might.

The apples started falling on all sides, rebounding like balls. Maurice retained a cry. He was already advancing to warn her that those apples represented the red hearts of the dead, and that it was impious and dangerous to touch them; but she seemed so joyful, so amused by her game, that he was gripped by a sort of shame stronger than his terror. His throat taut, his arms dangling, he stayed there, immobile, gazing at her.

What ravage in those apples! What ravage in those hearts! Here, she bit, there, she picked. Her precious little ankle-boots trampled. The marks of her beautiful teeth, cruel indentations, remained in the wounded fruit, immediately thrown down into the grass. In a few instants, they were strewn all around her. Then, without turning round, without seeing the child who was contemplating her, she went out through the little door at the back, returning to the unknown from which she had come, to her father, to Paris, to the life that was waiting for her.

And, gazing beneath the devastated branches at the remains of the accomplished sacrilege, perhaps the child understood that his heart was, fundamentally, only one of those apples, forever wounded. He understood that it was better not to be indignant, not to be astonished, and not to speak, since the hearts of the dead were doubtless as unfortunate and fortunate as his, for having been bitten profoundly, in spite of eternal annihilation, by the young, unconscious and fatal teeth of amour.

THE STICK
(*Le Journal*, 8 October 1907)

IT was a Sunday in October in the life of Princesse Patricia
when she found herself alone with her lady companion in
the middle of a capsized and crepuscular street in the port of
Honfleur.

Why had her excursion taken her to that remote corner of
the world, far from her after-season Paris, far from her flirta-
tions, her hunts, her arts and her fêtes? What auto breakdown
or fantasy brought her, at a belated hour, to that little seaside
town, reeking of tar, brine and hay?

Her beautiful satisfied eyes squinted in the twilight at the
old gabled houses, at the four-hundred-year-old Lieutenancy,
still standing in the middle of the port, at the vehicles, the
masts, the bushy hills that formed the horizon of almost every
Honfleuran street. It seemed to her, for a moment, that she was
living in some old master painting. She advanced, astonished,
delighted and silent, proudly holding her head high in the
midst of a turbulence of long mauve and violet veils tormented
by the sea breeze.

The rainy sky was fleeing obliquely, the sunset ended. The
Sunday strollers were going home, fishermen in their tight new
jerseys, fresh and well-coiffed young women, neat old couples
unsteady on their feet, families with children, decked out in

garish cheap clothes. The traditional hour of the last meal was approaching. The streets were emptying.

Perhaps the lady companion, shivering a little and feeling hungry, had a desire to imitate those people and go back to the hotel for dinner; but she followed the princesse step by step, with the resigned expression of those who are accustomed to the caprices of the great.

As they arrived at the darkest part of the street, where the houses, even more curiously sculpted, leaning toward one another, seemed to be trying to join up at the top, a compact assembly replete with cries and insults made Patricia recoil at first, and then attracted her.

"Let's go see!" she decided, with anguish and bravery.

Her heart was already hammering merely on looking at the somber and agitated group of common people: haggard women, snotty children and drunken men, scarcely discernible, with which she was about to mingle her ineffable elegance. But her knowingly cultivated imagination of a modern young woman whispered:

It's necessary not to miss this! What a slice of life, these people who are abusing one another, and are perhaps going to kill one another, in this dark little maritime street!

That is why, upright and authoritarian, she advanced in the flapping of her veils, followed by her fearful companion, and, in a few strides, found herself in full tumult, in the eddies of some forty people accumulated there.

Approved by the crowd with nods of the head, two fishmongers, their fists on their hips and their breasts loose in their rude blouses, were hurling insults with twisted mouths at a man who could be seen leaning on the sill of his window on the first floor of a thirteenth-century house.

Patricia rounded her magnificent eyes, trying hard to understand what it was about. The special argot the harpies were using disconcerted her. Certainly, she had already made the "grand dukes' tour" and knew many words, but there were expressions like *Sacré sacrat! Vieux croc! Sale cat-houant!* and *Vieux piant!* which remained quite obscure for her.

Suddenly, however, she understood.

A second person had just appeared at the narrow window of the house: a bony profile with a ridiculously long nose and hair drawn into a shapeless chignon, the bust of a poorly-built woman . . .

As soon as she appeared, the whole crowd vociferated with the grave and singsong intonation particular to Normans; fists were extended toward the impassive man. Patricia discerned that he had just brutalized his wife because she had given two francs to her son, that he had locked himself in the room with her in order that no one could come to her aid, and that he was a bad man who did not even have the excuse of being drunk.

The strange vulgarities overlapped in a guttural and gasping chorus. The man had folded his arms. His big red drooping moustache could be distinguished; his broad shoulders striped the background of intense shadow against which he stood out. He looked at the accusatory crowd without saying a word, with an ironic and triumphant expression. Leaning beside him, his wife was also looking into the street.

Then, as the rage of the two fishmongers was exasperated, he pronounced tranquilly: "Go and take your two daughters home, Mère Loriot, who are carrying on amours in the town."

There was muffled general laughter. He added: "And you, Mère Morin, go and get your son-in-law out of prison, where he's expecting you!"

One after the other, without adding anything further, the two women each went to their doors and disappeared. The man continued. Each one got a packet. Some shut up and went away, like the women, others responded. In a few remarks there were many obscure stories, old and salty, which were strung out, swarming like vague and nasty forms in the damp evening air.

However, a woman younger than the other two raised her head at the back of the crowd and, her eyes full of challenge, with magnificently vulgar gestures, recommenced abusing the man at the window from below. She was broad and red-faced. Large curls of colorless hair flew over her forehead. Patricia, who found herself next to her, saw at close range that face trembling with anger and audacity, those bright eyes that had no fear. She was seized by a sort of respectful and confident admiration for that masterly creature, who must already have seen a great deal in her life, and whose generous indignation was able to pour out so many extraordinary insults in such a short time. She regretted not being able to understand fully the strange language that was being spoken beside her, which prevented her from following completely all the phases of the drama.

It was for that reason that she did not understand why the beaten wife, suddenly animated, began to speak vehemently in her turn. But what she did understand, along with the entire crowd, was the man's reply. Abruptly, seized by fury, he shouted: "Wait! You'll see . . . !"

And before anyone had time to look away, he bounded into the depths of the room and came back with a big stick in his hand.

It was positively like a Punch-and-Judy show in the dark square of the window; the stick was raised and came down. The blow on the bony face with the ridiculous nose was audible. The woman uttered a horrible scream, the scream of a murder victim, which tore through the night.

Then nothing: she had disappeared.

Had she fallen to the floor, dead? A great clamor rose up. Patricia, her respiration cut off, tottered. Was it possible that she had seen such a thing with her own eyes? How had that man been able to strike like that with his stick, full in a human face?

Tears of anguish rose to her eyes. Around her, the crowd growled. The lady companion, in utter distress, repeated incessantly in a hoarse voice: "Let's go home, Princesse! Let's go home!"

One might have thought that a danger was hovering at the height of that window.

It was then that the man reappeared, placidly, and leaned on the sill again. Behind him, the silhouette of the woman was perceptible; she was sponging her face. She was not dead.

She approached, showed with a gesture the cut on her head and her eye, already swollen. An exclamation of pity rose up toward the unfortunate woman. Her sobbing voice pronounced: "It's to protect my child. He doesn't give him anything to eat. And worse, see: it's me who gets the plums!"

Patricia could not get over hearing the woman employ such a ludicrous term to describe her own injury. Sadly, she thought: *That woman talks about her husband as if he were an inevitable force of nature, like fatality . . .*

And without laughing, shaking her head thoughtfully, gazing at the poor ridiculous face, the poor bruised face: *It's her who gets the plums . . . in fact, true Monsieur's plums, those . . .*[1]

Then her anguish went on: *What can be done, what can be done to save that poor woman locked in with her assassin? Perhaps, by speaking softly, the man might understand something?*

Controlling as best she could the distress caused to her soul by the scandal and making her stifled voice firm, Princesse Patricia took a few steps and stopped under the window. The delightful timbre of her speech seemed to caress the violent night in which such things had happened. Calmly, she asked: "Monsieur, why are you beating your wife?"

The crowd had fallen silent in order to listen to that surprising thing. Astonished gazes peered at the beautiful stranger who was taking such an interest in the stories of poor folk.

---

1 This wordplay does not translate. I have rendered *prune* literally as "plum," although it refers figuratively to a black eye; a *prune de Monsieur* is, literally, an Orléans plum, but figuratively a black eye inflicted by a wife-beater.

Suffocated momentarily, the man quickly regained his equilibrium. He was seen to quit the window swiftly. A moment later he was in the street. Patricia saw that ruddy male face nose-to-nose with her own. In the attitude of a fighting cock, neck forward, he looked her in the eyes. The lady companion, her hand over her mouth, her eyes bulging, recoiled as if she wanted to sink into the houses.

"What's it got to do with you?" the man said.

The princesse examined the brute carefully. A slender nose palpitated above the thick moustache. The green-tinted eyes, as if phosphorescent were brooding an intractable soul, an irredeemably brutal and pitiless soul, but a certain native mockery nevertheless refined the general expression of that face. The tall stature, the astonishing broadness of the shoulders, impressed the princesse for a second time.

However, she was not afraid. The adventure was too extraordinary. Her overexcited nerves sustained her. Facing the adversary, a subtle rage possessed her.

"You're not ashamed?" she breathed, her teeth clenched. "Striking a woman in the face like that! You're a criminal! Look how you're stirring people up!"

He folded his arms. "People?" he mocked. "People? It's animals that I'm stirring up!"

He looked the princess up and down. "And you're worse! If I paid you next to nothing it'd still be too much. All this is cheap meat!"

The people drew nearer, with indignant *ohs* and *ahs*, interested, wondering how the dialogue might end.

Patricia sensed that she was pale with shame and astonishment. It was the first time that anyone had dared to insult her, the arrogant aristocrat who, in her life, has excited so many amorous hatreds, so many desperate furies.

The man, seeing that she was nonplussed, continued: "It's because you're from Paris? I've been there before you, to Paris. You weren't even born when I was there!"

And that unexpected remark surprised the princesse so much that she could not help laughing.

"But what you're saying there," she said, coquettishly, "is extremely gallant."

The man did not understand. He was in the rhythm of insults, unable to expect anything but insults. His nose wrinkled with fury.

"Gallant!" he repeated. "Gallant!"

And, enveloping her with a provocative gaze, he spat out, like the final phrase: "You've doubtless been educated, you. You've been to school. But that doesn't prevent you being more stupid than my . . ."

The final word was lost in a general exclamation. Patricia was surrounded. To speak in that fashion to a lady! That seemed to upset the people more than anything else.

As for the man, perhaps weary, he headed slowly toward the port, abandoning the game.

Then Patricia started questioning the people around her. What she had just seen confounded her.

Everyone replied to her at once. A little girl declared in a shrill voice that the man beat his wife every Sunday, because it was the only day when they saw one another.

"But don't the police ever intervene?" asked Patricia.

"Oh, he only beats her before nine o'clock," said the people. "At nine o'clock the curfew sounds, and then it would be disturbing the peace . . ."

Returning in silence to the hotel, side by side with her lady companion, who was still trembling. The princesse had her bad day eyes. A revolt was fermenting within her against those crazy things. She felt humiliated in her femininity for having seen a woman mistreated in that way. She did not take any account of the personal insults received; what revolted her incessantly was the sinister Punch-and-Judy show, the poor bony face cut by the blow of the stick. Her pride reared up at that memory, her pity sobbed. In an instant, she measured all the savagery still distributed in the civilized world. How many defenseless women, in the depths of cities and the countryside, were suffering such treatment? The poor things! The poor things! Did they not have enough feminine dolor? Was it necessary that they give birth, raise the children, toil like beasts, and still receive blows?

The princesse clenched her teeth; her long eyelids fluttered to retain tears, for the plight of her poor sisters, at that nocturnal moment, suddenly wrung her heart.

Fundamentally, she said to herself, *don't all men, left to themselves, become similar brutes quite naturally? Are they not complete and malevolent animals, unleashed at liberty in the peaceful flock of women?*

A bitter and menacing smile passed over her lips involuntarily, presaging imminent revenges. She, the beautiful, the young, the rich, the omnipotent felt invested henceforth with a kind of duty toward all the poor, all the ugly, all the weak women who buckled under male malevolence. Her head bowed in the black wind that stirred her veils, while her diabolical smile became more emphatic, she whispered:

"How right we are to make them suffer!"

But when she went to bed, as the lady companion got ready to blow out the candle and retire, she suddenly saw the princesse sit up in the hotel bed, all white in the perfumed lace of her long chemise. Aberration was reignited in the young woman's dilated eyes, just as it had once been in the depths of the retractile eyes of complicated and cynical empresses. Almost imperceptibly, as if fearful of hearing herself, Patricia murmured:

"Tell me, dear, if I had you send word to him, do you think he would come tonight?"

THE PHANTOM IN THE ROSE
(*Le Journal*, 15 October 1907)

WHEN the orphaned young man recovered his senses, he simply believed that he had undergone a second operation after his six months of illness.

If he was still deafened by a kind of ringing sound and his skin was crawling, was it not a residue of the effects of chloroform?

When, lungs full of that stupefying sweetness, one begins to lose consciousness in anesthesia, it seems that one's being is dispersed like a vapor throughout the world, and that the first effort one makes on recovering consciousness is, so to speak, an effort of reassembly.

The young man could not discern things yet, but he was sure that when he opened his eyes, he would find himself lying in his bed. The beautiful face of his fiancée, his only family, would be leaning over him anxiously, and around that beloved face he would distinguish the décor of the room where he was suffering, a strict, tidy room, fitted out in accordance with the customs of sanitaria. The nurse would also be there, who would take his pulse, and then the intern, and then a few faces of friends . . .

However, he was in no hurry to recover his sight. He felt that he was plunged in an ineffable wellbeing. No more illness, no more fever. An interior smile beatified him entirely. For a long time, his tenderness was exhaled thus, mute, blind and motion-less, sweeter than incense, toward the fiancée whose presence he sensed, close by. Then, his consciousness becoming increasingly determinate within him, he ended up extending his will, and finally emerged victoriously from the limbo of slumber.

Had he truly opened his eyes?

With stupor, instead of rediscovering his habitual pillows, his bedroom, and his servants, he observed that he was standing up, plunged in the obscure corner of a room that he recognized as the drawing room of the Château d'Aspille, where, every year, his fiancée's family came to spend the beautiful season.

The day was declining. A sunset bloodied the autumn en-tering like a tide through the ancient window-panes. Shadows were gathering in the curtains; the lamp was not yet lit. The young man saw his fiancée sitting in an armchair beside the large fireplace, in which the flames were dying. She was leaning on her elbow, her chin in her hand, staring fixedly at his eyes.

His astonishment was such that he did not even think of asking her a question. He stayed there, without speaking and without moving, his eyes looking into his fiancée's, and little by little, with an immeasurable terror, by various evident and imperceptible signs, he understood *that she did not know what she was looking at.*

He wanted to cry out, to call her by her name. His will formulated: "Mathilde?" but no sound was audible. Had he become mute, then?

However, the young woman had shuddered. Her hypnotized gaze became animated, her hands fell back. She murmured, as if in response to the young man's appeal: "Jean."

With all his soul, he precipitated himself toward her; but as he commenced the gesture of extending his arms, he perceived that he could not see those arms.

He had no arms; he had no body; he no longer had any-thing. He was invisible.

A flood of maddening thoughts unfurled in the young man's mind.

I am, however, awake . . . I am, however, reassembled. I can see, I can hear, I can feel . . . I exist! And yet . . . my fiancée is sitting there; she is looking at me and cannot see me . . . Is it because . . .

And suddenly, the truth, the implausible Truth fell upon him like the blow of a sledgehammer. He had just perceived a petty detail: his fiancée was in mourning.

Then, his voice, which could no longer be heard, pronounced, slowly:

"I'm dead . . ."

✳

How long did he remain absorbed in the horror of that discovery? How long did he strive, without being able to succeed, to remember the circumstances of his demise?

Now, with a sad curiosity, he examined the situation.

This, then, is death, he said to himself. One retains alive the senses and understanding, but their envelope is no longer here. It's elsewhere, in the ground. Why am I not above my tomb? I don't even know where it is. Why have I recovered consciousness here? For I'm conscious; but it's only passive senses that remain to me This is it: one can see; one can hear; one can feel; but one no longer has anything active, for example, talking, or grasping. It isn't the will that is lacking, but one is like a man who has had his legs amputated, who feels that his feet are cold . . .

He looked sadly at the darkening window panes, and mused:

The park of Aspille is there, with its yellow trees buzzing with wasps, its autumnal valleys, its meadows, so green, where the month of October is beginning to scatter red and russet heaps. We walked there, Mathilde and I, for an entire season. How ingenuous and affectionate we were! Nothing was more innocent than the deep gaze of my little promise; and I, in spite of my desire and the frequent opportunities that were offered, respected her with a sort of embarrassment. What is there more redoubtable than an innocent gaze? Today, when I'm delivered from my maladies, cured of life, I feel so light, so healthy! How I would love to walk with her again! I haven't retained any memory of the tortures of my illness. Nothing remains to me but an extreme tenderness for the woman who cared for me, a sort of emotional weakness, of candid chastity, an entire poetry that perhaps wasn't in my character. Alas! Alas! It would be so good to live . . . !

Night had fallen completely around the young man; an opaque, starless autumnal night. Suddenly, a shrill exclamation of joy and terror brought him back to himself.

"Maman! Maman!" cried the insensate voice of Mathilde. "Maman, I can see Jean, I can see Jean! He's there in the corner. I can see him! It's him! He's come back . . . ! Maman . . . !"

A noise of overturned chairs. The young woman has stood up in the dark. A door opens, a lantern blinds the darkness. The mother, very pale, has precipitated into the drawing room

"Still all alone and without a light!" she reproaches, sharply. Then her voice softens. "My poor child . . . you'll end up making yourself ill . . ."

She hugs the distressed child against her, whose teeth are chattering.

"Maman," Mathilde stammers, "he was there . . . in the corner . . . I assure you! It's your lamp that has effaced him . . ."

The mother looks at her child fearfully. She is doubtless thinking: *The child is going mad!*

And for a long time, holding her against her shoulder, she speaks. Jean listens avidly. How he is regretted! He learns in what fashion he was extinguished. He has been dead for a week. Only today has all the distress of the funeral begun to calm down. His last words were a request to be buried in the park at Aspille. The body was transported there. That is why these ladies are here.

An incalculable gratitude for Mathilde fills his soul. He tells himself that it is doubtless the strong sentiment that he has for her that is maintaining him alive like this, in spite of death. Then, drawn by his desire to be nearer to the sobbing child, he has been displaced. His vacillating being, which no envelope any longer maintains, is floating hither and yon in the room, as uncertain as a child's balloon. That is perhaps why phantoms prefer to fix themselves in corners. At length, he will learn the practicalities of his new condition.

After much groping, he contrives to remain almost tranquil beside his darling. At that moment, her head buried in the maternal lap, she collapses and abandons herself to a bitter spasm of grief. As the phantom, subtler than a breath, has brushed the nape of her white neck, the young woman turns around, and for a second time, without being aware of it she plunges her streaming gaze into that of her fiancé.

*

The next day, at dawn, the young man found himself at the foot of the bed of his inconsolable friend. Had he slept? He had woken up at the same time as her, and as she was about to commence her toilette, by virtue of a charming sentiment of delicacy, he turned to the wall again.

Once her toilette was finished, he followed her downstairs, witnessed her breakfast, listened to the day's conversations, visited his own tomb by the side of the child in mourning, and returned to the château. When night fell he went to sleep, as he had the previous day, to wake up the following day at the foot of the bed.

At length, the days succeeding one another monotonously, the phantom became bored. One morning, while he was gazing with indifference at the pretty demoiselle, who was having a bath, he started to reflect.

Fixed regarding his new destiny, was he not beginning to envisage things in a slightly different manner? He was certainly no longer in the same phase of emotion as before. The poeticizing effect of the illness seemed to be considerably attenuated. As a phantom, he found himself similar again to what he had been in the human condition as a healthy man, neither more sublime nor more demonic. Was he not, save for the flesh, composed of the same elements?

Gradually, his egotism regained the upper hand. He found that life as a revenant could be quite agreeable: no hunger, thirst or desire; no needs at all. An extraordinary lucidity. Death was a total castration. It rid the flesh, once and for all, of the demanding and, in sum, rather uncomfortable, flesh. Now that he no longer had a body, the young man revaluated things. In truth, three quarters of his tenderness for Mathilde had evaporated with his sexual apparatus. Who would ever have suspected such a thing? What a revelation regarding the so-called sentiments of the heart! Fortunately, he had died before marrying. After six months of honeymoon, he would have been very unhappy.

Had he not already had enough of this family life in which one wept all the time? Ideas of independence came to him. He would travel the world. He would see everything, he would hear everything, and remain invisible. What an amusing and risk-free existence! What liberty!

Adieu, my darling! he thought, with some irony. Sure that it was not his tenderness, as he had imagined at first, that was maintaining him in a conscious state, since he had just perceived that he no longer loved his fiancée, he could leave. He therefore saluted the young woman mentally and, traversing the closed window, he found himself outside.

But a new surprise awaited him.

After having spun for a few moments with two or three leaves detached from the large chestnut tree he felt himself, in spite of his will, imperiously caught by an inexplicable magnetism. He was like an animal on a leash pulled back by an abrupt gesture. Violently, he traversed the window again, but found himself back in the room.

Stupefied, he tried to emerge for a second time, and was brought back to his place for a second time.

Am I free? he said to himself, with anguish and revolt.

But Mathilde's large eyes, while she dressed herself mechanically, gazed into the distance with an expression so lamentable that the phantom fiancé divined that she was thinking of him with adoration.

Conceit consoled him slightly; then, in consequence, his mind, singularly apt in argument, was suddenly enlightened; but the new proposition that he found made him shudder terribly.

If it isn't my tenderness, he reasoned, *that enables me to remain, in spite of everything, living in close proximity to that young woman; it must be hers, her posthumous tenderness—let's say her regret—that has reconstituted me entirely near to her. I'm a part of her, as her own sentiment is a part of her. I am, therefore, linked to her in a fashion narrower than her shadow. It's because her chagrin evokes me that I return; it's because her eyes still seek out mine that I can see; it's because her voice speaks to me that I can hear; it's because her heart appeals to me that I can feel. The experiment presents me with the proof. I believed myself disengaged from all attachments, as light and fantastic as a fay, but I felt the leash harshly as soon as the first efforts to escape. I'm very humiliated. Already I was projecting to abandon my fiancée in an ugly fashion, and I discover that I depend on her. I'm not my own master . . .*

He concluded gravely, brought back to the austere reality:

Are the regrets of the living, then, the only veritable revenants, and the only oblivion of the dead forgetfulness in the hearts of humans? Unless one remains immortal by means of some work that reminds the living of them incessantly, it's necessary that the deceased are forgotten some day. One inscribes on tombs in vain the fallacious assertion of eternal regrets! Sooner or later, the phantom disaggregates; that temporary condensation, due to the warmth of regret, is dispersed again. And it's then that the dead die . . .

He gazed at his fiancée, so pale in the black dress that she had just put on. And like a child requesting protection, frightened, ashamed and submissive, he begged: "Mathilde, Mathilde, never forget me! Mathilde, don't allow me to disaggregate! Mathilde, regret me forever!"

At those mute words, the young woman, believing that she was opening her arms to emptiness, began passionately to embrace the spirit that was speaking to her, and with the voice that made her mother anxious, she sobbed all alone in her room, in the midst of the charming disorder of her toilette: "Jean, my Jean! No, no! I'll never forget you, I swear to you! I swear to you . . . !"

Seasons passed. For three years, the mourning child and her mother had not quit the château, but, for nearly eight months, the phantom had felt less evident from day to day.

Doubtless, the magnetic thought of the young woman, which resuscitated him, which sometimes went as far as enabling him to appear, in glorious bodily form, was slackening. For, after having, for interminable months, followed his fiancée step by step, witnessed the cares that she lavished on his sepulcher, heard his name cried in her sobs, the unfortunate young man saw her posthumous flirtation cooling in disquieting fashion. Every morning, time seemed to chip away a piece of the poor glorious body. Hearing and sight were becoming vague; understanding was weakening. Little by little, the specter was no longer anything but a thin vapor confounded with the morning and evening mists. He was dispersing in the general melancholy of the autumn that was once again tinting the beautiful park of Aspille crimson.

He did not suffer from that state of affairs, for his consciousness was almost obliterated. He sensed himself simply living in the fashion of trees, clouds, water and the air of the weather. He had forgotten his name, forgotten his lover, forgotten his past condition of an organized being. And doubtless, enveloped in the great formless soul of things, he would have been extinguished in that fashion if, on one beautiful afternoon of the after-season, a little ray of sunlight had not woken him up once again with a start from the annihilation into which he was sinking. This time, he found himself endowed again with human intelligence, buried and as if incorporated in a rose flowering above his own tombstone.

What's happening to me? his mind formulated, at first.

Then the memory of his life and his death returned to him abruptly.

"Ah! Mathilde, Mathilde!" he sighed. "So it's you, now then, who are abandoning me? See the condition to which you've reduced me! And why, now, having resumed the rhythm of thought, am I plunged like a bee in the hollow of this mortuary rose swaying next to my sad cross? Doubtless you've just thought about me forcefully; doubtless your heart has just identified me with this rose . . . ?"

He was not mistaken, for, an instant later, he saw the young woman, very sprightly in her blue dress, advancing toward the rose and toward him. A young man was following her, a living man, nicely turned out, probably her new fiancé.

"You see," she said. "I told you so. This is the last rose of the season, and it's on his tomb that it has grown. Poor Jean!"

A few tears appeared in her eyes. The phantom in the rose was overwhelmed. Never had he felt closer to life. The petals in which he was buried lent him a new flesh, odorous and fresh. And now he felt tortured by a sudden and violent jealousy because of the young living man who was accompanying Mathilde. With all his borrowed perfume he exhaled himself toward her, in a breath so provocative that she appeared to understand, and, almost fainting:

"This rose is so strong," she said, with coquetry. "I want to kiss it. There's a little of Jean in it . . ."

She advanced the lips that Jean had never taken.

Then, under that passionate mouth, quivering entirely with a carnal passion, the phantom who had become perfume, was engulfed with a supreme surge into the breast of the young woman. Thus, he was the first to possess her. For an instant more, conscious, intoxicated by pride, he saw the eyes of his little promise, which capsized, and he heard her moaning sigh.

But the new fiancé had also seen and heard. That is why, imperious and gentle, he leaned toward her as she sighed and applied his peremptory kiss to the mouth swooning on the lips of the rose.

Traversed as if by a sword by that first amorous embrace, Mathilde tottered. The past, the present and the future were abolished at the same time for her. Jean, completely forgotten, sensed that he was finally being annihilated in the universal breath of life. Killed by the kiss of the living, his phantom swirled for a second, disaggregated and vanished. . . .

Death had just died.

THE FEW STEPS
(*Le Journal*, 5 November 1907)

H E is a private gamekeeper, dressed in green velvet, brass buttons ornamented by the heads of game animals, a kepi, and gaiters. He is busy, with the gestures of a housekeeper, in the little forest manor where his master, Monsieur de Valgue, has just arrived unexpectedly, in the middle of the week of All Hallows. It is necessary to make up a fire, do a little cooking, sweep and dust, serving as maid and valet de chambre. No staff has been brought, and the gamekeeper has no wife or daughter to help him.

"If Monsieur had come alone!" he says to himself. "But there's his lady friend . . ."

The lady friend is a blonde from Paris, very well dressed and not yet twenty-two. A little fresh flesh in order to forget that one is growing old, a little thirteen-sou profile that costs very dear; for Monsieur de Valgue is about fifty-five, a wheedling and unhappy age, devoid of illusions, even devoid of irony, at which one is not astonished by paying far more for amour than it is worth.

His good eyes, whose gaze has often suffered, understand, without there being any need to talk about it, the sad eyes of the gamekeeper. By taking him into his service he once saved him from a bad situation: debts, seizures and the entire cortege of poverty. That benefit has brought them closer together. And then, each of them has had misfortune in his life, like almost everyone, and that creates an entente between people. In addition, their troubles have had certain resemblances, since here they both are, wrecks of their youth, having arrived at almost the same age without a companion, without children, their hearts empty of the tenderness necessary to humans, especially when they grow old.

In order to try to fill that lacuna, Monsieur de Valgue has mistresses. As for the gamekeeper, he has a dog, an old dog from his young days, now so extraordinarily old that his color and form are indefinable. He loves that dog, however, like a family.

As the morning advances, the gamekeeper becomes annoyed with the fire, which will not catch in the dining room fireplace. He knows the petty dry tone in which the temporary mistress of the house will lament if she comes down too soon. In two days he has already reddened and paled several times at the insulting observations of the young woman, who, being of base extraction, is imbued with an obtuse and obnoxious authority—for the vulgar woman, who has a love of commanding, will never know the supreme aristocracy of being able to be served with charm. And as Monsieur de Valgue seems to be more dangerously smitten than usual with his new mistress, the gamekeeper cannot complain about the affronts made to his dignity as a man of probity, blunt and susceptible.

Indeed, he hears the light step of which he is afraid coming down the stairs, and the silky rustle of moving skirts. The poor man's heart begins to beat faster. Fortunately, she has not come into the room. Through the windows blurred by drizzle he sees her, with precaution, lifting up her skirt and going round the puddles, walking in front of the manor: a little tour before breakfast.

Then the gamekeeper respires. Calmer, picking up the tongs, he kneels down patiently in front of the fireplace . . .

And while there are no witnesses there is an encounter beneath the trees of the avenue, between the young woman and the old pooch.

✳

She advanced under cover. The moist wind, coming from the left, tormented the stray wisps around the beautiful straw-colored chignon and the cheek full of the first youth, as smooth and bulbous as a rose petal. A scarf was flying. The little ankle-boots, as they came down, caused twigs to crack and crushed yellow, red and crimson leaves lost by the dramatic branches. The fatal perfume of autumn impregnated the windswept countryside, which was bruised in its entirety like one of those sanguine leaves.

As the unusual walker was making errand-girl reflections in her blonde head on the subject of autumn, she suddenly uttered a little scream.

She had just walked over an object in the grass. An apparition loomed up before her. What was the beast looking at her, embarrassed in its long ears, vacillating on its clawed paws, with discolored hair, peeled by a horrible mange? A hoarse, disarticulated bark frightened her. The dog, disturbed in his slumber, wheezy and valetudinarian, made as if to leap upon her.

Executing a rapid about-turn, forgetting the puddles, releasing her skirts, she started running, believing that she was being pursued, and on the threshold of the door, she fell, disheveled and quivering, into the arms of Monsieur de Valgue, who had just come down.

The tone in which the young woman recounts the adventure can be imagined. A flame has risen to her face; the aureole of her light hair gives the impression of whirling. She has the swollen heart of a child and the bilious gaze of a fishwife.

It is a consternating breakfast. The unfortunate gamekeeper, assailed with harsh words because of his old dog, chews his large moustache in order not to explode. Monsieur de Valgue doubtless would not fail to defend him, but unfortunately, he is gazing at the mouth that is saying filthy things, a red moist cherry, so tempting that he has a desire to stand up and bite it. He does not even jump when the Megaera with the rosy cheeks suddenly makes this unexpected pronouncement:

"It's necessary that that dog is put down today!"

The gamekeeper has gone white. His eyes seek those of Monsieur de Valgue, who once understood everything. But Monsieur de Valgue has lowered his eyelids.

Now, a cortege was marching over the yellow, red and crimson leaves. The gamekeeper, at the head, had his rifle on his back and a spade is his hand, pulling his dog behind him on a leash, an old carcass, all bristling, snuffling and gasping. Closing the march, Monsieur de Valgue had his head bowed. Leaning on the sill of a window in the manor, the young mistress of the house is watching.

The pretty female animal has stuck stubbornly to her idea of revenge. The death of the dog is necessary to the petite beauty in order that she become tender and cheerful again. There is also, on her part, an unconscious rancor against the game-keeper, who, in spite of everything, allows it to appear in his attitude that he does not consider her to be a lady. Humbly, he had, however, come to beg and plead for his old comrade in solitude and sadness, for that remaining witness of a time that was doubtless happier. Monsieur de Valgue had also tried to bend the obstinacy of her blonde head, promising to keep the dog locked up, making excuses—and then, was the poor old debris not about to die of old age? Was it not necessary to respect his few remaining days?

An entire eloquence had been expended, tears in lamentable eyes on the edges of eyelids wrinkled by dolorous life. But those ineffable things cannot touch an individual devoid of nobility when she is still new and cruel, in the manner of infancy, when she has no pity, simply because she has not suffered. It is necessary for the human soul to have measured all joy and all suffering for itself in order to begin to comprehend their depth. As long as the self has not felt them, they are only foreign things. That is why egotism, of which so much ill is spoken, is, in sum, the basis of all great sentiments.

Thus, the dog had to die. His teeth clenched, the gamekeeper marched toward the place chosen to kill the animal and bury him. His entire being revolted against that act, but he could not say a word about it, because he was a poor man who had once been saved from destitution. How heavily, at that moment, his master's benefit weighed upon his soul! What a burden gratitude is! What a gag over the mouth, and handcuffs on the wrists!

They had reached the foot of the agreed tree. Angrily, the gamekeeper began to dig the grave. Attached closely, the dog had sat down. His head was so low that his long ears were trailing in the grass. A desolate gaze immobilized his eyes, blue-tinted by old age, and his expression was so humanly and so infinitely sad that one might have thought, in truth, that he understood everything that was happening.

Around him, a few leaves swirled before settling. Monsieur de Valgue's moustache was trembling. The gamekeeper dug without saying a word.

Poor old companion of my life, so it's your grave that I'm digging today, and yet you're not dead, you're sitting here watching me do it. It's me, therefore, who raised, trained and caressed you, and sometimes struck you when it was necessary, me, who has cared for you for twenty years, who is going in a little while to take aim and shoot you! Oh, when I was a man of thirty, cheerful and full of enthusiasm, and you were a young dog with shiny fur, sharp teeth and a slender figure, do you remember our beautiful hunts? When the game rose in the dew-soaked grass you bounded like a panther, and often I nearly hit you when I fired. Is it possible to think that you can do no more, that you had only to die of old age, perhaps this evening, crouched against my fatigued legs, but that, in a moment, you're going to perish of a violent death, to roll in the grass under my rifle shot like a hare or a rabbit? Look at your grave, my poor old fellow! Humans were not worthy of your confidence! Will your master have loved you for twenty years to finish in fratricide . . . ?

The ditch is sufficiently deep. The gamekeeper has raised his head. Large tears are rolling from his eyes. He throws the spade away, picks up his rifle, and then he looks at Monsieur de Valgue, and then his dog. A momentary silence reigns between the three beings. An immense emotion seems to shiver in the moist wind. But in the distance, at the window, a little woman is leaning, and that little woman is the figure of fatality.

Then Monsieur de Valgue, darting a last and futile glance toward her, finally pronounces the sentence of death.

"Shoot!" he says.

The gamekeeper does not even think about embracing his dog one last time. A thousand thoughts whirl in his unfortunate brain. With a rapid, jerky movement he shoulders his rifle and takes aim.

The dog is in the same attitude, sitting at the end of his rope, head down, his eyes still dolorous, not looking at anyone, and his ears trailing. The rifle trembles in the gamekeeper's hands. He fires . . .

What cries! What heart-rending cries torn from an old, worn-out throat, which ought not to have the strength any longer to howl thus! The gamekeeper, too emotional, has missed his shot. The dog, wounded in the shoulder, turns rapidly round his rope, one paw in the air. His head has straightened up for those frightful cries, his poor jowls drawn back over his worn fangs,

Monsieur de Valgue has turned his eyes away. The spectacle of an instant: the gamekeeper has fired a second shot. The dog falls, curling up, in the attitude of the hares of old. A trickle of blood flows from his mouth. He is no longer crying out now, but his eyes are open immeasurably, as if in the immense stupefaction that the assassination has caused him. He is not yet dead.

Then, before those eyes, which are following his movements, the gamekeeper seems to go mad. He seizes his rifle by the barrel, and with furious blows he strikes the mute dog. As soon as the first blow, the animal is dead, but the man continues, his jaws clenched, with an insensate fury. Red pulp begins to stain the butt of his rifle, to spring forth around him, splashing, as if to heighten the October leaves, already so ardent . . .

Autumn and blood . . .

A gust of wind passes, molests the branches, stirs heaps of dead leaves at random. There is murder in the air!

I've just killed with my own hands the old friend who loved me, and the old friend watched me do it with his poor animal eyes, which no longer understood anything. The old friend has seen me kill him . . . There's murder in the air! Ah! Ah . . . ! The burden of gratitude is on the ground! Now I have killed, I'll kill the man who once saved me. Today is the day of destiny! To kill someone like a dog, *they say. Indeed! A fine blow of the butt on the head of Monsieur de Valgue! The beautiful pulp that will spring forth! The bitch at the window will see that! And doubtless she'll go next, the slut! I'm alone here, she can scream! Defenseless, defenseless! Like the dog. You'll be well avenged, my poor old friend. I haven't dug the grave for you alone!*

The gamekeeper turns round abruptly, the rifle-butt raised, his face livid. He is splattered with blood. A horrible expression contracts his cheeks, flares his nostrils and twists his mouth over his bared teeth. For an instant, the butt remains raised; but it falls back.

The master is no longer there.

Has he been sickened by the spectacle, or is he in haste to return to grace with his mistress, or is there a more mysterious cause that, without him really knowing why, has made him take those few steps in retreat just before the gamekeeper turned round?

Now, as if gripped by stupor, the gamekeeper remains there, looking at the distant back of his master, who is drawing away through the branches, returning to the manor. Then, gradually, his faces relaxes and, with an unsteady step, he goes to lean his shoulder against a tree, passes his hand over his sweat-soaked brow, and finally lets his stained rifle fall into the bloodstained grass.

※

That evening, at table, Monsieur de Valgue's young lady friend was cheerful. Her triumph rendered her good humor to her. By turns, with the secret pride of women, which is one of the joys of their cunning life, she looked at the two fellows with gray moustaches with whom she had reckoned, all alone in the depths of a forest, making them do exactly the opposite of what they had wanted.

How stupid men are! she repeated to herself once again. *They were stupid enough to kill their dirty dog in order obey me, and now, this evening, here they both are, enchanted!*

But she only thought that because she could not comprehend the significance of the glances exchanged between the two males, whose eyes, every time they met, said in their tacit language:

The irreparable has passed between us today, but, thanks to a few steps taken a little sooner, it has not been accomplished. So, it is as if both of us have returned from the dead, and we are fully enlightened.

We shall never speak about it, but we know now that, in spite of its horrors, in spite of its sorrows, life is still a good thing; for, in spite of the young women of Paris, does not the delectable and mute understanding of two old hearts like ours make existence worthwhile anyway . . . ?

THE DUCHESSE'S LESSON
(*Le Journal*, 5 December 1907)

THE two sons of the widowed Madame Perlier de Servières, leaning over the table that is reserved for them at the end of the drawing room, are playing the *jeu de l'oie* while waiting for the dinner bell. Around them the furniture, authentic Louis-Philippe, is variegated by those ridiculous little rugs, antimacassars and receptacles for odds and ends that are the patient handiwork of sage provincial ladies. Outside, through the casements blurred by autumn, is the bristling and black Norman countryside, where the moonlight is commencing . . .

The two children, fourteen and twelve years old, are lymphatic of complexion, faded in their tresses and meager in their gestures. While they play, their distracted ears perceive scraps of the conversation of their mother and their aunt, sitting by the fireside. There are the customary reflections on the present epoch with which those ladies accompany the little thrusts of the needle they give to their respective embroideries. From time to time, one hears: "Poor France!" or even: "Fortunately, there is still nobility in the world!" Or there are those anecdotes, retold a thousand times, about some great family that no one in the house ever knew, but whose genealogy and alliances they know by heart. Aunt de Tarne, especially, possesses her armorial like a d'Hozier,[1] and not an

---

1 Charles-René d'Hozier (1640-1732) established the *Armorial général de*

hour passes without her reciting entire chapters of it, in the manner of a catechism.

At the moment when the children, absorbed in their game, are about to start arguing, as is their habit, calling one another "Monsieur" and pinching their lips, the farmer comes in, introduced by an old domestic, and, very emotionally, recounts that a broken-down automobile has stopped at the entrance gate and that the mechanic has come to the farm to ask whether, since it is the only habitation for two leagues around, they can offer accommodation to his lady employer, lost and without provisions, who is dying of cold and hunger on the road.

The two ladies have dropped their needlework; the children, intrigued, have drawn nearer. They look at one another with amazement. It is the first time that such an adventure has happened.

"How does she seem, this lady?" sighs Madame de Servières, finally, in the midst of the general hubbub.

"My God, Madame," says the farmer, "I didn't see her very well, because of the dark, but she smells good! She's in an auto as if she were at home!"

The two ladies have exchanged glances, then lowered their eyes. The same thought has just crossed their minds. Certainly, charity commands them to assist this traveler, but what if the perfumed stranger is a *creature?* What a scandal for the house, what a spectacle for Philippe and Gontran!

Suddenly, Aunt de Tarne has an inspiration.

"Go and ask this lady to give you her card," she says.

They wait with agitation, murmuring. In the kitchen, the domestics are talking in low voices. The whole house seems to be in upheaval.

Finally, the farmer comes back, carrying the card. And as Aunt de Tarne has taken possession of it and has brought down,

---

France—34 volumes of text and 35 volumes of armorial bearings in color—which became the definitive index of the French peerage, although inevitably incomplete.

in order to decipher it, the spectacles perched on her gray head-band, she utters an exclamation.

"Divine Providence does well what it does," she declares. "Read, my dear. This traveler is quite simply Duchesse Jacques de Hongueville. What an honor for the house, and what a lesson for Philippe and Gontran, to see at close range one of the greatest names of France!"

She hastens to continue: "This Duchesse Jacques is a very young woman. She was born Rancy, her mother was Mademoiselle . . ."

But no one is listening any longer. Madame de Servières swiftly straightens up a few antimacassars, and then runs to the kitchen to inform the staff, to check the dinner, to order that a tablecloth be set out and that the silver fruit-dishes should be brought out. Philippe and Gontran smooth their faded hair with a furtive gesture and get ready, with the unconscious emotion of young males, to see at close range this great name of France who is a very young woman.

As soon as she had taken her first steps in the drawing room, and her first glance at the aunt's Second Empire headbands, the duchesse understood the attitude that she ought to adopt. She therefore dropped the lorgnette that she was about to aim and inclined her supple figure ceremoniously, lowering her chestnut-hued and well coiffed head; she illuminated with a smile her fresh-cheeked face with a proud nose, beautiful blue eyes, lightly made up, and bowed all round, most insistently in the direction of the aunt.

The turned-up wings of her hat quivered, her long furs spread a gust of subtle perfume; and in her exquisite voice, which emphasized the words, she commenced a well-turned and suave speech of apology, recounting that she took a hired auto from Paris that morning, whose mechanic is nothing but a donkey; and, above all, she thanked the benevolent hostesses who have consented to receive thus a stranger gone astray in the country.

The ladies protested warmly. Armchairs were advanced, apologies were offered in advance for dinner. And Aunt de Tarne, in order to put the stranger at her ease, was already reciting the genealogy of the Honguevilles.

It was also the aunt who sustained the conversation throughout dinner. She had finally found ears worthy of her knowledge! Madame de Servières did not say much, supervising the service with anguish. As for Philippe and Gontran, they forgot to eat, in order to contemplate with round eyes and open mouths the ravishing person with the troubling gaze, the enameled fingernails and the beautiful perfumed fabrics. They scarcely heard the delectable remarks, the turn of which, so personal and so frank, had made the duchesse such a reputation for wit in Paris.

Who, then, around that tablecloth, could have suspected that the young woman with such a grand air, witty and becoming, was hiding beneath such an exterior, by means of a discipline long acquired, the furious anger with which her little feet were quivering under the table?

The hired mechanic, however, who had already conducted her once or twice to her dangerous rendezvous outside Paris, seemed on this occasion to have broken down deliberately in that remote area, although it would only have required a few more hours to reach the town where she was awaited. A disaster; she would miss her entire affair, not to mention that she would not be back in Paris in time for her absence to pass unperceived.

Now, suddenly, without knocking and without being announced, the mechanic came into the room. Aunt de Tarne stopped dead. Everyone looked at one another. The mechanic nevertheless took off his cap, because of the magnificent tips that the duchesse gave him. Without bowing to anyone, however, he commenced, in a voice like an angry wasp:

"I said that it must be a fly in the carburetor . . . but now it's necessary that I wait for daylight to see why it's taken a bad turn . . ."

At those words, Madame de Hongueville's eyes darkened. And because modern young duchesses sometimes have words devoid of mildness when they are no longer watching themselves, the little grand dame, forgetting where she was and all discipline, thumped that table and screeched:

"You, my lad, get me the hell out of here, you hear me?"

Grumbling, the mechanic fled to the kitchen. The duchesse, having recovered, saw the petrified faces that surrounded her. She shook her head prettily, coughed once, and said, gracefully, turning to Aunt de Tarne:

"Absolutely the character of my great-grandfather! As you were saying just now, he couldn't master his outbursts . . ."

✳

The duchesse departed in the morning without encumbrance. However, there was a further alarm in the house, because she has asked the chambermaid to run a bath for her toilette, saying that it was her habit to bathe every day. Aunt de Tarne, on being told that, raised her eyes to the heavens, crying: "Are the mores of today so relaxed, even on the part of honest people? Take her the footbath, my girl, that must be what she's asking for."

On the whole, however, everything went well. Philippe and Gontran, invited politely, climbed into the auto with the duchesse in order to indicate the road to the mechanic, as far as the turning. However, they came back after an hour, overexcited by their first excursion in an auto, and said that the duchesse had not ceased to be angry with her chauffeur. At that news, the aunt and the mother shuddered, but they recovered quickly on learning that the duchesse had spoken through the window with her head outside. In that fashion, whatever she had said, in the midst of the noise of the engine, the children would not have heard anything. Eyes were lowered after an oblique exchange of glances, and no one mentioned it again.

A week went by. The passage of the duchesse did not seem to have left any memory to anyone. Since the great lady had come, though, Aunt de Tarne no long recited the armorial.

One evening, however, after dinner, as Philippe and Gontran were playing the *jeu de l'oie* in their habitual place, Madame de Servières and Madame de Tarne suddenly heard, in the middle of the eternal dispute of every evening, this horrifying remark from Philippe:

"To begin with, Monsieur, you're nothing but a filthy swine!"

And before they were able to open their mouths to complain, Gontran had replied: "I'm not afraid of you, you know! Don't be such a pain in the neck, or I'll give you a thick ear!"

THE FUTILE ROSES

(*Le Journal*, 19 December 1907)

IN the unusual drawing room into which he had just been
introduced, amid the faded cameo furniture, the moth-eaten
carpets and the eighteenth-century windows, the missing small
panes of which had been replaced by pieces of paper, the young
man looked around in the commencing dusk. His curiosity
increased more and more. On the road of his remote region,
his auto had broken down amid the last fallen leaves, at the very
end of an avenue invaded by grass, which had led all the way to
this dilapidated château. Was he really to be accommodated for
the night in this singular abode?

What would the mother he had quit that morning in Paris
have said if she had been able to see him standing in this drawing room of ghosts? She would doubtless have thought that
such an adventure could not fail to happen to her eccentric
child, to the one who, since his thirteenth year, had been called,
in the humorous manner of the great Japanese painter: "the
young man fond of music."[1]

Suddenly, he retained an exclamation. There, above the man-
telpiece, was a modern painting! It was a portrait of Alexandra
Jadiska, the celebrated cantatrice who had died ten years ago,

---

1 The reference is to the painter Odilon Redon, who was equally renowned
for the influence of Japanese painting on his work and for his love of
music.

for whom he had had, from his fifteenth to his eighteenth year, one of those furious secret passions that sometimes ravage the hearts of adolescents.

Leaning in the shadow in front of the unexpected portrait that reminded him of such a recent past, forgetful of the time and place, he was absorbed by his memories. He saw her again on the triumphant evenings when the hall of the Opéra seemed to crumble under the stamping feet and the cries of admiration of an overwhelmed crowd. Never had Europe admired a more sublime female voice. Like himself, a poor young man mad for music, the entire world doubtless desired to fall at Alexandra's feet.

What exalted sobs, in the course of those evenings, had shaken the humble unknown child! What nights of anguish had been his! When the Polish woman advanced on to the stage, with her admirable Oriental eyes, her beautiful inspired gestures, when her breast had swelled, when her eyelids had fluttered as if in a dolorous spasm, her loud voice, her woman's voice, had coiled around souls; her voice was the female serpent that fascinates, which attracts, and by the embrace of which one is doomed forever . . .

A door opens suddenly; the young man, awakened with a start from his dream, turns round, very troubled.

"Bonsoir, Monsieur!" says someone with the hoarse tone of an old colonel.

And he sees, in the obscure room, advancing toward him, enormous and buxom, a woman clad in a bizarre floating crimson dress, with gray back-combed hair around a pale and puffy face. In that colorless fat, two dark eyes are sunk, emphasized excessively by kohl, whose gaze is singularly hard.

In the home of what surprising old whore has he run aground?

He tries to collect himself and does his best to recommence his apologies and explain his breakdown; but she interrupts him at the first words.

"I know," she said. "I'm pleased to receive a stranger, although it's the first time it has happened."

She rolls her *rs* forcefully. The young man is disconcerted. He becomes confused in his thanks, catches his feet in the rugs, and ends up finding himself, without knowing how, sitting facing the lady in a dining room even stranger than the drawing room.

A large fire is blazing in a vast fireplace. An old maidservant silently brings, in ancient and chipped crockery, a rustic farmer's repast. Then she disappears . . .

As soon as the first mouthfuls, in order to break the awkward silence, the young man stammers a few words about today's adventure. But the fat woman, without a word, considers him while he eats, with a fixed and categorical stare. An anxiety seizes him under the gaze of those Oriental eyes, deep-set in the pale fat of her face. Then, suddenly he finds in his mind a subject of conversation that might perhaps interest the lady.

"You have in your drawing room a very fine portrait of Alexandra Jadiska," he says.

Emerging from her mutism, the lady has shivered violently.

"Ah! That interests you?" says the hoarse voice—and its intonation is so menacing that the young man finishes losing countenance. Without knowing why, internally furious at profaning his dearest secret by delivering it to this fat equivocal Turk, he starts talking volubly about his memories, about his amour, about his obsession, about his despair on the day when he learned about the death of the cantatrice. He has stopped eating. His voice trembles. A sob rises to his throat. And suddenly, he interrupts himself. The fat woman has just risen to her feet abruptly.

260

Upright, pale and voluminous, her eyes strangely somber, she advances toward the frightened young man and puts her hand on his shoulder.

"Look at me," she says.

He has stood up in his turn, tipping over his chair. What is wanted of him in this disquieting house?

The fat woman has picked up the poor light that illuminates the room. She holds it up to her bloated face and says: "I'm Alexandra Jadiska."

Next to the dying fire, sitting facing the petrifying Alexandra, the young man had not wearied of listening to her. Now, he knew. She had told him everything; her voice suddenly lost in her glory, her unfruitful secret attempts to find a cure, her pretended death, so well simulated and so artfully contrived that even her family had been deceived, and no one in the world had known about the irreparable misfortune. He knew about the languor in which she was patiently allowing herself to die, of obesity, hoarseness and despair, in this lost old dwelling, the sole retreat in which she had been able to hide her devastated life.

"It's here that I shall be buried," she continued, breathlessly. "I've taken precautions a long time ago in order that, when the hour comes, all the authorizations are in place. My farmers know the corner in which I am to be placed, without a cross or a stone, in order that no one will ever be able to discover my grave . . ."

The young man, astounded, watched that creature sweeping before him in whose soul, as if in a wine suddenly shaken, the entire lees of ancient suffering had been stirred up. He scarcely dared interrogate her; it was with a certain terror that his mind groped in that feminine darkness.

Suddenly, the wandering eyes seemed to abandon the invisible. Alexandra, leaning forward, plunged her gaze directly into that of the young man.

"How you would have loved me!" she murmured.

And without waiting for his response, in a heart-rending divagation, her husky voice sobbed:

"Yes! Even ridiculous and fat, as I am now! For you don't know that, during my last years, I had become almost as bad as today. Well, people loved me even so . . . they loved me enough to die of it. My voice threw them all to their knees before me . . . Listen! This was my last triumph. It was known in Russia that I particularly loved roses. One evening, one of the Grand Dukes, while I was on stage, had my dressing room filled with them, to the extent that one could no longer get into it. They were overflowing all the way to the stairways. And what roses! It was the middle of winter . . . a true miracle . . . and I was such as you see me. I'm telling you the truth . . ."

Her eyes were streaming.

"Now, I have nothing more of a cantatrice than the diaphragm; but the voice has gone . . . it has gone."

She coughed horribly, her throat labored; then, agitated by a somber vehemence, her forehead thrust forward, her gaze deep-set:

"And yet it's me, me that you heard . . . it's my song alone that came from this corpulence that disgusts you . . . it's here that my voice was, here in this hoarse throat, in this disaffected breast . . ."

With an impetuous, unexpected movement, she tore at the red creases that covered her neck.

Troubled and tremulous, the young man had stood up. A breath of the divinity of old had just passed over him. He approached Alexandra, still sitting in her armchair, and, with an involuntary movement, fell to his knees before her. Was he not finally finding himself at the feet of his amour? Once, he had

had the entire world for a rival. This evening, she belonged to him alone.

"Alexandra!" he murmured, without raising his buried head. The voice of old was singing in his memory.

Gently, she caressed the young man's hair. A long frisson ran through him. He raised his head. Then, he no longer saw before him anything but an obese woman with gray hair collapsed in an armchair, ridiculous, with her dress unfastened over an enormous bosom . . .

He had stood up. She understood.

And, extending an indifferent hand to him, she resumed her glacial dignity.

"It's getting late," said her broken voice. "I'll ring for my old maidservant, who will take you to your room. And tomorrow morning, the farmer will put you on the right road."

Having returned to Paris, the young man spent a deranged year.

A regret, a sort of remorse, tormented him. It augmented with such violence that, without knowing exactly with what goal, as soon as autumn began to bite the trees again, he took the road to the desolate château again.

He arrived there one afternoon. His auto was entirely filled with roses, magnificent roses brought that morning from Paris. Would they be as beautiful as those of the Grand Duke?

His eyes dilated by virtue of having gazed at so much faded countryside all along the road, he descended from the vehicle and, leaving the roses behind him, he penetrated into the park. But the shutters were closed, the door bolted. The young man knocked, called out, searched. At the farm he found the two old people sitting in their house. They looked at him with their uncomprehending eyes, and finally decided to speak.

"Madame is dead," they said. "It took her shortly after Monsieur's departure. We had her buried in accordance with her instructions . . ."

For a long time the young man wandered in the park illuminated by the rich palette of autumn. The leaves fell. He searched in vain for the funeral place of the woman who had doubtless died because of him.

Then, taking armfuls of the roses he had brought with him, he threw them at random in the yellowed pathways, in front of him. Would not the wind, which knows how to transmit pollen, be able to discover the deceased, in order to bring her that belated final homage?

"What mythology," the young man murmured, weeping, "will be able to transform the divine voice of Alexandra Jadiska into an autumn nightingale, whose desperate song will be able to enchant motionless moonlit nights?"

And as little by little on the horizon, the last diurnal sky was attained by the stars, the sudden screech of a barn owl from the depths of the trees interrupted his speech. And one might have thought that, in truth, from the depths of the tomb hidden under the leaves, the voice forever lost, by means of that ironic hoarse sob, had just replied to his question.

THE GHOSTLY MARINER
(*Le Journal*, 7 February 1908)

THE soul of a fisherman lost at sea wandered for nights and days over the waters. It was in pain because its body lay without sepulcher somewhere in the mud. It had not yet been extracted like those of other drowned fishermen, those brought back to port dragged behind the boats like the wooden reservoirs in which crayfish were accumulated.

Devoid of color or weight, the soul roamed, invisible, and walked over the sea. For a long time it allowed itself to be bobbed like a buoy over the waves of the Channel. It had almost lost consciousness. It was scarcely quivering when a hasty seagull traversed it with an abrupt wing in passing. The weather was calm and fine, and perhaps it would have lived all of its eternity in that placid state if, one afternoon, a gust of wind coming from the sea had not pushed it in the direction of Honfleur.

As soon as he recognized his town from afar, the dead fisherman said to himself, joyfully: "One might think that I were returning home now!"

And, recovering consciousness fully, he started looking around.

As he passed along the estuary, he did not see anyone except Louis Ternier, the great hunter of Honfleurian water-fowl, who, with his slender silhouette and his bright eyes, resembled some gull lingering on the edge of the marsh. Then, as the wind continued to push him, he suddenly found himself at the entrance to the harbor.

Here are the winter coasts, blue in fine weather; their hump-backed form is visible. Here is the town, irregular and gray, the lighthouses and the basins. The soul in pain doubles the jetty and approaches the quay . . .

Oh, to see all the comrades again busy among their salty sails and their wet masts, unloading writhing nets, swarming fish with silvery bellies! To hear the good voices of old calling to one another from boat to boat, while women sit on the parapets watching, surrounded by their red-cheeked brats!

The dead fisherman mingles with the groups of mariners. No one suspects his presence. And suddenly, no longer able to stand it, he places his phantom hand on a broad shoulder in a blue jersey, that of the owner of his boat, a tall fellow who liked him a great deal. The owner, who is standing slightly apart, turns round, his face benevolent, his eyes laughing, and sees nothing. An astonishment passes over his beardless face.

Then the phantom, laughing, cries: "Hey boss! I've come back now! I'm Budet, your matelot!"

His voice resonates so loudly that everyone raises his head. The owner has recoiled, his eyes mad. A second of horror. Then, like a flock of curlews surprised by a rifle shot, the fishermen run away in all directions, uttering frightened cries. All of them, as they run, make the sign of the cross. The women have gathered their kids and are making off, embarrassed by their skirts.

"Budet has come back! Budet has come back!"

All the voices howl at the phantom. In two minutes, the poor ghost has made a void around him. And he makes such sad reflections!

They've all left me here on the quay, he thinks, *and I can't go up to one without chilling his blood. Everyone would make the sign of the cross as I approached, as if I were thunder to polish them off. It's only been four months, though, since we were working together.*

Then, suddenly taking stock of the situation jovially:

It doesn't vex me, all the same. They're working and I'm strolling. I can't do as much as if I were alive.

He sets forth again, more slowly. The wind is no longer pushing him, and his will is tottering. Should he go, as a silent spirit, to see his wife and children? Should he enter the closed dwelling, in order to listen, to see whether they were talking about him, whether they regretted him a little? A dread stops him. He has so often seen the wives of mariners take up with another man a fortnight after the disappearance of their own. Oh, what an unfortunate condition is that of a wandering dead man without a sepulcher!

Having arrived at his door, the dead fisherman listens for a while. To begin with, he is afraid that his voice might send his entire family into convulsions; then too, he would like to know at whom his wife is shouting so loudly. There are three brats wailing, as on days of great dispute. No, he won't wait for the end of the quarrel. He turns round abruptly, and with a gesture of unadmitted cheerfulness, concludes: *She wasn't always comfortable. Now I'm rid of her forever.*

Lightened by the sentiment of his liberty, he contemplates the little old town of his birth, so sweet to his gaze, the human life around him, so tempting. They do not know their good fortune, those who are coming and going without thinking about it; it does not know its good fortune, that dog rummaging in rubbish with its moist nose and sharp teeth of a living being!

The dead fisherman, having become melancholy again, leaves Honfleur in order no longer to see the spectacle, and plunges into the countryside. The winter night is already falling, a vigorous Norman night scented by grass and labored earth; the moon is about to rise, another revenant, in order to give form again to things eaten by shadow.

One by one, under the nascent light, the erased forms reappear. The windows light up under the slate and the surly thatch.

267

The bread will soon be dipped in the soup. The housewives are already bent over the hearth, their heads above the fire, among the sausages and the ham hanging to the right and left of the pothook. One can only see the broad taut backsides of those farmers' wives.

The dead fisherman approaches doors like a beggar, and gazes. No one would suspect his presence if the dogs, which might be able to see the invisible, did not bristle in their barrels, barking furiously at the impalpable vagabond. Already, elder sons are coming out, cudgels in hand . . .

Go away quickly, poor phantom; the dead are intruders among the living.

Will the dead fisherman regret the sea, on the round waves of which he floated like a buoy? There, at least, he was not disturbing anyone.

But he quickly pulls himself together.

Those who eat, he says to himself, *are well off, but there are so many who go hungry every day. That's happened to me many a time. Now I have my sufficiency, since I'm never hungry!*

Laughing all alone under the moon, he returns to the il-luminated town. The meal time is long past. The chimes of nine o'clock have unleashed the heavy toll of the curfew over the rooftops.

How am I going to pass the time? he asks himself, with a hint of anguish.

Suddenly, the sound of the bell inspires the phantom fisher-man. Has not the ringer of the curfew, the blind bell-ringer of Sainte-Catherine, been his friend for a long time? He re-members the first day of their amity: he a matelot, in his blue jersey; the other, a bell-ringer, in his dull jacket. What an idea he had had, the naïve Budet, to climb up the bell-tower of Sainte-Catherine, the independent bell-tower placed alongside its church like a lid alongside its box, the Gothic windows of which, encumbered by flower-pots, gleamed in the night like a giant night-light!

"What do you want to see?" the bell-ringer had said. And, turning to Budet a face with closed eyes, a hermetically blind face: "For that, it's necessary that I go up before you, for you won't see anything without me."

That speech had struck Budet so much that they had immediately become friends.

Now the dead fisherman is at the door of the bell-tower. He waits for the end of the curfew before knocking. Is it for a revenge for his blindness that the bell-ringer rings for such a long time? Curfew, extinction of the light . . . With what joy he blinds the town every evening, that bell-ringer devoid of eyes!

The last stroke has just died away in the sky ecstasized by moonlight. The dead fisherman knocks on the door. Is his idea not good? He has said to himself: *The bell-ringer can't see anything, so I can talk to him without chilling his blood. He'll be astonished that I've come back, but it's not difficult to explain to him that . . .*

And now he is explaining:

"They said I was drowned, I think, when I was carried by the tempest to England. It was necessary to come back, which took time. I don't want to go home his evening because of the children and the wife, who'd take me for a ghost. Tomorrow, in daylight, it'll be better to tell them that. Excuse me if I'm disturbing you . . ."

The bell-ringer, who has never seen anything but darkness, is not astonished by the invisible fisherman, and invites him in, without suspecting that he is a specter.

"Sit down, Budet, poor fellow. I have our friend the great organ-blower with me this evening, who is blind, like me. We're going to celebrate your return by all three of us getting drunk, although it's not our habit. You'll lodge here tonight, and tomorrow you'll return home."

Here they all are at table. Budet recounts everything that has happened to him in England and the others laugh as much as they can. But every time one of them wants to touch the specter on the shoulder, he cries immediately: "Above all, don't touch me, England has given me the mange!"—with the result that the two blind men spend the night with their terrible guest without any suspicion of his nature.

But as phantoms cannot drink, Budet watches, desperately, the two comrades swallow coffee after calvados and calvados after coffee. They think that they are drinking with their guest, and are unaware that they are emptying his glass themselves, by turns. He listens to them singing; he sings too, but without enthusiasm.

Oh, this funereal sobriety! With what jealousy he sees the cheeks of the blind men redden!

There it is, he says to himself. *They've both had a little pot too much, and I, for want of being a beast, have watched them. I've come back, yes, but I'm dead. And I'll never, ever be drunk . . .*

And as, for a fisherman of Honfleur, not being able to be drunk is irreparable, the inconsolable specter takes advantage of the moment when his two companions are beginning to snore in order to leave silently through the closed doors of the bell-tower. And in the moonlight, like someone committing suicide, he goes straight toward the sea.

Because, he says to himself as he runs, *I can renounce comrades, the wife, the children, and eating, but if one can't get drunk on land, one might as well be a drowned fisherman.*

A PARTIAL LIST OF SNUGGLY BOOKS

MARCEL SCHWOB *The Assassins and Other Stories*
BRIAN STABLEFORD (editor)
   Decadence and Symbolism: A Showcase Anthology
BRIAN STABLEFORD (editor) *The Snuggly Satyricon*
BRIAN STABLEFORD (editor) *The Snuggly Satanicon*
BRIAN STABLEFORD (editor) *Snuggly Tales of Hashish and Opium*
BRIAN STABLEFORD *The Insubstantial Pageant*
BRIAN STABLEFORD *Spirits of the Vasty Deep*
BRIAN STABLEFORD *The Truths of Darkness*
COUNT ERIC STENBOCK *Love, Sleep & Dreams*
COUNT ERIC STENBOCK *Myrtle, Rue & Cypress*
COUNT ERIC STENBOCK *The Shadow of Death*
COUNT ERIC STENBOCK *Studies of Death*
MONTAGUE SUMMERS *The Bride of Christ and Other Fictions*
MONTAGUE SUMMERS *Six Ghost Stories*
GILBERT-AUGUSTIN THIERRY *The Blonde Tress and The Mask*
GILBERT-AUGUSTIN THIERRY *Reincarnation and Redemption*
DOUGLAS THOMPSON *The Fallen West*
TOADHOUSE *Gone Fishing with Samy Rosenstock*
TOADHOUSE *Living and Dying in a Mind Field*
TOADHOUSE *What Makes the Wave Break?*
LÉO TRÉZENIK *Decadent Prose Pieces*
RUGGERO VASARI *Raun*
JANE DE LA VAUDÈRE *The Demi-Sexes and The Androgynes*
JANE DE LA VAUDÈRE *The Double Star and Other Occult Fantasies*
JANE DE LA VAUDÈRE *The Mystery of Kama and Brahma's Courtesans*
JANE DE LA VAUDÈRE *The Priestesses of Mylitta*
JANE DE LA VAUDÈRE *Three Flowers and The King of Siam's Amazon*
JANE DE LA VAUDÈRE *The Witch of Ecbatana and The Virgin of Israel*
AUGUSTE VILLIERS DE L'ISLE-ADAM *Isis*
RENÉE VIVIEN AND HÉLÈNE DE ZUYLEN DE NYEVELT
   Faustina and Other Stories
RENÉE VIVIEN *Lilith's Legacy*
RENÉE VIVIEN *A Woman Appeared to Me*
TERESA WILMS MONTT *In the Stillness of Marble*
TERESA WILMS MONTT *Sentimental Doubts*
KAREL VAN DE WOESTIJNE *The Dying Peasant*

CPSIA information can be obtained
at www.ICGtesting.com
Printed in the USA
BVHW030942081020
590605BV00001B/107